CLOUDED WATERS

Books by Dianna Hunter

Clouded Waters, a novel, 2023

Wild Mares:
My Lesbian Back-to-the-Land Life, 2018

Breaking Hard Ground:
Stories of Minnesota Farm Advocates, 1990

CLOUDED

A Novel

WATERS

DIANNA HUNTER

HOLY COW! PRESS
Duluth, Minnesota
2023

Please note: The characters in this book are entirely fictional.
Any resemblance to actual persons living or dead is entirely coincidental.

Author photograph by Deborah Anderson.
Cover photograph © copyright by Sara Pajunen and used
with her permission.
Cover and book design by Anton Khodakovsky.

Printed and bound in the United States of America.

ISBN 978-1737405160 (*paperback*)
      978-1737405177 (*ebook*)

First printing, Fall, 2023.
10 9 8 7 6 5 4 3 2 1

Library of Congress Cataloging-in-Publication Data
Hunter, Dianna, 1949- author.
Clouded waters : a novel / Dianna Hunter.
Duluth, Minnesota : Holy Cow! Press, 2023.
LCCN 2023010086 (print) | LCCN 2023010087 (ebook)
| ISBN 9781737405160 (trade paperback) | ISBN 9781737405177 (ebook)
LCSH: Women newspaper editors—Fiction. | Mines and mineral resources—Fiction.
| Mesabi Range (Minn.)—Fiction. | LCGFT: Ecofiction. | Lesbian fiction. | Novels.
LCC PS3608.U59255 C58 2023 (print) | LCC PS3608.U59255 (ebook)
| DDC 813/.6—dc23/eng/20230413
LC record available at https://lccn.loc.gov/2023010086
LC ebook record available at https://lccn.loc.gov/2023010087

Holy Cow! Press projects are funded in part by grant awards from the Ben and Jeanne Overman
Charitable Trust, the Elmer L. and Eleanor J. Andersen Foundation, the Lenfestey Family
Foundation, The Woessner Freeman Family Foundation, and by gifts from generous individual
donors. We are grateful to Springboard for the Arts for their support as our fiscal sponsor.

Holy Cow! Press books are distributed to the trade by Consortium Book Sales & Distribution,
c/o Ingram Publisher Services, Inc., 210 American Drive, Jackson, TN 38301.

For inquiries, please write to:
Holy Cow! Press, Post Office Box 3170, Mount Royal Station, Duluth, MN 55803
Visit *www.holycowpress.org*

DEDICATION

For my wife, Deb, my blood family, and my chosen family who provide daily examples of loving authenticity and support.

And for Starr and Luna. Without them, life would not be one-tenth as hairy or half as fun.

ACKNOWLEDGMENTS

My spouse, Deborah Anderson, deserves tremendous credit just for putting up with me and my absent, distant gazes as I wrestle with words, technological faux pas, and all the mundane tasks that come with creating and distributing books. Thank you for being a wise reader, sounding board, advisor, and partner—and most of all, for loving me through everything these nearly thirty years.

Thank you, Jim Perlman, publisher and proprietor, and the rest of the crew working with Holy Cow! Press, for taking on this novel, believing in it (and me), and seeing the book through to a conclusion that I hope makes us all proud. I especially thank my copy editor, Felicia Schneiderhan, for turning her considerable talent, skill, and experience to this project.

Pamela Mittlefehldt, my attentive, wise, and encouraging reader, saw me through multiple drafts of *Clouded Waters*. She is simply the best at helping draw unrealized meaning and direction from raw and half-baked ideas. Sara Pajunen, self-described composer-improviser and audio-visual artist who grew up on the Mesabi Range, provided the cover photograph that felt, from the first look, custom made for this novel. Many readers gave their wisdom, insight, and precious time to help clarify, correct, augment, and nudge this book toward its printed form. Thank you, Doris Malkmus, Nicole Elysian (who also advised me about the ethics of massage therapists), Molly McCarthy, Cathy Klaber-Hartl, Patti Berg, Martha Benewicz, Charlene Brown, Christine Jenkins (who read and responded and then mentioned the novel to Jim Perlman), and Lisa Kane (who doubled as technology mentor).

I · A SPRING DAY

THE YEAR BEFORE the virus arrived, an ordinary winter and dark spring fell upon the town of Iron, Minnesota. On an April morning in the ancient, watery place that we now call the Mesabi Iron Range, Susan B. Ellingson thought she had endured enough gray and frigid days to last the rest of her life. This one felt like just another in a long string of good ones to stay indoors, and that was fine with her. Her work relationship with Gwen Groveland was never better than when they settled at their desks on a dismal morning, riffing ideas and writing in the dim, natural light.

SB (as most people called her) loved Gwen, but not in the way that some of the more suggestive citizens of Red Stone County might have thought. True, SB did know what it was to love another woman romantically, erotically and soul-stirringly, and once she'd figured it out, she'd almost never felt the need to make a secret of it. With Gwen, though, she shared a bond rooted in work and everyday, mutual interests. She counted Gwen's friendship as a major blessing and almost enough to sustain her.

Right then SB needed sustaining. These were the hard and lonely years of her widowhood and empty nesting. As for the empty nesting part, she hadn't put much store in that overused figure of speech until the past September. Before then, she would have dismissed the old saw, claiming it stereotyped and did an injustice to the hens of the world, not to mention the human mothers, but her circumstances had changed. Her daughter, Arte, had graduated from the university a year earlier and found work in Wisconsin, and then Skye, SB's son, took wing to study visual arts at a private college in St. Augustine, Florida. SB found herself living with Lil, her Labrador retriever, in the large and comfortable apartment above her newspaper office on the main street of Iron, the mining town where she'd been born. She'd been raised in that apartment above the newsroom and press shop, and she had raised her own family there. Now, in the living room that used to vibrate with human voices, the only talk she heard most days was her own. Her words bounced off the walls and fell to the floor. She tried not to dwell on her losses or her loneliness, but sometimes she felt like she expended more energy yearning for her absent people than doing anything else.

Thankfully she had the *Union Voice*, the newspaper her immigrant great-grandparents bought from a collective of Finnish union organizers during the First World War. In the age of disinformation, contested truths, and the decline of print journalism, SB felt the press of history riding on her shoulders. She struggled to pay the bills, but she had no intention of letting the *Voice* go broke or toothless on her watch.

"Did you see today's tweet?" Gwen asked archly, stretching about as far as SB ever heard her go toward high passion over politics.

"There are so many tweets," SB answered. "I don't know how you keep up."

"This one's got to do with us," Gwen explained. The irony in her grin became visible as she swiveled her chair and looked SB in the face. At sixty-seven Gwen was crow's-footed, cropped-haired, and recently retired from the city library's reference desk. She dressed as she pleased in idiosyncratically matched styles and palettes, and often went so retro that she became fashion forward. She mixed patterns long before it became a thing. That morning she sported a vivid floral print, striped pants, and a long, denim vest with an array of pockets that looked best suited for holding seed packets and gardening tools.

"He says he's canceling the Forest Service study," Gwen explained about the tweet.

"What?" SB asked. "You mean our mining study? The one the tribe and the resort owners lobbied and pushed for?"

"The very same," Gwen told her.

"Can he do that after they won that court order requiring it to go forward?"

"Apparently he thinks he can," Gwen said.

"Geez," SB responded. "Everything about this has been so fraught. He'll probably take it all the way to the Supremes."

"Could be."

"I wonder what the chances are," SB mused. "I suppose it'll cost the locals a fortune."

"I think that might be the strategy. Browbeat and bust them right out of court."

"Stay with it, will you?" SB said, feeling her lips pull uncomfortably tight. With so much at stake, she needed to get this story right. "You know the drill. Flesh it out. Talk to some of the clean water people and some of the pro-mining people. Talk to the lawyers and some of the Crooked Lake Band leaders. See if anybody from the Forest Service will comment."

"And the White House?" Gwen asked in a smart-alecky voice.

"Sure, what the hell?" SB said. "Send a tweet."

Titles being what they were, SB listed herself on the paper's masthead as Editor and Publisher and Gwen as City Editor and Senior Researcher. In practice, they both did all of the research and reporting that SB didn't buy from news services or get free from volunteer stringers who were happy to accept a byline in exchange for chronicling the fishing, sporting events, weddings, school happenings, and other goings on that sparked local passions.

SB had relied on Gwen's research help since ninth grade, when Gwen arrived as Iron High School's fresh-faced rookie librarian. The two of them knew how to flourish together in silence, so, as often happened, they let their conversation transition into one of those no-harm, no-fault disconnections. While Gwen keyboarded at her desk, SB started an email inquiry to the outreach director of the Minnesota Environmental Safety Commission. If anyone knew the story behind the study that the president claimed to have cancelled, it would be Latelle Washington. Out of respect and fear of screwing up, SB deliberated over every word of her message.

"Latelle," she started and then had second thoughts. She didn't want to give the impression that she was trying to diminish the director's status or trade on their acquaintance. SB saw email as a fragile and dangerous medium. Writing so concisely made tone nearly impossible to convey. One badly chosen word or missing qualifier could blow the message and put the whole conversation on tenterhooks.

She revised to the more formal, "Director Washington, could you share your wisdom with me . . ."

She deleted that sentence, too, and began again. "Could you share your insight for our readers on what has happened to the Forest Service study on the safety of copper-nickel mining in the Iron Range watersheds? We're trying to make sense of the process that appears to have led to the environmental study's cancellation."

SB guessed Latelle to be roughly her own age—a little over fifty. SB had watched her operate for years, learning the science and politics of her job until she had mastered them almost as well as the public relations. In the process, Latelle had climbed the bureaucratic ladder and connected with a rich network of earth and water scientists, public office holders, union executives, mine owners, directors of environmental nonprofits—the whole range of so-called "stakeholders" in the business of extracting natural resources from the earth. Not bad for an outspoken, round-bodied, supposed outsider from the north side of Minneapolis.

Once SB had weighed and rewritten to her satisfaction, her impulse was to close with, "Call me anytime. We can take your comments on or off the record."

She scratched that, too, knowing that Latelle's official email account was vulnerable to internal reviews and open records requests.

SB went with the much less directive, "Looking forward to hearing from you."

That way Latelle could respond officially or call SB from a private phone. Or she could not respond at all. Whatever message Latelle did or didn't send would carry some kind of meaning. The trouble would come in trying to decipher silence if that's what SB got.

She understood that they both played relatively small roles in a struggle that had become titanic. The world's tech-hungry consumers clamored for electronic devices that required copper, nickel, and trace rare metals, and the miners in Red Stone County needed jobs, wages, and homes for their families. The mine owners—their geologists, lawyers, and engineers anyhow—had been sniffing around Iron for half a century, drilling core samples, looking for copper and nickel, finding them, and seeking permits to mine. Naturally the mining companies wanted to blast and dig and start profiting from the expenses they'd incurred, but they'd run into a very big problem. The ore veins ran through sulfide rock that had the unfortunate property, when exposed to water, of interacting chemically and releasing toxins like acid, lead, mercury, and arsenic into the watershed.

Water, by nature, had to run. Rain that fell near Iron washed across the remnants of a two-billion-year-old, eroded mountain range that had once stood taller than the Rockies. For centuries the Dakota had called this place home, and then the Anishinaabe who named the hundred-mile long, iron-bearing formation inside that prehistoric range Misaabe Wajiw (in English, something like "Giant Mountain" or "Big Man Mountain"). It was the newcomer Europeans who kidnapped Misaabe from the oral language and pinned it down, using it for their own purposes. You could see it spelled every which way, as it was now on maps of the Mesabi Iron Range, road signs on Mesaba Avenue in Duluth, and the ore cars of the Duluth, Missabe, and Iron Range Railway.

One thing hadn't changed.

From the high points of the old range, snowmelt and rain diverged across a three-way continental divide. Water descended along gravity-driven routes through wilderness, rural lands, flowages, and cities, carrying essential minerals and pollutants alike to Hudson Bay, the Mississippi River, the Labrador Sea, and the North Atlantic by way of the St. Lawrence

Seaway and Lake Superior (the great Gitche Gumee), which by itself held ten percent of the world's fresh water.

SB had watched the champions of copper-nickel mining and the champions of water wrestle since she was a child. She had seen the balance between them tip back and forth. The struggle still played on through social media spats, letters to the editor, talk radio harangues, court filings, legislative hearings, permitting battles, trials, public meetings, demonstrations, and news reports. So far no mining company had been allowed to dig for copper and nickel on the Range, but a local corporation called BeneGeo pressed hard to get started.

SB reread her message to Latelle Washington one last time before hitting Send. Afterward, she stretched her arms, straightened her back, and looked at the clock. Another twenty-minute chunk of her life had just slid down the tube labeled "writing."

She said to Gwen, "I need a break. How about you?"

2. LATER THAT DAY

FROM HER PERCH at the publisher's desk, SB gazed across the newsroom and through the *Voice* building's lobby windows at a slice of downtown Iron. The main drag, Mesabi Street, stretched from west to east in front of her, its gray pavement wide enough for diagonal parking on both sides, as if the town could afford all the elbow room in the world. Brick buildings, mostly two stories tall, lined both sides, except for the substantial edifice directly across the street with its dun-colored, Beaux Arts façade. The First Miners Bank had shut down after the high-grade hematite ore ran short in the '80s and everyone learned that its officers had not secured enough collateral to back the loans they'd made to the suddenly failing local companies.

The high-grade ore ran out completely during SB's second year at the University of Minnesota, which everyone called "the U." Eventually some of the U's engineers found a way to concentrate iron from the lower-grade taconite ore into pellets of high enough grade to sell to the steel mills back east. By then nearly half of Iron's fifteen thousand people had left town. Most of the downtown businesses had closed, and the landlords who didn't lose their buildings ended up leasing storefronts to tattoo parlors, secondhand shops, video rental establishments, and dollar stores. When global demand for steel raised taconite prices, big box stores sprang up along the U.S. highway. SB stayed put and watched deferred maintenance and fierce, seasonal thaws and freezes take their tolls on downtown Iron. The *Voice* building stood as an exception. SB had made sure its brick façade sported a fresh sandblasting and tuck-pointing job that held off the elements and showcased its Art Deco flourishes.

She was congratulating herself on her management and budgeting skills when a stranger opened the front door and walked into the lobby. She had a striking face, noticeably alert, canny eyes, and ruddy cheeks bounded by a shaggy mane of collar-length, gingery brown hair. There was an air about her—an energy—that struck SB as robust and appealing, but she pretended not to notice. She got up casually from her seat, taking care to seem as professional and indifferent as she could. She approached the counter with an air of nonchalance that was purely an exercise in acting as if.

In her head, she heard her daughter's voice warning, "Don't go there, Mom. Don't assume anything. You don't even know how this person identifies."

When the language and concerns of her children flowed through her mind, the advice sometimes proved amazingly perceptive. This time, though, SB felt pretty sure it was just a window into her own anxieties.

She said as casually as she could, "How can I help?"

The stranger gave a smile that looked both open and tenuous. It showed just a glimpse of a gap, an intriguing sliver of empty space, between her top front teeth. Yes, SB thought, "her" most likely. Leave the pronoun discussion for later, as if there would be a later and as if there would be a pronoun discussion, which there surely would have been if Arte had been present and involved.

Gwen was watching and holding her mouth in an amused-looking curl. She shifted her eyes back to her computer screen as soon as SB noticed.

"I was wondering about a business ad," the woman said, elevating her pitch uncertainly at the end in a way that made SB want to rush in and provide some direction.

"Display or classified, do you think?" SB asked.

"I don't know," she answered with a shrug. "I've never done this before. I've always managed to find new clients through social media or word of mouth." At this point she interrupted herself and looked like she was consciously shifting gears. She stuck out her hand—awkwardly, SB thought—and said with a game smile, "I'm Merle Byrne by the way. I'm new in town. I have a therapeutic massage business."

SB introduced herself, too, and said, "I'm the publisher." Afterward, she thought she might have sounded too full of herself, so she added, "Otherwise I'd probably be able to help you much more effectively."

Merle Byrne exhaled a gust of air that doubled as a chuckle. She said, "I'm sure you'll manage somehow."

SB laughed, though she hadn't been completely kidding. Advertising might have been her bread and butter, but it wasn't her bailiwick. Her advertising manager, Dave Maki, was the real expert, but Dave was on the road at that moment selling space in the upcoming *Range Summer Fun Edition*, a tourism and real estate advertiser that brought in half of the *Voice's* annual net profit. SB depended on Dave, but she also prided herself on at least a rudimentary knowledge of every part of her operation.

She said to Merle, "Suppose you tell me what you're thinking."

"I'm looking for some new clients," Merle explained. She was sounding a little more relaxed.

"Good start," SB said, "Tell me more."

"I've been a massage therapist for twelve years, and it just got to be time for me to make a change, I guess. I wanted to get out of the city, so when I thought about it, I realized that I had some long-term clients around here. They used to drive into Duluth to see me, so I figured I could rebuild my clientele with them as a base. I took the leap. Bought a house and a little land a few miles out in Willow Township. Moved there with my dog. Now I need to find some new clients. Any ideas?"

"Maybe start with a display ad and then switch to a listing in our service directory," SB said. "We could write up a news story about you for our business section, too, at no charge. That way we can put together a reasonable package."

"Sounds good," Merle said. The gap showed up again when she smiled.

"We'll need a photograph," SB said.

"I don't really have a good one."

"If you don't mind, I can snap a few."

By the time Merle went out the door, SB had her ad copy, email address, credit card payment, business card, phone number, a few head-and-shoulders shots to sort through, and the name and breed of Merle's dog, Bernie, a part-bred collie.

Gwen chirped from her desk, "Merle seemed nice."

"I thought so, too," SB said.

"And capable." Gwen added convincingly.

"Hmm," SB hedged. "I wondered for a minute about the massage thing."

"Really?" Gwen's brow knit in puzzlement for a few seconds. "Oh, you mean whether she was legit?"

"Yeah, but she seems like the real deal."

"I'd say so," Gwen told her. "I think you can let that one go. Are you planning to make an appointment?"

"For what?"

"Oh, come on," Gwen pushed back. "What do you think?"

"Massage, you mean?"

"No," Gwen retorted, "psychotherapy."

"I'm thinking about it."

"What's there to think about?"

"I don't know. I guess for one thing you've got to let your guard down to get the most from a massage."

Gwen stared over her glasses. "Isn't that one of the best things about it?"

"I don't know. I need to think about it, I guess. Maybe yes."

"Jeez! Don't work too hard at it. You sound like you're about to blow a few brain cells."

SB just shook her head.

She was still mulling over the encounter that evening, after supper in her apartment. Her rooms stretched the length and breadth of the second story of the building, which itself had been framed with some of the last posts and beams cut from the climax, white pine forest—trees so mature that their canopies blocked sunlight and competing species from the forest floor.

The building had been a woodshop and lumber storage warehouse before the pine ran out, and the Finnish miners bought the place from foreclosure to house their scrappy little newspaper. SB's great-grandparents developed the living quarters and added the windows trimmed in red oak, the birch built-ins with leaded-glass doors that graced the dining room, and maple boards that ran across all the floors in clear, luminously varnished, fourteen-foot lengths, the likes of which could not be bought any longer, except from an architectural salvage dealer. Such maples no longer existed.

When SB got up to clear the dishes, Lil took it as a cue to put on a display of prancing.

"You're shameless," SB chided.

She snapped a leash on the dog's collar and allowed her to lead them down the back stairs and out the door that emptied into the alley behind the building. The clouds had cleared, and in the distance, SB saw the sun sinking in the direction of a stand of third-growth woods that framed the far shore of Kettle Lake. As far as SB was concerned, the lake contained the living, beating heart of town. Carved and filled by the receding glaciers of the last ice age, it was little more than a pond but big enough that its water was the reason the lumbermen had built there in the first place. Iron started as a refilling station for the steam locomotives that pulled trainloads of white pine to Chicago, Seattle, and locations in between.

On their way to the foot-beaten path that circled the lake, Lil steered SB through mown grass, wild meadows, and thickening woods, until they came to the stretch that ran for maybe half a mile around the circumference of the lake. The sunset was just beginning, and a small breeze rippled the water's mirror, creating a reflection of a reddish, impressionistic sky behind the feathery-looking umbers and mauves of maples and poplars just starting to swell into bud.

She spotted Casper Karlsrud and his springer spaniel too late to avoid an encounter. On the circular part of the path, the only escape would have been to make a one-eighty turn, and such an obvious reversal would have conveyed a signal that she couldn't afford to send to the cranky, politically shrewd Red Stone County Commissioner. Besides, Lil had seen them, too, and was already leaning into her leash, pulling and squealing for Karlsrud's attention.

Bent over, arms extended, he chittered, "Hey there, Baby Girl! Come and see me, Lil! Come on now!"

SB had watched his springer, Algernon, grow from a pup, and she grieved to see him becoming ancient and lame in the much-too-fast way that dogs do. The man was in his early seventies and not aging well, either, by the appearance of him. SB owned to herself that she looked older, too. Every time she caught a glimpse of her face in a mirror, she looked more creased and careworn than she expected, but Casper's sallow face and unnaturally dyed black hair struck her as a case study in venality and self-harm. Shadows languished around his eyes, frown lines descended like troughs from the wings of his nose, and a cigarette protruded from the corner of his mouth, looking like a port for rapid delivery of toxic gases.

"We grow into the faces we earn, you know," Grandma Ragna Ellingson had told SB many times. Ragna was not an immigrant but second-generation and a functionally bilingual businesswoman who spoke English with a Norwegian accent.

Ragna had suspected Karlsrud of various frauds and schemes, and so had her son. Whistleblowers handed Kjell Ellingson a few bits of information, but he never was able to get his hands on enough solid evidence to take a story to press. SB would have loved to surpass her father in that way, but all of her leads had fizzled, too, and she'd decided that Casper was no longer worth the effort.

She cringed as she watched him slip a biscuit from his pocket and hold it just beyond Lil's reach, hyping her excitement and asking repeatedly, "Who's my baby? Come get some love, Precious Girl!"

When he finally delivered the treat and Lil wolfed it down, SB felt humiliated by extension. She offered a hand to Algernon and, with deliberate subtlety, brushed the soft black-and-white fur away from his eyes.

"How are you doing these days, Old Fella?" she asked. "Still getting around, I see."

"He's a stoic guy," Casper answered gruffly. "He's toughing it out."

"Dogs are great that way, aren't they?" SB said, looking for her exit strategy. The commissioner had a tendency to steer perfectly pleasant conversations into abrupt, angry twists of subject. She hoped to avoid dealing with Commissioner Hyde.

Karlsrud stubbed out his cigarette against the smooth bark of a young maple and replied balefully, "I wish people were more like dogs."

She hoped to leave it there and agreed with a grin.

Casper's returned smile could have doubled as a grimace.

"Oh, look how dark it's getting," SB said. "We've got to get going."

She clicked to Lil and stepped fast, waving goodbye as they broke into a trot for home. They were nearly there when her phone chimed, and caller ID came up, "Latelle Washington."

SB touched the green icon and offered, "Hello."

A voice in a distinctive, tenor range replied, "SB?"

"Yes. Hello, Latelle," SB said.

"Let me get something straight right from the start. Are we off the record?"

"We can be."

"Well then we must be."

Jesus, did she have to make it sound so ponderous?

SB said, "Okay."

"This is for background only," Latelle clarified. "I'm not to be recorded or quoted, not even as an anonymous source. No 'someone who is familiar with the matter,' or anything along that line. Is that clear?"

"Yes. Sure. Agreed," SB said. She had arrived at the back door of the *Voice* building, holding the phone and leash in one hand while she felt in her pocket for her keys with the other.

"I'm certain you know that this whole thing is dangerous for me. And the study is a federal matter. Nobody here has seen the president's order. We don't know if there is one."

"Right," SB said, leaving it there in the truncated way a person does when she wants the other party to know she's present, listening, and waiting for them to go on.

Latelle elaborated, "The scuttlebutt is that the preliminary results don't look too good for BeneGeo's plan, and there's some problem with one of the investigators. A lot of people think the administration is trying to kill the study to speed up the approval and keep the facts from coming to light."

SB let herself and Lil inside. They passed by the door that led into the back of the newsroom and started up the stairs.

She asked, "Is that based on speculation, or do you think it's reliable information?"

"Some of both probably," Latelle said. "Our people talk to their people. You know? Our projects and interests interconnect at lots of levels. Things get said that can't always be verified. I wish I could be more specific."

"And what about the investigator?" SB asked, boosting Lil from behind to keep her ahead on the stairs. "What happened there?"

"Again, I can only speculate. What I hear is the person hasn't been responding to phone calls or electronic queries."

"Is that unusual?"

"Within the research circles, yes. They tend to be all about sharing information and working collaboratively. Some people think it's exceedingly strange that this person has fallen off the radar."

"Who is the person?" SB asked, entering her kitchen.

"I can't tell you that or anything more specific."

"Can you tell me if it's a federal employee or a contractor?"

"No, and I should probably end this call right here before you get me to go any further," Latelle said. She put a no-nonsense emphasis at the end of her sentence that left SB feeling she had no alternative but to accept.

"It's your call," she said. "Thank you for reaching out."

What a day! In honor of nearing its end, SB uncorked a cheap red blend she liked well enough. She poured herself a full glass before she sat down at the kitchen table to write notes detailing what she remembered from her conversation with Latelle. She loved the fuzzy edge the wine started putting around everything as she wrote. She hoped it would float her to sleep eventually. She also hoped it would help her stay in the current moment, which was hard to do when she was home alone and trying to keep her thoughts from carrying her too far.

She spent too much time remembering, and it made her feel like she was staring into the Time Machine folders on her laptop screen, trying to retrieve an old piece of writing that she had over-revised and wanted to return to its original freshness. The past could feel like gazing into layers of infinity, and sometimes she felt weirdly comforted by the overwhelming vastness and intangibility of everything. Keats gave her that in high school English. She wanted love and loss to sink to nothingness in the face of geologic time and twenty-first century astrophysics, and sometimes she could let it.

What she wanted most of all was for grief to join the inexorable flow and pass her by, but she couldn't make that happen. She remembered too much.

Like her wife.

Like the great love of her life.

Like Ramona.

3 · LATER THAT WEEK

S B LEFT FOR WORK in the evening with a canvas bag slung over her shoulder. She slipped out the back door and closed it behind her while Lil sat crestfallen, staring through the narrowing gap. The evening air felt soft and warm, and as she walked, SB sensed her body loosening from the clench of winter. She took the long way around to the Carnegie Library, looping through the edge of old downtown. On such an evening, she would have preferred to follow Lil down some green path on a nose-driven walkabout. But duty called, and when it did, it called most ardently to SB Ellingson.

Amid birdsong, new grass, and budding dandelions, she walked with steady purpose, stealing envious glances at kids without jackets who squealed and chased each other around old, wood-framed houses. This part of Iron dated to the time of the city's founding—the second founding, that is. The original Iron had sprung up around the state's first open pit mine on the far side of Kettle Lake. When the mine owners discovered that their ore vein ran under town, they loaned horses and skids to the property owners to make sure that they all moved their buildings to the new location.

Nearer the library, cars sat bumper to bumper along the curb. SB had hoped for a good turnout at the meeting, but she worried that people might have been put off by the news release. She thought she recognized Latelle Washington's stilted prose:

> The Minnesota Environmental Safety Commission invites citizens to attend an informational listening session on the future of copper-nickel mining proposals in Red Stone County. This moderated event will include presentations by experts and an opportunity for questions and comments from the audience.

The library had perched on the very same street corner since 1905, when its namesake, Andrew Carnegie, gifted it to the city. Carnegie, John D.

Rockefeller, and J.P. Morgan had all held business interests on the Range. Local iron helped the robber barons of the last century's Gilded Age pile their fortunes higher, and now that the city had built a new, digitally wired public library on the edge of town, the city council had decided to repurpose Carnegie's gift as a community center. Approaching the squat old sandstone fortress, SB heard a buzz of voices rising from an open basement door.

Downstairs, people spilled across rows of folding chairs and into the aisles and edges. They leaned toward each other and yipped and yapped in packs of twos, threes, fours, and more. SB recognized many. Some appeared too involved in conversation to notice her. Others nodded. Some made small talk.

Rocky Russo, the weathered horsewoman who boarded SB's mare, grabbed her elbow from an aisle seat and said, "I want you to meet a new woman in town, Merle Byrne. She boards with me, too."

"Hello again," Merle said shyly from her seat beside Rocky.

SB made a face that probably looked more standoffish than she intended. "What kind of horse?"

"Buckskin gelding," Merle answered. "You?"

"Sorrel mare."

In SB's peripheral vision, Cherise LeDoux closed in, holding a sheaf of papers. The thirty-something, always carefully put together communications director for the mining company, BeneGeo, showed plenty of form in a skin-tight pantsuit with three-quarter-length legs and sleeves. SB didn't get why adults in the twenty-first century wanted to dress like Pee-wee Herman in 1985, but her flight into judgment was interrupted when someone grabbed her from behind. She felt herself pulled into a bear hug and nearly toppled backwards into a familiar-scented cloud of Canadian Club and rosemary shampoo.

Alberta Desjardin's voice rasped like a saxophone in SB's ear, "My favorite daughter-in-law!"

SB really had no choice but to relax and go with whatever Alberta had in mind. An escape attempt most likely would have upended both of them and shown a disgraceful lack of consideration for her elder.

"Berta," SB said, "when did you get home?" The affection in her voice was both genuine and strained with embarrassment.

Alberta held fast and rocked SB from side to side. "Late last night or I would have called you."

"You should have called anyway," SB said. "You can call me any time."

"And I have sometimes, too, you might remember," Alberta said, loosening her grip. "I figured I'd see you tonight."

Set loose, SB turned and took in her mother-in-law's face—the brown eyes, alert and glowing with enjoyment of a good tease, the long, balanced curve of her cheeks against the striking arc of her dark hairline. It was a compelling face, a face to be admired and reckoned with, a face very much like Ramona's.

The thought brought SB a momentary tug of grief, but she pulled herself back to the present moment and asked in a voice as cheerful as she could muster, "How are you? Is everything okay?"

"Oh, hell yes," Alberta said. "And you and the kids?"

"Good," SB said. "Arte has landed well, I think. The farm seems to be working out. And Skye—what can I say? He checks in once in a while."

"Young man in his prime," Alberta chuckled. "Last thing he wants is Mom and Grandma, right? You and I should get together and download one of these days. Tonight, I've got the grandmothers here—or more like we've got each other."

Alberta glanced to the side, and SB followed the direction of her gaze. The elders clumped together there along the far aisle, talking and looking around in their hand-sewn, appliquéd vests that served as both banners and uniforms. In their handiwork she caught bright images of animals, kids, sky, and water.

"What are you ookomisan planning for us tonight?" SB asked about the grandmothers.

"Your pronunciation still stinks," Alberta laughed. "I suppose you want me to give up our element of surprise to the press, huh?"

"Why not?" SB shot back. She reached into her shoulder bag, pulled out a notebook, and pretended to get ready to write. "Let's see," she said. "The grannies say there'll be a surprise. What is it, Alberta? When, where, why, and how?"

"Let's just say you'll have to wait and watch it unfold," Alberta winked. "I gotta go join my warrior women. That's ogichidaakweg if you want to try to learn it."

Into the spot vacated by Alberta, Cherise LeDoux sidled closer and flashed SB an inquisitive expression.

"Family," SB shrugged.

"We've all got them," Cherise replied with what sounded like genuine empathy.

SB had known dozens—maybe hundreds—of PR directors, but she didn't know this one well. Cherise had only arrived in the last year to help BeneGeo push the new mine through—at least that's the assumption SB had made based on the timing.

"I've got a few fact sheets and documents for you," Cherise offered in a chipper voice. "We could go over them after the meeting if you have time."

"Better give them to me now," SB said. "This could go long."

Cherise didn't offer the documents that easily. She said, "I thought you might have questions."

"I'll call you if I do," SB said, trying to leave no wiggle room.

"I guess that works," Cherise told her before handing over the papers.

Up front, TV crews from Duluth had set up lights. On the grandmothers' side of the room, two somber-looking, dark-suited strangers stood together with their arms crossed over their chests. The slighter one wore mirrored glasses, and the beefier one raked the crowd with hard, narrow eyes. SB thought she could make out the bulges of concealed weapons under their jackets. They worked security for BeneGeo, or she missed her guess.

On the other side of the room, she noticed the reassuring bulk of Sheriff Walker Hayes, at ease in his khaki and tan uniform. He chatted with two blue-outfitted, city police officers, his pistol, baton, and Taser clearly visible on his belt.

From the podium, Gwen caught SB's eye and directed her with a tip of the head to a chair in the first row. SB pulled off the sign that read, "RESERVED FOR UNION VOICE." She sat and jotted down the names of groups whose presence she had noted. Clean Water Now, Indigenous Lives Matter, Iron Miners Union, Resort Owners for Wildlife, Save Our World, Mining Forever, Hunters for Wilderness. The Warrior Grandmothers stood in a loose huddle around Alberta, whose back, by then, was turned to SB. She saw, on her mother-in-law's vest, a cut-and-stitched circle of humans holding hands, three grownups and two children. They stood on the back of a giant turtle.

A gust of breath rattled the sound system, and Gwen's voice boomed, "Testing! Testing! Can you hear me in the back?"

Someone yelled, "You're good, Gwen!"

"I know I'm good," Gwen cracked Mae West style, "but am I loud enough?"

The crowd twittered and hooted, encouraging her to give more lip.

A red-cheeked man took the seat beside SB. She knew him by appearance and reputation, but mostly through his writing. She had published Chase Monahan's work many times—letters mainly, treatises submitted online in defense of water and wilderness. When they first met in person, she remembered, he looked exactly as she expected, with intense, electric blue eyes and wild, auburn hair that had recently grayed to a distinguished-looking strawberry roan. She nodded to him as she felt in her bag for her digital recorder.

BeneGeo's sleekly coiffed CEO, Holton Skibo, sauntered into the room through a side door. He climbed the three steps to the stage, followed by the rickety Commissioner Karlsrud. They took seats at the speakers' table, near Latelle Washington and a bland-looking younger man wearing a gray cardigan sweater and an open-collared shirt. The dark-suited security men worked their way forward and took positions by the corner of the stage. The local law enforcement officers separated into three different sections of the room. SB sketched the layout and labeled the positions of the various players.

She switched on the recorder as Latelle took the podium and gave a booming, "Welcome, everyone!" When the room quieted, Latelle continued, "I want to remind you how it's going to work tonight. First, we'll hear from our speakers. After that we'll have comments and questions. If you want to speak, you need to sign up over there with Gwen, and most importantly, please remember that we are considering difficult decisions about a future that we will all share. Remember we are in this together. Let's treat each other with respect."

SB took notes. A bad microphone wire had once cost her a front-page story, and she never forgot the lesson. She wrote:

> *L calm. HOW? Voice clear, plain, even. "We are near the end of a long study process . . . Safety Commission must perform our mandated twin role to promote mining and protect the environment."*
> *Moans. Someone yells, "That's an impossible contradiction!"*
> *Someone else: "Mining Forever!" Clapping. Booing.*
> *Shouts: "Save our water!" "Get real!"*
> *Sweat on L's brow?*

Latelle broke through the noise with a deep and sonorous voice. "Please remember, people . . . everyone . . . You will get your chance to speak if you sign up over there with Gwen. In the meantime, keep in mind that, whether we like it or not, the legislature mandated a twin role when they created the MESC. By law we must support mineral exploration, research, development, and production as well as looking after the environment. Now we find ourselves at the end of a long study. We have followed a mandated research process, and we are hearing from many voices. Your comments and questions tonight will become part of the evidence we've gathered. If you take your turn and speak when called on, you will be heard."

Groans of suspicion rose and dwindled. Monahan's leg began to twitch. Containing all that sturm und drang must be one hell of a challenge, SB thought. And as Latelle was introducing Casper Karlsrud, SB snapped a burst of images.

In range of the microphone, the commissioner cleared his throat and croaked a hoarse, "Hello." His voice clarified some as he went on. "I sure am proud to be here tonight, and on behalf of the county commissioners, I want to tell you how excited we are to start cutting through all that red tape to clear the way for BeneGeo, its hard-working CEO Holton Skibo over there, and you miners."

Wild cheering and applause interrupted him. Karlsrud grinned and stretched out a hand to direct the audience's attention to the CEO whose fine suit jacket traced the lines of his torso so perfectly that SB thought it surely had been custom tailored.

"Look at Holton Skibo over there," Karslrud told the crowd. "Doesn't he look sharp? Well, he's more than that, too. He's a good man and a real leader, and BeneGeo is a great American company. You've followed their history here. You know they were founded here. They're headquartered here. They buy and spend here. They pay their taxes here, and guess where their workers are going to live and spend their wages once they get the mine going?"

"HERE!" voices answered from seemingly all parts of the room.

"That's right!" Karlsrud said, looking gratified that he'd managed to spark a call and response from his typically tight-lipped constituents. He went on, "Between the workers and the company, they're going to bring millions and billions into our local economy, so whatever they need, we're going to make sure they get it. Isn't that right?"

Some in the crowd cheered. A few grumbled. SB noticed a lot of shifting in the seats. She gathered that most people weren't ready to breach the barricade of cool, rigid restraint, but they were thinking about it.

Karlsrud gestured toward the CEO again. "Just say the word, Mr. Skibo! We trust you, and we trust BeneGeo. You've studied this whole thing to the nines. I've read your plans, and I can't find a single fault with any of it. We're going to clear the way!"

"Give 'em hell, Casper!" a lone voice cried from the union crowd.

And then a high, thin waver from one of the Warrior Grandmothers, "What about the water? What about all those heavy metals?"

"I hear a little noise out there," Karlsrud said, sounding dismissive and insincerely sweet. "Let me tell you, BeneGeo has consulted the best experts anywhere. The last thing they want to do is hurt the water. That's all taken care of in the plan."

"Disgraceful," Monahan hissed to no one in particular. "They've showed us no plan."

Shouts of protest rose and were drowned out by a chant of "Mining Forever." The din brought Latelle Washington back to the microphone, banging the lectern for order.

She introduced the ESC's environmental compliance officer next. SB didn't catch the young man's name and resigned herself to picking it up later from the tape. He swallowed, hesitated, and generally looked uncomfortable. Then he summarized, weighed, and qualified until SB lost the thread and only snapped back to attention when he started talking about a new method of storing the waste. He described folding the tailings into a mineral mix, stacking the mix on a waterproof liner, and topping the pile with dirt and plants. She made some notes.

The young man concluded, "Mix and Separate shows promise in addressing environmental concerns, but of course there's more testing to be done." After that, he looked hugely relieved and sat down.

Holton Skibo brought a cool kind of swagger to the podium. He struck SB as a man who was used to being heard, taken seriously, and accommodated. She had grown up with men like him, and based on watching her father and grandfather operate, she surmised that Skibo believed himself clever and connected enough to find a way through any setback without losing status, face, or money. In other words, he was a white man securely launched from a family with resources.

"Thank you, Commissioner Karlsrud," Skibo began. "I'm proud to be here tonight to speak for BeneGeo."

A few in the crowd hissed and grumbled, but once again the mining crowd drowned them out.

"As most of you know," Skibo went on, "we are based right here in America."

"Did NOT say local," SB noted on her pad.

"What we do at BeneGeo," Skibo continued in an assured and mellow flow, "is explore and mine for minerals to meet America's needs. We're the future. We keep the tech boom growing and create jobs for American workers. We understand your concerns about safety, and we only want the best for you and your families because we understand what you're facing. We're raising families, too. We want prosperity and safety for Red Stone County, for America, and for the environment."

The cheers started up again, and Skibo raised a downward facing hand to quiet them. "I know that some of you worry about mining waste," he went on, "and let's be honest. We have to admit that, in the past, in some countries overseas with political corruption and poor regulatory structures, some copper-nickel mining operations have done more damage than they should have been allowed to do, but we're going to do it right here. Our new mine will be the safest copper-nickel mine in the world."

"That's a pretty low bar, since they've all leached poisons," Chase muttered.

"We're ready to mine," Skibo told the crowd. "We have capital in place. We have tech companies lined up, competing to sign contracts with us right now. We want to start hiring. We want to start mining. We just need to get our permit approved."

"Screw the government! Get it going!" a gruff-voiced man yelled from the back of the room.

The dissonance and caterwauling erupted again. SB turned and saw the man on his feet, pumping a fist in the air. She thought she recognized him. The name took a few seconds to float up in her memory—Kent Nowak, if she remembered right, a coarse-boned, scruffy-haired miner who showed up fairly often in the court records section of the *Voice*. She wondered how many other miners in the room hoped that people didn't assume Nowak spoke for them.

Latelle was on her feet again, drowning out the noise with the help of the sound system. "People," she thundered, "we must have order! We'll hear from all of you if you sign up to speak. Now let's quiet down so the public comment section can begin."

She called on Arno Toivola, president of the Iron Miners local. SB knew him from childhood. He had grown into a tall and affable man with a gangly, ropy-muscled body that had never quite filled out to match his broad shoulders.

He said, "You all know how important mining has been to Iron since day one. Like a lot of you, me and my family go back more than a hundred years, to the lockouts, strikes, and head-bangings when the companies fought our unions toe-to-toe. We were here when the ore ran heavy, and we stayed after the good ore ran out. We've got taconite now, but we know that's not going to last forever, either. We just want to keep a roof over our heads and make a future for our kids, and BeneGeo's got a plan for that. Nobody wants to spoil the water. Let's give 'em a chance."

A parade of union members followed, and then Jason Bjornstad, a blond and sun-browned resort owner, got up and said, "Really? Come on, Guys. We run a family business here. My wife and kids and I work just as hard as you all do. We put money into the local economy like you, and we can't do that without clean water, healthy fish, and woods. Those are the reasons people come up here. Without the tourists, we'll go broke, and the money we bring to town will dry up and disappear."

After Bjornstad finished, Latelle called for Marilyn Bednar. A middle school teacher with a serious set to her jaw and a heavy frame both fore and aft, she drafted through the crowd with the bearing of an ore boat under load on Lake Superior.

"The resort owners are like selfish children," she began. Whether her explicit insult was due to strategy or tone deafness, SB couldn't tell. She listened, fascinated, as Mrs. Bednar went on. "If they get their way it'll be at the expense of the rest of us. Think what mining could mean to the School Trust Lands fund. Ever heard of it?"

Bjornstad yelled from the floor, "Only about a thousand times—most of them from you, Marilyn!"

SB knew the history as well as anyone. After the U.S. government impounded the homelands of the Dakota and Ojibwe, Congress granted eight million acres to the new entity called the state of Minnesota to hold in trust forever, collecting user fees from mining and logging companies to fund the public schools. As so often happened in the government's dealings with the First Nations people, forever didn't prove all that long. Less than half the land remained in trust on the day of the meeting. Mrs. Bednar said she was talking about three-and-a-half million acres.

"BeneGeo will pay three billion dollars into the school trust over the life of their mine," she claimed. "Think what that could mean for our kids!"

SB made a note to check the figures.

A butt-numbing parade of environmentalists, public school students, parents, hunters, more miners, and more resort owners marched to the podium and talked. By the time Latelle called Chase Monahan to the microphone, SB's legs had fallen asleep.

Monahan leapt off his seat and began talking before he reached the podium. He projected his voice effectively without a microphone and with an ease that appeared to come from plenty of practice.

He pointed at Holton Skibo sitting behind the speakers' table and spoke in an accusing tone, "That CEO over there talks about the safest copper-nickel mine in the world."

SB noticed the suited-up BeneGeo men adjust their postures toward Monahan before he reached the podium.

Under the lights he switched to an earnest tone, "That's not really saying much, is it? Because there's never been a nonpolluting copper-nickel mine anywhere in the world. This kind of mining isn't like the iron mining we know, folks. I don't need to talk down to you. It's been widely reported. You already know these things if you've been following the issues."

SB heard grumblings from various parts of the room. Someone shouted, "Fake news! You lie!!"

Chase went on, "This is real, and it's not business as usual. The heavy metals that are going to leach from that mine waste are poisons. It's not *if* but *when*. That's the most important thing we need to remember. We're talking about lead, arsenic, and mercury. Neurotoxins. If we do this, we *will* poison our water. We *will* poison our fish, and we *will* poison our children's brains and nervous systems. That should be all we need to know since we love our children. Case closed. Right?"

He left it there, and a good-sized chunk of the crowd cheered wildly while another sizable portion tried to drown them out. Neither gave in until Latelle hurried back to the podium and banged again for order.

When she could be heard, she announced, "Alberta Desjardin is our last speaker."

Alberta and the grandmothers swept to the front before Chase had a chance to sit down. They intercepted him and wrapped him in a semi-circle open to the crowd.

"What is going on?" Latelle demanded from the speaker's table. "One at a time, Ladies! Where is Alberta Desjardin? That's who I called for."

"I'll speak from here," Alberta shouted. She had something like a blanket in her arms that she was unfolding.

"Speakers must come to the podium," Latelle insisted.

"This quilt represents how we're all connected," Alberta continued as SB shot a photo and one of the grandmothers held up the quilt to give the crowd a look at rich colors and a border of vines and flowers—a traditional Anishinaabe beading design reinterpreted in fabric. Inside the border, SB saw a circle enclosing a mini universe of sky, earth, water, green plants, wild animals, and children.

Alberta said, "We're not separate. Whatever happens to one of us happens to the rest of us, and we thank you, Chase, because you reminded us of that tonight." She arranged the quilt around his shoulders like a cloak, adding, "Your words are strong and clear. We honor and encourage you. What happens to the water happens to all of us."

From behind, Nowak groused, "Oh, for god's sake! Who cares what you old bats think? Shut up and fly back to the Res!"

The crowd grumbled, and someone shouted, "Sit down, Nowak! Blow it out your sloppy hole!"

Latelle announced with frowning finality, "This meeting is adjourned. If anyone has further comments, you can submit them electronically on our website."

SB took her time. Outdoors, the night air had turned chill, and a half dozen union men stood around the library entrance chatting. Only a few parked cars remained. Halfway home, she looked around and found herself alone on the street in the faint light cast by a quarter moon and a few widely spaced streetlamps. In the quiet, she heard a car engine grow gradually louder from behind. When the driver slowed and pulled beside her, she felt a rush of adrenaline before the passenger window came down and she made out the auburn curls and piercing eyes of Chase Monahan, leaning across the seat.

"You run a smart little paper," he said.

She stood staring, too annoyed to respond.

"Did I scare you?" he asked. "I didn't mean to. I admire your guts. It's just that I had something to tell you that I couldn't say in there."

She waited for him to go on, letting her silence add to the evening's chill.

"Sorry," he said. "I wondered if you'd heard about the missing water scientist."

She thought fast what to say. "I've heard some rumblings. No specifics. No name."

"Cheryl Solem," he told her. "She's a PhD hydrologist who lives off the grid in Moose Horn Township. You know that unincorporated village up north that never got power lines run out to it because the houses fell between the service areas of two electric co-ops?"

"I've heard of it," she said.

"Bunch of old hippies, environmentalists, and sustainable growers," he told her. "Friends up there tell me that Dr. Solem's been working under contract with the Forest Service and MESC. She's supposed to evaluate this BeneGeo tailings disposal plan, and she's dropped out of sight. They don't know what's happened to her."

"Have they talked to Sheriff Hayes?"

"They have," Chase answered, "but he didn't take them seriously. He told them adults have a right to go missing once in a while. He said she probably just went on a little get-away or is having a fling of some kind."

"Well, that sounds fairly reasonable," SB said. "Walker's a decent man. He knows the law."

"Maybe so," Chase told her. "But her friends say she was expecting some test results from a researcher up in Ontario, and she was all about getting that data. She expected it might change everything. She wouldn't have left before it arrived."

SB didn't know how much to trust Chase. His story sounded sketchy enough that she could follow it a long time and come up empty. Then again, it could turn out to be the story of her lifetime.

She said, "I guess I could talk to Sheriff Hayes."

"Good," he said, "but whatever you do, watch your back. We're playing against some big boys here—some really big boys."

"We always are," she told him.

4. DEADLINE DAY

FRIDAYS ALWAYS CALLED for a stern spirit and plenty of caffeine. SB and Gwen needed to finish all of the writing and editing and lay out the week's copy online in the columns Dave Maki had left for them to fill around the ads. SB added an extra scoop of dark roast to the coffeepot's basket before she sat down to put her to-do list on paper.

The definite first item was to call Walker Hayes and set up a face-to-face. She needed to get to the bottom of the missing scientist thing—if it was a thing. She had to plan how she could put it to Walker in a way that would leave it hard for him to stonewall her the way Chase claimed Walker had done to Cheryl Solem's neighbors.

She found the Sheriff's private line in her contacts, touched the listing, and reached his recording. Disappointed, she disconnected without leaving a message and selected the public line. A dispatcher answered.

SB recognized the voice and said, "Morning, Jill. Is Walker in?"

"Hi there, SB," the dispatcher replied cheerfully. "He's out 'til afternoon. Can somebody else help you?"

"Thanks, but probably not this time."

Such familiarity didn't stretch SB's sense of professional boundaries at all. She liked to keep business conversations as casual and personal as possible. She didn't like to appear too concerned with her own importance. She got more information that way.

She asked, "When do you expect him back?"

"Two-ish. Maybe later. He's in Duluth for a meeting."

"Much appreciated," SB acknowledged.

"Glad to help," Jill responded.

And then the coffee pot had filled enough that SB could pour herself a cup of the strongest, earliest brew. The first sip hit her taste buds with such a satisfying bitterness that she let it slosh around on the back of her tongue awhile before swallowing. Braced by the promise of caffeine, she fetched her notes from the shoulder bag left lying collapsed on her desk and started reading. Once she'd downed a few more swallows and felt a growing buzz, she puzzled over where to start.

A description of the scene at the library maybe? Contending voices from the crowd? Holton Skibo's claim that BeneGeo had discovered a way to mine sulfide rock in wet country without polluting the watershed? The BeneGeo angle opened the door to the rest of the story more effectively than the others, she thought. It raised questions and begged for evidence and explanation. She could see herself fitting the pieces together from there, so she got started.

Gwen came in wearing a light wool jacket, her hair electrically charged and standing in unruly clumps. She brought to mind some rogue, inscrutable genius.

"Am I interrupting?" she asked.

"As if you could," SB answered, suppressing a grin.

Gwen smoothed her hair with her hands and chirped in a purposefully comic way, "I thought I'd show up and try and get some work done."

"A worthy goal," SB replied, just then realizing—thanks to the diversion of Gwen's arrival—that she had let herself get too far past due for a muscle stretch and a second cup of coffee.

"I need to move," she complained. "Can I get you a cuppa?"

"I don't know," Gwen said. "Did you make it your usual strength?"

"What do you think?"

"Got white stuff?"

"Yes."

"Then I'll take a chance on half a cup with cream."

"Done," SB said. When she returned with two mugs in hand, she asked, "Can I run some thoughts by you?"

Gwen gave her a quizzical look.

"About last night," SB clarified.

"Oh, goody," Gwen said. "That's what I was hoping!"

"Casper Karlsrud really did show himself to be a major tool for BeneGeo, didn't he?" SB asked. "Or was I the only one who got that impression?"

Gwen shook her head. "That old hustler was right in there pitching. I just don't get his lack of concern for the possible consequences. He's got kids and grandkids. It's hard to believe he's not getting paid off by someone."

SB nodded. "My dad always thought so, but he never could get enough proof to go to press with a story. That would be a gratifying one to write if it ever happened."

"You know what they say in the mystic circles," Gwen said. "Before you manifest it, you have to imagine it."

"Watch out," SB told her. "You're starting to sound like my mom."

"Ah, Nikki," Gwen said affectionately, "or I should say Artemisia? She stood out around here in a way that I think we needed."

SB let it lay there, and Gwen followed suit. They both knew that SB still had a lot to work out about her mom.

In chronological age, Gwen fell between SB and Artemisia, whose parents had named her Nikki Makinen. SB and Gwen had been young together, even though SB hadn't realized it at the time. Gwen was a twenty-something rookie reference librarian when SB came to the city library looking for help with her middle school research projects. In SB's eyes, Gwen looked like an experienced and sophisticated older woman. SB assumed Gwen only cared about her out of charity and some sense of duty to fulfill the terms of her job. Looking back, SB realized that the difference in their ages mattered less and less, and sometimes she even admitted to herself that Gwen may have seen some sparks of promise in SB's character and work. Still, she continued to see Gwen as wiser and more accomplished.

"You've followed the local water studies pretty closely, haven't you?" SB asked.

Gwen replied with a drawn-out and inquisitive, "Yes?"

"Do you know any of the researchers?"

"I've met a few of them here and there. At meetings mostly," Gwen answered.

"Does the name Cheryl Solem ring any bells?"

"Sounds a little familiar," Gwen said. "Why do you ask?"

"Apparently she's a hydrologist who worked on the Forest Service study of the BeneGeo waste storage plan, and she lives near here," SB told her. "I've talked to people who think something might have happened to her. They say some of her friends and co-workers haven't heard from her in a while. They think she's disappeared."

"Who thinks that?" Gwen asked.

"Chase Monahan for one, and, off the record, Latelle Washington told me that something seems wrong with one of the researchers on the study. She wouldn't say more. She'll deny the whole thing if asked."

"I'll bet she would," Gwen said. "So, you put one and one together and got two. What does Walker say about it?"

"Nothing so far. I haven't been able to reach him yet. Chase just gave me Cheryl's name last night after the meeting. He says Walker blew off the neighbors and wouldn't take a missing persons report. He trailed me with his car in the dark and crept up slowly. A little too noir for my taste."

"Of course it was," Gwen said. "He's a complicated one. So intense! I can't decide if he reminds me of some Cecil B. DeMille version of an Old Testament prophet or Ted Kaczynski. There's so little difference in some ways. Alberta seems to like him, though, doesn't she?"

"I don't know," SB said. "I suppose he served her purposes last night. My guess is she came with a plan to honor the person who put up the best fight for clean water. I'm sure she admires Chase well enough on some levels, but it's got to rankle her that he's a privileged white guy who wants to save the world that privileged white guys appropriated from her people in the first place."

"I imagine Chase thinks he voluntarily gave up his privilege when he moved to the woods and learned to get by on a shoestring," Gwen said.

"As if," SB said. "The man definitely has a gift for words, though." She had published a few of his essays and all of the letters he'd submitted to the *Voice*. Dozens of them.

"He's also a man of action," Gwen said. "That group he started keeps getting bigger."

"Did you sign on?" SB asked.

Gwen scrunched her face dismissively. "Just to keep an eye on the followers."

"By Any Means makes a nice allusion," SB said, "and BAM's the best acronym I've heard in a long time."

"So the guy's been to college," Gwen replied. "Maybe BAM isn't the most calming message to send from either side at this particular time."

"You might be right," SB allowed, but as far as she could tell Monahan's people acted like reasonable grownups. They did their homework and showed up when it counted. The only explosions they'd caused so far were the kind that snapped between people's synapses.

She asked, "Do you really think he might be dangerous?"

Gwen shrugged. "He means well, I think, but I get the feeling he bears a little watching. Probably no more than those BeneGeo goons or Casper Karlsrud or Kent Nowak—or blooming Marilyn Bednar for that matter—or a whole lot of other self-appointed know-it-alls I could name around here."

"I'm not sure if that's supposed to make me feel better or worse," SB told her.

"Well, if you need me to weigh in on that, you're in trouble." Gwen stated unequivocally, and then her face drooped into a look of concern as though she might have suddenly tumbled to the idea that SB could be papering over a lot of anxiety.

"Bednar caused you and Ramona a lot of trouble, didn't she?"

"You could say that," SB said. "She shot her mouth off to anyone who'd listen, claiming that we were abusing our kids by being open lesbian mothers. Oh, and by the way, asking who the fathers were, and didn't something seem awfully questionable about the adoptions and the joint parenting?"

"I know I don't have to tell you how wrong that was," Gwen said, "or that you've chosen a tough profession."

"I know it comes with the territory," SB told her.

"How about now? Are you doing okay?"

"Mostly," SB lied. "I'm not losing any sleep."

"Aren't you?" Gwen asked.

"No," SB said, unsure why she felt the need to sidestep Gwen's empathy.

Part of it was that SB hadn't exactly chosen her profession. She had come to grips with her inheritance. She might have made different decisions at certain points if she hadn't been born into so much luck and whiteness. Her great-grandparents came through Ellis Island at the tail end of the lumber boom when loggers had just about obliterated the supposedly inexhaustible white pine forest and loads of high-grade iron ore started replacing wood in the freight trains heading east. The Ellingsons had managed to bring a small family nest egg, and they used it to buy the nearly bankrupt *Union Voice* from the Finnish unionists who had run afoul of the iron and steel interests by working with the Wobblies to organize miners and oppose the First World War. History was on the Ellingsons' side. The demand for arms spiked steel prices, and the spin-off prosperity brought new readers to town and spurred the Ellingsons' advertising revenue. During the depression, her grandparents bought Florida real estate, and steel boomed again during the Second World War. SB understood why some people might see her professional position as a gift of fortune, an unearned advantage.

She saw it that way herself, but also saw it as an accident of birth, a burden that she really didn't have the courage to lay down. She felt grateful for the work of asking questions, parsing through answers, and putting words together to convey what she'd learned. She knew better than most how much flak came with the territory, even though she acknowledged that her work was fair game and subject to potshots. She would always be one reader's truth-teller and another's enemy of the people, and she'd learned to toughen her skin and put up with a running commentary of outside judgment that never stopped. She got through it by hanging onto the idea that words couldn't hurt her if she didn't let them. She'd be fine as long as her critics stopped short of using sticks and stones. Unfortunately, such restraint had started to seem less and less a sure thing.

"What about BeneGeo?" she asked Gwen. "Do you think this new drying process they claim to have developed could really work?"

"I would say doubtful," Gwen answered. "I can look into it some more."

"That would be great," SB said. "Find out who the experts are. Call a few of them, and try to get some comments. Check for anything you can find on Cheryl Solem while you're at it, and look into Chase Monahan, too, will you? I'll stand the expense of background checks. You know the drill."

"I do, indeed, Boss."

"Ha!"

A ding alerted SB to her email. She had ignored a number of electronic summonses all morning, but this time she sighed and said reluctantly, "Sounds like I'd better give some attention to my devices."

"Me, too," Gwen said. She slid her chair back to her desk and switched on her computer, and they both fell into silent work.

Of the sixty-four emails in SB's inbox, one caught her attention. According to the time stamp, Latelle Washington had sent it at 5:13 a.m. SB pictured the outreach director in her budget motel room on the U.S. Highway bypass, sleepless after moderating the contentious meeting, drinking bad coffee, and catching up on correspondence.

She had written:

Thank you in advance for your usual careful and thorough coverage, SB. If you need more information or if I can answer any questions, please feel free to contact me. I know I can always rely on your accuracy and discretion.

SB replied:

Thank you for your follow-up, Latelle. A few questions do occur to me. For instance, what more can you tell us about the MESC's "twin role"? In practical terms, how do you balance the interests of mining against the need to protect the environment? In the end, what do you think the balance will look like in this case? Will the agency be asking for more details about BeneGeo's planned new method for handling mining waste? Will you look for a way to continue the cancelled environmental study on your own, or will you accept its cancellation?

"Let's see how she manages to wiggle around that!" SB said to Gwen.

Gwen looked blank, and SB waved her off, saying, "Sorry. Talking to myself. Only sixty-three emails to go."

5. ARCHAIC MESSAGES

DAVE MAKI, A WHITE-HAIRED, self-identified "proud Finlander" with a trim comb-over and a build that resembled a fire hydrant, walked in the back door carrying a tabloid-sized newspaper.

He went directly to SB's desk and, with a sweeping gesture, laid an unfolded copy in front of her, crowing in a good-humored way, "Behold the mock-up of the summer tourism edition!"

Beneath a full-color photo of the Minnesota governor and his grandkids mugging in a boat during last year's fishing opener, the banner splashed in all caps:

RANGE SUMMER FUN EDITION

"Looks great!" SB said, feeling the heft and smiling at her advertising manager. "From the feel of it you've kept us afloat for another year, Dave."

"Glad to do it," he said proudly. "It's my livelihood, too, you know."

The stories inside the tourism edition featured hiking trails, art festivals, and summer activities across the Range, but they mostly just provided filler linked to the ad copy that paid the bills. Dave had done his job. He'd hit up businesses in every little town and gathering spot in the area, and he'd brought back advertisements for lodging, real estate, wilderness guides, concerts, and whatever else the locals wanted to showcase to their summer visitors. From May to October the travelers crowded in from all over, looking, as SB saw it, for whatever cachet they could still find of the great boreal wilderness—even as it succumbed before their eyes to overuse, climate stress, invasive insects, and fires. Merle Byrne's black-and-white photo, her gingery hair and the tiny gap between her top incisors reduced to surprisingly similar shades of charcoal gray, appeared on page twelve, along with a story that emphasized her exodus from urban humdrum to a little piece of northern paradise. SB felt pretty sure it would attract the attention of twenty-first century wilderness seekers who wouldn't want to burn too much gas traveling to get a good rubdown.

Her phone dinged, and when she looked at her screen she laughed aloud.

"What?" Gwen said, cranking her neck with curiosity.

"My daughter sent an email," SB answered.

"Arte? I thought she claimed she'd never use such an archaic platform."

"She swore she'd be embarrassed to do it. As you know, my daughter has been dissing my technological backwardness since she was in middle school."

"Maybe she's maturing."

"I hope so, and I hope that's all."

Arte wrote:

What's up? Kinda quiet here. Rainy. So there's time to email. We'd like to get the legumes in the ground, but it's too wet right now. Noah and Ashley are worried the beans will mildew. (The dry beans are the seeds. Did you know that?) Anyway, Noah says we'll definitely treat them with an organic fungicide before planting. Ashley says we should just wait for the waxing moon. She says the sun will come out by then, and the soil will warm up, and the beans will sprout before they have time to molder. Noah puts on his Man of Logic voice, "We'll have to rely on soil science." But I think they'll probably end up doing both since Ashley is pretty strong willed and says she inherited a Kabbalistic soul from her grandmother. Does that mean I have a Dianic Wiccan soul thanks to Artemisia or a spirit-filled soul thanks to Alberta? lol! Don't worry. There's no evidence of either so far. Know what, though? I'm considering a visit home once we get the crops planted. Would your prodigal daughter be welcome for a few days? I can bring the best pork you've ever eaten and some early greens from the tube shelter if we're lucky.

That last sentence delighted SB. She imagined how satisfied Arte must have felt to find herself in a position to make such an adult offer. Her daughter had gone into a deep psychological dip after her first post-college job went belly up. She'd managed to land a position teaching English as a Second Language to migrants and refugees in San Diego. She'd felt so lucky about it and so excited, and then the whole project fell through in the uproar over closing the border and rounding up her potential students for deportation. After the bad luck, Arte brooded, questioned herself, squeaked by on part-time gigs, and looked a long time before she found the paid internship at Hog Heaven Farm. The growers who employed her, Noah and Ashley Sunberry, operated a community-supported, organic pork and vegetable operation in the hills around Madison, Wisconsin.

Of course, SB had run a full background check on both of them. In the photos on their website, she saw a couple of early-end Millennials, just enough older than Arte to show signs of the early wear and sun exposure that crinkle the smooth skin around the corners of the eyes and mouth. Noah's tall and rawboned build contrasted with Ashley's smooth-shouldered plumpness. Together they embodied what looked like a comfortable counterbalance. They stood embracing side-by-side in a robust field of greens and in the hog barn surrounded by pink, smiling, pig faces pressed between the boards of pens. In the farmyard they posed with a child who looked to be about two years old. Boy or girl SB couldn't tell, but the kid's robust and contented look gave her the impression that the Sunberrys were doing a good job parenting. Their background checks revealed a late payment to a veterinarian and another to a feed store, but nothing that looked nefarious. She thought she could trust them with Arte. And now the email arrived.

SB answered right away:

You're welcome here any time, kiddo. You know that's unconditional and always will be, right? Just let me know when. And if you need any help with travel money . . . well, I get that you're probably doing just fine on your own, but you know . . . I'm mentioning it just in case I can help. Lil sends wags. Me, too!

At the end, she allowed herself a double heart icon despite the fact that she didn't want either of her children to know how much she missed them and longed for their company. After a certain age, ardent mother love was pretty much a universal turnoff, and she was determined to avoid it.

Gwen broke the silence to say, "I'm meeting Chuck for lunch at one. Can I bring you something, or would you like to join us?"

"Oh, that might have been fun," SB offered distractedly. "Just say hi for me, though, will you? I think I'd better grab something here."

She found Gwen's husband good-enough company. He was fine to look at—silver-haired, tall, and as angular as a long-distance runner. A retired high school principal, he had plenty of brain cells at his disposal, but he devoted an awful lot of them to subjects that didn't interest her much.

"Too bad," Gwen said. "I was hoping you'd help me steer the conversation away from his golf game this morning and the Twins' standing in the American League Central."

"You're on your own with that," SB said. "If I came, all I'd want to talk about would be mining waste and multinational corporations."

"I guess it's all for the best then," Gwen said with that familiar ironic grin.

SB shared a cold sandwich with Lil, then locked up the office and let the dog take her on a quick walk. She was back at her desk, scrolling through photos from the previous evening's meeting when Cherise LeDoux popped in. SB got up and met her at the counter.

The PR director smiled winningly. Her sleek, blond hair gleamed under the fluorescent lights. She said, "I brought you the information I promised you last night."

"Oh. What do we have here?" SB said, looking over the sheaf of papers.

They appeared much the same as the night before, only this time some of the pages had tabs with labels on them.

Cherise launched into what she seemed to hope would be just a beginning, "To start from the top and work down, there's a news release covering what happened at last night's meeting . . ."

SB interrupted brusquely, "I'll take a look at it if you'll leave it."

"Overall, we thought it was a big success," Cherise declared with far more zeal than seemed necessary. "People had legitimate questions, and they got answers."

"I've got it all on tape," SB said. She kept her words spare and made sure to promise nothing. No one was going to tell her how to approach a story.

Cherise remained undeterred. "Don't you think Holton Skibo is impressive? Did you know he's a Minnesota boy educated at St. Olaf and the Carlson School of Management?"

"I think I read that when he was hired," SB said. "Local boy makes good, huh?"

"It might be a nice angle," Cherise suggested. "I really think he understands how Minnesota works. I tucked a copy of his resumé in here."

"I'll look at it," SB said. "Did you happen to tuck in anything about that new waste storage method he touted last night?"

"Oh, Mix and Separate?" Cherise said. She paged through the stack of papers. "I had a feeling you would ask about that. I brought a copy of the updated permit application we filed with the MESC. It's all public record, so I thought I'd save you the trouble of requesting it from the agency. It's a promising technique. I included an article about it from *Mining Today*, too."

"What sort of tests did you run?" SB asked. "Can you get me those?"

Cherise looked her in the eye and sounded genuinely sorry as she answered, "The details of our tests would be proprietary. I can tell you the results are looking very good, though. We expect quick approval."

"How quick?"

"You know, it's hard to say for sure. That's up to the agency."

"What with the Environmental Safety Commission's twin role and all? Do you expect that's going to help speed things up?"

"Well," Cherise said, "we do expect them to help us with technical expertise as well as verifying the safety of our plan, but don't quote me on that just yet."

Her gaze floated toward the wall, SB noticed, and fixed on a watercolor that Skye had painted for his high school senior project—images of a bee in a flower, a kaleidoscope of images actually—repeated and fractured and subtly varied. Skye had spent hours and hours applying wax and layers of paint in varying thicknesses to keep the edges distinct and deepen the colors. Cherise looked entranced.

"Who did that?" she asked.

"My son," SB said.

"He's good!" Cherise said. "Is this college work?"

"High school," SB said.

"He must be way ahead of his peers!" Cherise said with what seemed like genuine admiration. "He knows what's going on, doesn't he? He chose such a current subject. And look at the detail and color saturation! That's not easy to do with watercolor."

SB said, "I didn't know you were such an aficionado." She hoped she didn't sound too flabbergasted about discovering this surprising facet of Cherise.

"No, not at all," Cherise replied. "Not really. I'm just a dabbler."

"A pretty well informed one, it seems," SB allowed, feeling somewhat chastened for having written Cherise off as an intellectual lightweight.

When Cherise left, Dave Maki came over and said to SB, "Please don't take offense, but is there any chance you could fine tune your skepticism a little on this mining issue? The merchants and miners are going a little wonky on us. They're wondering whose side you're on and why they ought to give us their business."

"I'm surprised at you, Dave," SB said, "You know I don't look at it as being on anybody's side."

"I know," he said, "but that doesn't exactly convince everybody."

"What kind of flack are you getting?" she asked.

"A few of them are talking about withdrawing advertising," he said.

"How serious are they?"

"Remains to be seen," he shrugged. "Mostly bluster probably. So far so good."

"Keep telling them the truth," she said. "We're doing our job, digging up facts, covering all sides, and sharing what we learn."

"Will do," Dave said with a sigh. "If it's any help, I want you to know I'm behind you. It's just tricky when you're trying to sell a product that people aren't sure they need these days anyway, and then they take offense at what they read in it."

"I hear what you're saying," she assured him.

At two o'clock, she tried Walker Hayes' private line.

"Now's as good a time as any," he told her when she asked if she could see him.

Since Gwen wasn't back from lunch, SB put the closed sign on the door, got in her car, and drove uphill along Mesabi Street, roughly a mile to the county law enforcement complex.

"What can I do you for?" Walker asked when she entered his office. She'd known him since grade school and had watched him mature from an awkward boy, big for his age, into a thick muscled and capable man. He kept a lot inside, because of professional ethics and self-preservation, she guessed. She didn't like to push him beyond his comfort zone, but there were times when she got better information from him if she did. The difficulty lay in knowing when to use which approach. This time she decided to get to the point.

"I need to ask you what you know about a missing woman."

That got his attention. His eyebrows lifted with heightened interest, and she took it as an acknowledgement that he knew exactly what she was talking about. She decided to confront him with the facts as she'd heard them.

"Her name's Cheryl Solem. She's from Moose Horn."

Walker tried to pretend that he didn't know what she was talking about.

"Oh, that unincorporated village up north by the CN tracks?" he asked. "The place off the electrical grid?"

He leaned back in his chair and wrapped his meaty arms around his chest. In high school, he'd been curious and sharp, but he hadn't ever seemed to know what to do with his body. In late middle age, he'd grown into himself—an observant, composed, and by-the-book man.

"That would be Moose Horn all right," SB said. "That's the place."

"And what exactly makes you ask about this woman?" he said, adding unconvincingly, "Cheryl something?"

"People tell me about her," SB said. "I hear they tell you the same thing. Her neighbors tried to report her disappearance to you, and you wouldn't take their reports."

"Oh, for cripes sake," he griped, unfolding his arms. "I swear you can be so disagreeable sometimes, SB. If I say anything to you at all about this, it's off the record. Agreed?"

"I don't know," she said. "There must be something you can tell me for publication."

"About what again?" he said, putting on a sly grin. "I don't recall."

"Okay," she answered. "What the public records laws say is public information stays public. Anything else can be off the record."

"Off the record, I don't think there is a missing woman," he said. "I have no evidence to back up that idea."

"Didn't her friends ask you to file a missing persons report?"

"Yeah, but that doesn't mean it was the appropriate thing to do. They hadn't seen her in a day. That's all I know. She's an adult. She gets to go places without telling the neighbors."

"Did they say why they were concerned?" SB asked.

"Something about her work in research and mining, which doesn't quite add up to evidence of a crime or any kind of clear and present danger that

I can see. It's not like they're saying she had an abusive husband or a stalker of some kind."

"The neighbors didn't say anything more particular?"

"Not that I recall," he said with his lips pulled a little too nervously tight.

"Well, that's an evasive answer," she fired back. "Can you at least tell me who came in to talk to you?"

"I probably said too much already," he answered. "Why don't you just go back to your office and do your newspaper work, and I'll stay in my office and do my sheriff's work. There ought to be enough to keep us both busy and out of each other's hair."

"Well, I can't say I'll miss the company," she told him.

He pointed toward the exit.

Back at the office the 'Closed' sign was no longer on the door. Gwen sat at her desk behind her computer.

"I've got Cheryl Solem's address for you," she said. "It was easy enough to find, and she seems to be the real deal. She's got no criminal record, and when I cross-searched copper-nickel and mining waste, her name showed up as an author on all sorts of professional journal articles."

"Good," SB said. "I think I'll drive out to Moose Horn tomorrow and have a look around. I'll knock on a few doors and maybe talk to some neighbors."

"Well, there aren't many of them," Gwen said. "Half a dozen at most. By the way, I dug up some interesting dish on Chase."

"And?" SB said in a way that begged for elaboration.

"He tried to start an Aryan Nations group in high school and register it as a school club," Gwen said.

SB felt her eyes widen. "Seriously?" she asked. "Around here?"

"No," Gwen explained. "Out in Indiana where he grew up."

"Oh, former homeland of the KKK," SB remarked. "I suppose that makes a certain amount of sense. How did you find that out?"

"You know the web is full of gems if you're patient and curious enough to go deeper into the search results," Gwen answered. "It seems the principal told him absolutely not, and the whole thing would have never become public information except that Chase made a crusade of it. He took it to the school board as a free speech issue and acted as his own attorney. He told the whole story to the local newspaper. He was eighteen at the time, and they printed it."

"I have to admit I'm shocked," SB said. "I never would have pegged him as a white supremacist."

"It might have been just kid stuff," Gwen speculated, "trying to differentiate himself from his parents and spit in the face of the authorities, you know? Or maybe he was going along with some crowd that appealed to him at the moment. A phase. He could have done a one-eighty by now. True believers are noted for flip-flopping from one extreme to another."

"Maybe and maybe not," SB said sternly. "I don't know if people grow out of cruelty. Besides, you're the one who told me he bears watching."

"So he still does," Gwen said more casually than SB expected. "That hasn't changed."

Around seven SB quit proofreading and sent the file of Saturday's paper to the printer. The banner read:

Plenty of Voices at BeneGeo Info Session

Beneath, she'd arranged a montage of her photos from the meeting, with Alberta and the grandmothers front and center, caught at the moment they wrapped the quilt around Chase Monahan's shoulders. She put the press release from BeneGeo on page two, credited to Cherise LeDoux, alongside a short story introducing a local water scientist who worked internationally on the issue of copper-nickel mining waste. She thought mentioning Cheryl Solem's name in print might shake something loose somewhere.

6. A CHILLY SETBACK

ON SUNDAY MORNING SB woke with a chill. Her shoulders were uncovered, and when she tried to pull the blanket over them, she couldn't because Lil was nested on top. When SB tried to shove her over, she acted like dead weight, so SB burrowed deeper and wrapped herself in her own arms. She lay there awhile longer, trying to let herself float back to sleep.

After twenty minutes or so, she knew that she might as well get up. She went to the window, raised the blind to see what sort of day had dawned, and felt her mood plummet. It was the twenty-eighth of April, and a thin layer of snow covered the sidewalks and streets. Snow outlined the tops of the street signs, the electric wires, the lampposts, and the roofs and hoods of the parked cars along Mesabi Street. Downtown Iron sparkled like a made-for-TV Christmas movie set, which she would have found charming in early December. There was something about the early snows, but after five months of winter she could barely stand the sight of it.

She dawdled over morning coffee, and when she stood up and took her cup to the sink, Lil stretched and posed and rubbed against her pant legs until SB went to get the leash. She didn't want to go outdoors, but a dog deserved to have some agency in the world. Lil came in handy when SB needed a set of ears keener than her own and a fierce bark to back up her play, but the best thing about dogs was that they knew how to give themselves up to the moment—something SB hadn't managed to learn on her own.

Outdoors, the sky looked fierce and promising. The winds aloft were breaking the clouds apart and scattering their remnants. In the bright places on the sidewalk, the sun was already melting the snow. Lil set a course toward Kettle Lake, and SB followed, watching for spots that might prove slippery. On the path leading to the lake, robins and sparrows sang in the trees. Rabbits had left evidence of their overnight foraging, and Lil followed a trail of little pellets under a lattice of red osier dogwood.

Up ahead, SB spotted the commissioner and Algernon. She would have had time to take a spur trail toward the other side of downtown, but Lil had seen them, too, and pulled at the leash, yipping and making a show of anticipating her interaction with Casper.

As he and Algernon drew closer, Casper produced a treat with the usual fanfare, and once he had met up with SB and made Lil beg long enough to suit him, he said tartly, "I saw you at the meeting last Thursday."

"Hard to miss, huh?" SB answered. She meant to steer their interaction back to a lighter and friendlier place. Most of all, she hoped to keep it short.

He didn't read her signals or decided to blow right through them.

"I can't say I thought too highly of how you covered it," he complained. "What's with all the negativity about BeneGeo and the focus on the greenies and Indians? I never had to worry about the Ellingsons supporting this town's economic interests before."

"I don't know what you're talking about," she said. "I just report what's happening."

"Really?" he shot back. "Why does it look so obviously biased then?"

"I thought I conveyed what happened pretty accurately."

"By questioning BeneGeo's plans?"

"Questioning is part of what I do," she said. "I'm trying to get at the facts."

"The facts?" he said. "What about BeneGeo's facts? What about the miners' facts? What about that schoolteacher's facts? What about the fact that BeneGeo will pay billions in user fees to the state?"

"I'm trying to figure out what's true in all that," she said.

"True?" he said with a mocking chortle. "You always have been an idealist, Susie."

SB felt her hackles lift. No one called her Susie—or even Susan—anymore, except for her father and sometimes Alberta. And she hadn't thought of herself as an idealist since she didn't know when.

"Sorry you see it that way, Casper," she said. She planned to make a graceful segue toward parting, but he pre-empted.

"It's not just the way I see it," he said. "People around here are asking what happened to the *Union Voice*. The Ellingsons used to know what side their bread was buttered on until you and your so-called wife started running things." He ran a little short of air and gasped for a breath before he continued, "I'm telling you, Susie. You'd better hope that BeneGeo's plans sail through without a hitch because I would hate to see the people of this county blame you for spoiling their future prospects. And if you get your way, mark my words, their kids and grandkids will end up scattered to the four corners, and you're the one they'll hold responsible for it."

When he became too breathless to go on, she looked at him and countered, "And yet I have no political power." She thought about adding, "unlike you," but she could see from his open-mouthed glower that he had caught her meaning.

"You have the power of the pen!" he croaked. "And you'd better watch how you use it because hell's going to rain fire on you and your little snot-rag of a paper if you stand in the way of economic development on the Range!"

"Sounds like a threat," she said.

"A threat?" he asked, switching to that insincere, kindly sounding tone that SB found much creepier than his bluster. "I would never threaten you, Susie. That would be illegal. Let's just consider this a friendly warning. And now, if you'll excuse us, Algernon needs to get his old joints moving, and I've got better things to do than stand around and argue with a childish turncoat."

"Have a good day," SB said, matching his fake pleasantry as she tugged Lil's leash and whistled her into a sprint. She wanted to spark some endorphins and put a quick distance between her and the commissioner, even if hurrying away risked letting him know that he'd gotten to her at least a little.

Back home she called Gwen and downloaded what had happened. When she arrived at the climax, she told Gwen, "He says that if we don't say good things about BeneGeo, the pro-mining people are going to march on us with pitchforks and torches."

Gwen scoffed, "I wouldn't worry too much about that. It's more likely phones and selfie sticks these days, isn't it?"

"And they'll be posting videos of themselves denouncing us on our own website," SB replied.

"Right," Gwen said. "I think we can handle it."

7 ⋅ OFF GRID

O N MONDAY MORNING SB tapped Cheryl Solem's address into her
phone's GPS program. She also circled Cheryl's place on the paper
map in her county plat book just in case she ran out of cell coverage. Then
she loaded Lil into the back of her Subaru and set off for the mostly
unpopulated place identified on the map as the unincorporated village of
Moose Horn. On paper Moose Horn seemed like an inexplicable place
to put a village, but it had once been another train stop for the white
pine industry. SB kept a photo on her office wall of her great-grandfather
standing in a business suit beside some logger baron's stone house there.
Rumor had it that Sinclair Lewis got off the train at Moose Horn to
stretch his legs and decided to set a novel in a little boomtown modeled
after it. The village now consisted of the abandoned stone house and a
series of scattered homesteads lying generally north and east of Iron amid
thousands of acres of logged-over woods in various stages of second and
third growth.

In places the clear-cut woods had sprouted back thick and impassable
with volunteer poplar. Other stretches had been standing long enough to
transition from poplar to evergreens, maples, and birches. Their canopies
now blocked enough light to kill back some of the sun-loving brush and
partially open the forest floor. When the first loggers arrived around 1880,
SB had read, they found a carpet of pine needles and a canopy so dense it
completely blocked the sun. No one thought the massive forest could be
exhausted, but forty years later, the last load of white pine shipped from
the Iron Range town of Virginia. Nowadays the trees cut around Moose
Horn went mostly for paper and wood chips. The cabins, trailers, and
houses stood widely scattered and seemingly isolated.

At the railroad crossing where SB expected to find a sign announcing the town, she saw swamp-dwelling, raggedy black spruce stretching

to the horizon. She pulled over and tried to activate her maps program, but she had no cell signal. As best she could figure from the township map, Cheryl's driveway lay only a quarter mile ahead. SB drove on a little and found an opening with two dirt tracks marked with a fire number that corresponded to Cheryl's address. Up ahead the tracks curved and seemed to disappear, but she turned onto them anyway. Rounding the curve she saw the house, sitting in a clearing on a small rise. It struck her as well situated and sturdy, an older cabin, maintained with a new steel roof, satellite dish, and cedar siding that appeared freshly stained a dense, rich blue. In the fringe of underbrush, she saw a jaunty-looking purple outhouse with a slanted roof, and in the clearing beyond the house, a good-sized solar array, mounted like a billboard on a strapping stand.

Whatever else Dr. Solem might turn out to be, SB chalked her up as a manager with something of an artist's eye. She hoped to find the good doctor at home and have a chat with her. To know that she was safe would take a load off SB's mind. She parked in the shade, opened the moon roof, and left Lil with plenty of fresh, cool air. Then she walked up to the door and knocked. No one came, so she knocked again and then again—each time longer and harder than before.

Finally, she shouted, "Hello! Is anyone home?"

No answer came. She looked around. The door had a small window, but through it she could see only a wall mounted with hooks and an assortment of hanging jackets. She walked around to see what views the other windows afforded. Through the kitchen she got a look into the living room. She expected to see the accumulated stuff of an academic researcher encamped in limited space, and she did see overstuffed bookcases and a desk with papers and books stacked like rubble from a demolition. And then she saw the cat, an orange tabby, sitting on a windowsill across the room and looking back at her. While she watched it jumped down from the sill, stretched long in its own good time, and padded across the floor in her direction. She noticed no obvious disturbances in the room.

No open drawers. Nothing looked tossed. There was no sign of Cheryl Solem herself, prone, upright, or otherwise.

SB nearly peed herself when a man's voice demanded from behind, "Can I help you?" He sounded disdainful, the way people do when they mean to bring you up short and point out that you've overstepped your bounds.

She turned and saw that he appeared to be in his mid-thirties and nice enough looking—clean-shaven with longish hair and a rugged, casual look helped along by rumpled pants and the rolled sleeves of his shirt. She might have felt predisposed to like him if they'd met under different circumstances, but with him glowering suspiciously at her, she felt put off and on guard.

She told him straight out, "I'm looking for Cheryl Solem."

He responded derisively, "I don't think she's home, do you?"

"No, I suppose not," SB said, "Do you have any idea where she might be?"

"That depends on who wants to know," the man said.

"Sorry," she said, fumbling in her wallet for her business card. She knew that 'sorry' wasn't really the right word. She hated the habit that some women had of apologizing as if everything was their fault, but she understood that deference could be used to break tension when tension needed to be broken.

She handed him the card and announced, "I'm SB Ellingson from the *Union Voice*."

As he read the card, she noticed dirt under his fingernails and dried mud on his hands and forearms. Had he been gardening, or maybe digging in the ground for some other reason?

"Publisher, huh?" he said. "I suppose that's impressive."

SB shrugged. "It is what it is. I'm just trying to check on Cheryl."

"Why?" he asked, continuing to look at her skeptically.

"I got a tip from someone," she said.

"Who?"

"A concerned friend."

"What friend?"

"I can't say," she said. "The person's a source, and I protect my sources."

"Would that extend to me?" the man asked.

"I don't know," she answered. "Are you thinking about giving me some information?"

"That depends on what you want to find out."

"Okay," she told him. "For a start, I'd like to know where Cheryl is. Do you have any idea?"

He shook his head in a way that looked genuinely regretful. "I don't."

"Is that just for today, or do you think there's any chance that she could have gone missing?"

"Oh! So you know about that, huh?" he said.

"What I hear is that some of the neighbors—maybe you—tried to file a missing persons report," she said. "Can you tell me if I have that right?"

He let out a sigh of resignation. "My name's Paul. Paul Mattson. My wife and I are friends of Cheryl's. We live next door." He gestured with his head toward the woods, and SB saw a path that she hadn't noticed earlier. It was no more than a trickle of exposed soil and a few beat-down plants here and there, a wildlife trail, most likely whitetail deer, augmented by a little human foot traffic. Paul admitted, "We're the ones who tried to file the report, but the sheriff wouldn't take it. He said she hadn't been gone long enough and she had a right to travel and not tell us, and yadda yadda yadda. He didn't seem to think we knew what we were talking about, or he didn't want to take us seriously enough to listen."

"That's curious," SB said. "How long has she been gone?"

"About six days now, I'd say."

"And you've tried phoning her?"

"All the time. We've texted mostly, but we left voicemails, too, until her box filled up. So far no answer."

"Is that a long time for her to be gone without letting you know?" SB wondered. "Doesn't she travel for her work?"

"God yes," Paul said. "She flies to Ontario, China, Zambia . . . all over the place actually, but this time she didn't say anything to either of us about a trip. That's what's so strange. My wife and her are close. They talk to each other just about every day when she's home. And when she's gone, we check on her place and feed her cat. She does the same for us. You wouldn't think there'd be anything to watch out for around here, but these days you never know. People get damn mad. Almost everybody's addicted to something, bodies showing up in landfills and mining pits."

A surge of cortisol sent SB's anxiety spiking. A woman in treatment had killed Ramona. It wasn't on purpose. She was young and trying to get her life back together, but the script of what happened that afternoon was something that SB couldn't afford to run through her head right then. She pulled herself back together and hoped that she was managing to keep her face looking reasonably calm.

Paul went on as though he hadn't noticed, "Yesterday a couple of suited-up dudes were parked in the driveway. I heard the car pull in, so I walked over. They were in a honking big SUV."

"Any signage on it?" SB asked.

"Not that I could see," Paul said.

"What did they look like?"

"I couldn't make out much. The windows were so tinted. The passenger was wearing mirror shades. Looked like the driver might be a pretty big guy."

"Did they go inside?"

"I don't think they had a chance. They left in a hurry when they saw me. Why do you ask? Do you have some clue?"

"Maybe," SB answered. "Not sure. Do you?"

"No idea."

"Have you been inside?"

Paul's eyes took an abashed, sideways turn. He admitted, "My wife and

I thought we should check. We wanted to make sure Cheryl wasn't sick in there or worse."

"What about the cat?"

"He's fine. Cheryl left him plenty of food and water."

"So she knew she would be gone for a while?" SB wondered.

"Don't know," Paul said. He seemed to have relaxed enough with her that SB thought she might as well go for the big ask.

She said, "Would you mind letting me inside?"

Paul hesitated and then said, "I think I'd like to run that by my wife."

"Can you call her?" SB asked, forgetting about the cell service.

"I'll run home," he said. "Be right back."

SB took the opportunity to let Lil out of the car. She had just put her back inside when a petite, youngish woman appeared on the deer path. She was dressed in a knit top and yoga pants with blond hair tied back in a ponytail. Paul followed close behind her.

"This is my wife, Jessi," he said when SB walked over to meet them.

Like her husband, Jessi sported traces of dried mud when she held out her hand.

"You must be SB Ellingson," she said. "I've admired your paper for a long time."

"Thank you," SB said. "I don't get all that many kudos."

"Well, you should," Jessi told her. "Someone needs to tell the truth around here, and I'm glad you've got the guts to do it. Paul says you want to go inside."

"If it's okay with you," SB said.

"I don't suppose it would hurt," Jessi said. "I don't know what else we can do for Cheryl right now."

"That's what I was thinking," SB said as Paul dug into one of his pants pockets and produced the key.

At first, nothing inside changed her impression. After a while, her eyes fell on the printer and router.

"No computer," she said to both of them. "Is that weird?"

Paul gave a half shrug. "Maybe, but she could have easily taken it."

"She uses a laptop then?"

Jessi nodded, "Yeah, but she was expecting to hear from a hydrologist friend who's studying copper mining in South America somewhere. She said she had a lot of work to do with this friend. She was looking forward to it."

"She could contact the friend wherever she is, though, couldn't she?" SB asked. "As long as there's wireless, right?"

"Right," Jessi said, "but she told me she was planning to work here. She likes feeling removed from distractions. The quiet helps her think, and she keeps a lot of records and books that she needs here."

"I wonder if any of that stuff is missing," SB said.

"We wouldn't know how to tell," Jessi replied. "It doesn't look like anyone's searched the place."

"They certainly haven't tossed it," SB said, "but Paul might have headed that off. I'd like to talk to Cheryl. Could you give me her phone number?"

Paul exchanged a glance with Jessi and answered apologetically, "If we hear from her we'll run it by her. We don't share friends' contact info without asking them."

"Okay," SB said. "I respect a clear boundary." In this case, though, she couldn't say for sure that she would have done the same thing.

While the Mattsons walked her back to the Subaru, Lil barked in anticipation, and SB thought of something.

She asked, "Do you have a wildlife camera by any chance?"

"Yeah," Paul said. "We like to see what comes around at night. Neighbors down the road claimed they spotted a cougar last winter."

"Did you get any shots of it?" SB asked.

"Not yet," Paul answered, "mostly whitetails and crows."

"What would you think about putting the camera at the edge of the woods over here," SB said. "Maybe see what you can spot around Cheryl's house?"

The Mattsons looked at each other and broke into grins.

"Wish I'd thought of that," Paul said.

"Admit it," Jessi laughed. "The lady beat you to it."

"I have my moments," SB said, exchanging a sparky glance of mutual appreciation with Jessi. "Let me know if you see anything interesting."

Driving home, instead of going back the way she'd come, she turned in the opposite direction. Fifty yards or so along the township road, she noticed another fire number posted in the brush. A hand-painted sign behind it advertised:

MOOSE HORN POTTERY
HAND BUILT AND WHEEL THROWN WARE
PAUL AND JESSI MATTSON

That went a long way toward explaining the mud.

8. OTHER SIDE

FROM THE TOWNSHIP ROAD, SB took the state highway. She wanted to swing by Rocky Russo's place to check on the mare Rocky boarded for her. Rocky fed Mara and made sure she had water, shelter, and horse companionship. SB hadn't seen the mare for a month.

Her phone issued a series of beeps, and she knew right away that she must have driven back into cell coverage. With no traffic in sight, she pulled over onto the shoulder. She had texts from Arte, Gwen, and Skye. She didn't want to attend to any of them right then, but her sense of responsibility got the better of her.

Arte wrote:

> I'll have pork ribs, chops, and the best veggies you've ever eaten when I come home. Wouldn't a BBQ be sooooo good? You're the best, Mom!

SB expected that Arte meant for her to do the cooking. As far as she knew, her daughter had never barbequed anything. With luck she might be able to count on Arte to toss a salad.

Gwen wrote:

> I dropped off papers for you at the office. My friend at Wilson Library came through with some studies I think you'll find very interesting. Talk later?

Skye wrote:

> Whazz up, Mom?
> All good here. Just
> checking off my daily
> parental check-in.
> haha

SB sent thumbs up to Gwen, a heart icon to Arte, and 'lol' to Skye. Then she silenced her phone.

When she neared Rocky's pasture, she saw a dozen mares and geldings inside the fence, sunning themselves and foraging for the first appetizing bites of spring grass. Some she recognized as Rocky's brood mares, and the rest belonged to boarders like SB. Mara's red coat made her stand out. Amid her grey and brown companions, she looked as spectacular as fire.

On the driveway SB met Rocky dragging a low-slung piece of equipment behind an old gray tractor. They both slowed, and Rocky signaled for SB to roll down her window.

Dressed in men's jeans, a chambray shirt, and a cap with a bill long enough to shade her eyes, Rocky yelled over the engine noise, "Hi there, newspaper woman! How ya be?"

"Good," SB shouted back. "How about you?"

"Can't complain," Rocky said with a half-smile. "Seems like it's been a while since you've seen your Mara."

"I know," SB said with a guilty shrug. "Time slips away."

"Well, it doesn't wait for any of us, but there's nothing to worry about," Rocky said. "She's doing fine. Will you be graining her?"

"I plan to," SB said.

Rocky touched the brim of her cap in a gesture SB took as a parting salute. "I'll hold back her oats tonight then," Rocky hollered as she released the clutch and let the tractor roll past.

In the barnyard, SB parked beside a small green SUV that she didn't recall ever seeing before. In the tack room of the barn, where boarders stored feed and gear, SB reached into her cubby and pulled out a short rope and halter. She tucked them into the waistband at the back of her pants and covered them with the tail of her shirt in such a way that the mare wouldn't be able to see them. Mara required a certain ritual from SB before she would allow herself to be caught, and SB understood the rules. She got a pail from the tack room and dumped a scoop of oats into it. Leaving the barn with the pail in hand, she heard Mara nicker from the pasture gate.

SB shook the pail so that the oats rattled. Mara nickered more enthusiastically.

When SB got to the gate, she opened it just enough to ease through with the bucket held out in front of her. In the pasture Mara made a couple of gingerly approaches, poking her nose toward the oats and jerking away. On the third approach she stuck her head into the bucket and started gobbling the grain. Only then SB could slip the rope around Mara's neck and expect her to comply like a well-mannered riding horse. Only then, SB could put the halter on Mara's head, buckle it, and lead her to the barn. One false move, and the mare would have pranced out of reach, snorting with her fancy head and tail held high, and that would have been the end of it. SB would have had to come back and try to catch her some other time.

Inside the hulking, dark interior of the barn, the air felt cool and smelled of wood chips and last summer's grass processed through the horses. SB tied Mara to an upright post and left her to get a saw-toothed curry brush from the tack room. When she came back she worked it around Mara's neck in short, round strokes, brushing away bits of hay and bedding, along with remnants of the long-haired winter coat that Mara was in the process of shedding. The mare stood quietly and dozed some. After a while SB heard hoof beats and looked up to see a rider coming in at a slow walk on a buckskin gelding that carried his head low and his neck relaxed. The rider wore a helmet, and SB didn't recognize her at first. Another of Rocky's boarders, she assumed. They tended to come and go. This one was taking her time and minding her horse's needs, letting him cool down after his exercise.

"Why, SB Ellingson," the rider called across the space between them. "Hello!" she said amiably. She seemed pleased. "We meet again!"

On second look, SB saw that she was the massage therapist, her broad cheeks looking flushed and one wayward, ginger-nutty curl escaping under the rim of her riding helmet. Her name? SB searched her mental hard drive. Too much in there. She prepared to feel embarrassed, and then it came to her.

"Merle Byrne!" she said more emphatically than she had meant to.

"Good catch," Merle said with just a hint of a smile.

SB looked away and tried not to take Merle in too directly. There was something about her that just seemed so . . . so . . . what? Familiar came to mind. Dangerous, too, but only because of where SB's mind traveled in her presence. Merle's low-cut chinos and tailored shirt accentuated the thick, straight-waisted core of her body and the flexibility that allowed her to sit deep and balanced in the saddle. SB wasn't comfortable noticing any of it.

"Nice buckskin," she said. "He looks well exercised."

Merle nodded. "Your mare's gorgeous. I noticed her in the pasture. Rocky told me she was yours."

She stood in the stirrups, swung a leg over her horse's rump, and dismounted in one smooth, continuous motion. On the ground, she pulled off her helmet and said, "This is Dillon."

"Mara," SB said.

"We should take them for a ride some time."

"Sure," SB said. She wasn't really committing to it and didn't want to come off as negative. 'Sure' covered a lot of ground.

"The trails here are amazing, don't you think?" Merle asked.

"If you don't mind getting spooked once in a while," SB said.

"Is Mara flighty?"

"A maniac sometimes," SB admitted reluctantly. It was embarrassing, like having a delinquent child.

"Fight or flight," Merle said philosophically. "We've all got it in us."

"Wait a minute," SB said. "I thought we were talking about my horse."

Merle grinned as she unbuckled Dillon's saddle and pad. When she carried them into the tack room, SB untied Mara and started leading her toward the door.

She had almost made it outside free and clear when Merle called after her, "Are you leaving?"

"Work calls," SB said. "Never a dull moment. You know?"

"Hmm," Merle said, looking mildly puzzled. "What do you think about that horse ride idea?"

"Sure," SB said, "but I don't know when."

"We could call it 'work' if you like," Merle chirped, eyeing SB for her reaction.

SB found herself tongue-tied, searching for some clever and noncommittal response.

Merle jumped in, saying, "Look. Whatever you're comfortable with. Really. I'm just trying to make some new friends."

"Shoot me a text?" SB said.

"Give me your cell number?" Merle answered.

She called up a new contact and handed her phone to SB to fill in the details. In the car, SB replayed the scene in her head. She could have been more pliable. She could have returned Merle's overture. She could have answered more openly and generously.

She didn't see the pickup at first. She only focused on its image in her rearview mirror once it had come recklessly close, overtaking her at much too fast a pace. Its hood, no longer aligned with its grille, flashed a startling yellow against the rest of its wrinkled, gray body. She seemed about to be rear-ended when the driver goosed the engine and swung around.

He pulled even with her, and she saw a man she recognized as Kent Nowak, the drunk from the meeting, staring bullets at her and scowling in the driver's seat. He raised his middle finger and thrust it toward her at arm's length while he continued to run alongside, steering with his left hand. Up ahead she saw a hill coming, and they were racing toward it much too fast. She hit the brakes and wondered if Nowak would do the same, but he roared past, kicking up dust and gravel and disappearing over the crest.

Through the immediate danger, she stayed cool. Panic didn't set in until afterward, and then her hands shook so that she could barely grip the steering wheel. It was all she could do to turn the car around and drive away. She wanted to put as many miles as she could between herself and Nowak, so she decided to take the longer way home. She couldn't make herself stop checking the rearview mirror or thinking about what could have happened if they had met oncoming traffic at the crest of that hill. They both might have been killed. Skye and Arte could have been made orphans, and for what? She wondered how much he had thought about what he did and why he did it to her. Had he been watching her? Did he plan his actions or just happen into the situation? Did he know her story? Did he calculate how his actions could traumatize her? Did he know what had happened to Ramona?

She tried to take a deep breath and let it out slowly, willing her heartbeat to slow. After a while she started getting control. As she drove on, the more she thought about Nowak, the more she doubted that he had planned anything. Most likely he was just hapless and drunk. He had spotted her on the road and took advantage of opportunity. That was what people like him did, she thought, and she had to take into account that people like him were out there and could make it all end in just such an arbitrary way. One moment of rage, one stupid impulse, one misstep—your own, someone else's—and you could find yourself on the other side. People slipped away. It had happened to Ramona.

9. AFTER FRENZY, REASON

WHEN SB WENT DOWNSTAIRS to the office on Tuesday, she looked through the research papers Gwen had left on her desk. On the title page at the top of the pile, Cheryl Solem's name appeared as the lead author. SB turned to the executive summary and learned that the research team had studied a copper-nickel mine in Peru and found traceable levels of acids and heavy metals hundreds of miles downstream. Dr. Solem was a coauthor of the next paper, a study of run-off from a mine in the Copperbelt region of Zambia. A multinational conglomerate called CUNIBelt had been using a storage method there that sounded a lot like the waste disposal plan Holton Skibo had described as BeneGeo's newly developed plan. The system had failed in Zambia, and the researchers said they weren't able to come to a conclusion about what went wrong because the company had pulled its support from their project as soon as the preliminary results showed problems. The third paper pulled together research studies from three continents on the effects of sulfide-rock mining on groundwater. Of the seven studies included, Dr. Solem had a role in four. It looked to SB like Chase Monahan hadn't exaggerated. The mines in wet environments had polluted their surroundings, and once the acid drainage started, things got worse. Microbes that thrived in the acidic environments multiplied quickly and caused even more sulfuric acid to leech from the surrounding rock.

SB punched up Gwen's phone number and said, "Holy Cow! You did well!"

"Well, you know," Gwen replied proudly, "some women like big cars, big diamonds, and big other things. I just happen to like friends with big databases."

SB chuckled, "I might be developing a taste for friends like that, too. I take it you saw Cheryl Solem's name on these things."

"She was one of the search terms I asked my friend to use," Gwen said. "If she's not an author, she's a principal investigator or a primary source on all of those studies. I think it's safe to say that she appears to be one of the leading experts in the hydrology of sulfide mining waste."

"I wonder why we didn't know about her until now," SB said.

"We didn't look at the research ourselves until now, did we?" Gwen asked. "We were asking anybody with an opinion to comment on it."

"Well, we're going to report on all of this," SB said. "People need to know it. We're going to have to make sure we get our facts straight, though, or we'll be crucified. It's going to take a ton of work, and we'll probably get crucified anyway."

"Well, that makes it sound inviting," Gwen said. "Let's try to keep it in perspective, shall we? I haven't even started to contact the researchers, but it looks like we've got a treasure trove of experts named in these papers. We'll let them go on record as to what the facts are."

"I wish we could talk to Dr. Solem," SB said. "I'd like to get a measure of her myself."

"She teaches in the graduate hydrology studies program at the U," Gwen said. "Looks like she's got all the latitude and credentials she needs. She's a full professor, and she appears to raise enough grant money to drive her own research agenda and work with any partners she chooses. The papers I gave you are just a small sample of her work."

"Geez," SB sighed. "Chase might have been right about a lot of things. I've got to tell you about my drive out to her house yesterday and my talk with the neighbors. They're the ones who tried to file the missing persons report that Walker wouldn't take. They seem like straight shooters."

"Did you get inside the house?" Gwen asked.

"Yes," SB said. "The place looks okay on the surface."

"What does that mean?" Gwen said. "What about under the surface?"

"Hard to say. There was no computer, which probably means nothing because the neighbors say she uses a laptop, but there was no backup drive, either, and that struck me as really odd. I would have thought she'd need one to make sure she didn't lose any of her work to some electrical glitch or other—especially off the grid like they are."

"That's not a whole lot to go on," Gwen said.

"It's what we've got," SB told her. "Add the neighbors to your research list, will you? Paul and Jessi Mattson. Looks like they're doing business as Moose Horn Pottery."

"Sure thing," Gwen said.

"And can you check into those two BeneGeo security guys who seemed to be standing guard for Holton Skibo at the meeting? We've got to get their names somehow. Paul might have seen them in Cheryl's driveway. His descriptions were pretty sketchy, but it sounded like them."

"I'll ask around," Gwen said.

SB almost didn't mention the Nowak encounter. She wasn't sure it would help, but then she went ahead and said, "I should probably tell you something else, too. I had kind of a road rage thing happen on my way home."

"What?" Gwen sounded concerned.

"You know Kent Nowak, right?" SB said.

"You know I do, unfortunately," Gwen said.

"Right," SB said. "He pretended to try to run me off the road."

"What do you mean pretended? Are you okay?"

"Yes. No big deal." SB minimized, "It was a one-off."

"Did you call Walker?"

"I don't want to bother him with it," SB said. She felt very sure that it wouldn't be a good strategy at the moment, and she hoped that Gwen wouldn't try to convince her otherwise. "I'm going to need him for more important stuff."

"Huh." Gwen sounded unconvinced but willing to yield to SB's judgment.

That night, before bed, SB's mind ran back and forth over what she'd learned and what she still needed to find out about copper-nickel mining and the Cheryl Solem situation. A Facetime request from Kjell interrupted, and she accepted. The light wasn't good. Shadows deepened the recesses in her eighty-year-old father's craggy cheeks, but his expression looked relaxed. His skin had good color. He had clearly been getting sun.

"How are you doing, Susie?" he asked.

"Okay," she answered. "Just fine, in fact." She couldn't tell him everything. He always wanted to rush in and solve her problems.

"You look tired," he said.

The word she would have used to describe herself was "haggard." She had briefly taken in her own image in the picture-in-picture window and was trying to keep her eyes averted.

"And the kids?" he asked.

"All good. Full steam ahead, as far as I can tell," she answered. "Arte's back in love with her life, and Skye's doing his minimalist communicator thing. He's making plans to stay down there this summer. Wants to spend time with his friends from school instead of coming home."

"There must be a girl," Kjell said.

"Maybe." Her father's unquestioning assumption that Skye identified as heterosexual offended SB, even though she thought Kjell might be right about Skye's reason for staying in Florida. She said, "He avoids the subject."

"Sounds like it's about a girl," Kjell said, "Why don't I invite him up for a weekend? I'll tell him to bring a friend. I doubt he could resist an invitation to take the boat up the Intracoastal with Grandpa buying the beer, gas, and food."

"You're probably right about that," SB said.

"I'll let you know what I find out," he added.

"Okay," she said. "Is that why you called?"

"Oh, God no," he said. "I wanted to tell you I thought you did a fine job covering that so-called informational meeting. You're going to get some blowback for asking questions about the company line, you know."

"Nothing I can't handle," she assured him.

"That doesn't surprise me," he said. "Just remember that your dad's got friends and resources and a few tricks up his sleeve. Some of these guys might get uglier than you'd think. Just know I've got your back if you need me."

"Good to know," she said.

She went to bed around ten-thirty and lay awake for what felt like hours. She tried every deep, controlled breathing technique she knew and still found herself tossing from one side to the other. She toyed with reading *The New York Times* online and then turned to the channel guide on the TV remote, looking for something that might interest her just enough to keep her focused while lulling her to sleep. She tried a British drama on PBS.

After a while, she felt Ramona lying beside her, propped on one elbow. The familiar, physical presence of her wife—her steady breath, brown eyes accented with the ambient glow of streetlights, hair in unruly, dark tresses tumbling across SB's collarbone—brought SB to a keen and charged attention. She felt herself tremble. And then the scene changed to a place of green willow brush, water, and blinding blue sky.

"Plunge in!" Ramona challenged. "Let yourself rip!"

They were both young and sleek as otters, paddling in a pool so cold it awakened every nerve. SB felt the ecstatic rush of being one with the water and one with her smooth and slippery-skinned lover, but something made her feel uncertain.

"Come on," Mona urged. "You're okay! You can do it!"

SB felt reckless, exposed, possibly challenged beyond her limits. She didn't want Ramona to think of her as a coward. She tried to shake the nagging dread—of what? Maybe that someone might see them and wish them bad luck, or actually try to harm them.

"You always doubt yourself," Ramona told her. "You're better than you think, you know. Trust yourself. The water will hold you up."

Lil jumped onto the mattress then and flopped against SB like a bag of bones.

Awake again, SB hung onto the feeling of Ramona's nearness. She missed Ramona's physical presence. She missed the company, and she missed sex. She wondered if she'd ever have another partner. Would she even want to, if she found someone with potential? What if the woman couldn't measure up to Ramona? And even if she could, would SB be able to open herself to love again? She didn't think so, now that she knew she couldn't hold on to anyone or anything against the universal onslaught of change. No one could. To try at her age felt like a violation of the natural order, brave maybe, and beautiful in spirit, but doomed.

10. SATURDAY AGAIN

JACK BONO BUSTLED AROUND the newsroom like a squirrel, jawing with SB and the city paper carriers and taking up most of the mental space. He was old enough to be SB's uncle. One of Red Stone County's original hippies, he had migrated from Minneapolis in the 1970s to help found an anti-war collective on a farmstead north of Iron. Back then, her father laughed to tell and retell the story of how he'd decided to take a chance on Jack.

"He showed up looking for a job delivering newspapers," Kjell said. "He looked like a long-haired girl but seemed like a good enough guy."

Kjell still told the story and still didn't seem to get how retrograde it made him sound. SB remembered Jack's thick curls spilling from his head down his sideburns and along his jawline from his ears to the places where his cheeks met his chin. These days he was bald on top. His muttonchops were white and wooly, and he wore his wire-rimmed reading glasses low on his nose as he hurried around front to back, side to side, and in and out the door, greeting the city paper carriers, handing them bundles of papers, and helping them carry the bundles to their cars.

"City paper carriers" had become an outdated phrase that SB used from force of habit. Her grandparents and parents had employed people to deliver newspapers to rural mailboxes, too, but after the high quality, hematite ore ran out, the *Voice*'s earnings followed local mining revenues right into a deep, dark pit. Her grandparents turned the paper into a bully pulpit for finding a way to revive the Range economy. The unions and local politicians put pressure on state agencies, and a university engineer came to the rescue by working out a process to separate iron from the remaining lower-grade taconite ore. He crushed the ore, separated the iron with magnetism, mixed it with limestone and clay, and baked it into pellets that worked in the blast furnaces back east. Taconite revived the Range, but by the '80s higher-grade ore started coming in from overseas, and Kjell was forced to reduce the print runs from daily to twice a week. He let the rural carriers go and sent the out-of-town papers by mail. When SB and Ramona took over, some people had personal computers and then the Internet. Typesetting went digital. Printing, too. Online news proliferated. Subscriptions dropped, and advertising revenues fell. SB had to let staff go. Ramona stepped up and helped. Somehow they held on, but after the accident, SB cut the print run to once a week.

Jack had been a key man through most of it. SB watched appreciatively as he picked up a bundle in each hand to help the last paper carrier out the door. The young mother worked three jobs to piece together rent, childcare, and groceries. She came across as bright and willing to learn, and SB had spent some time thinking about whether or not she could afford to create a part-time, paid internship that might help her make ends meet. Nothing had come of it yet. Jack escorted her through the front door with a muffled comment that made her laugh.

Afterward, he said, "Nice work on the front page, Susan B."

"Thanks," SB replied. She felt some pride about it. She'd taken more trouble than usual to get the banner to sound just the right note of balanced scrutiny. She'd settled on, "BeneGeo claims CuNi mining safe, but studies raise questions." She'd drawn from BeneGeo's news release and the research papers Gwen had found.

"You know you'd better get ready to hear some wounded roars, right?" Jack said. "They're going to tell you how you've crushed their hopes and destroyed the future of the Iron Range."

"I wish I could say you're surprising me," she told him. "Seems like I'm always out to sabotage the Range in somebody or other's eyes."

"Keep letting it roll off your shoulders," he said. "You know you're not alone. A lot of us want to know a lot more before we sign off on something we can't undo."

"Good to know," she said.

"Remember who you are," he said, putting an arm on her shoulder. "Kjell will be proud, don't you think?"

"Dad always finds a way to sound supportive," she told him.

He gave her a squint-eyed look that she took as an invitation to say more.

"Dad's just Dad," she said, "a small-town big man like my grandpa. They've done some good no doubt, but they've helped themselves, too. I left their photos up in there in the office to remind me how I don't want to be."

The photos in the publisher's office, a small, inner sanctum walled off from the rest of the newsroom, showed Kjell and Erik shaking hands with mine owners, union executives, politicians, and celebrities like the Polka King, Florian Kowalski. The one that stood out most in SB's mind was a black-and-white of the two of them in fedoras and business suits, flanking Dwight Eisenhower when he headlined Iron's celebration of the state's centennial. The president's bald, white head resembled a baby's, and the rangy Ellingson men bookended him like a couple of fawning princes.

She said, "Everything must have seemed so easy to them."

"I don't know about easy," Jack said with an ambivalent smile. "The thing is that guys play in teams. What matters is you're on the team or you're not."

"I wouldn't be surprised to hear he golfs with Holton Skibo," she scowled. "In fact, I'd be surprised if Skibo hasn't already found some excuse to look up Dad in Bonita Beach and take him out to dinner or maybe even arrange a gulf cruise on some BeneGeo investor's private yacht."

"Kjell's not a bad guy, though," Jack responded. "He makes friends both up and down the ladder."

"Right," SB said. "I give him credit for that. He picked you. Saw you as a good bet right from the start."

"But?" Jack asked.

"But I just wish he was more aware of the advantages he's had without having to earn them."

"Is anyone ever fully aware of those things, though?" Jack asked.

Under his questioning gaze, SB felt surprisingly chastened.

"I don't know," she said. "Some of us like to think we try."

II. SCOOPED

W HEN SB PICKED UP her Sunday newspaper from the stoop at her back door, the banner headline stopped her short:

OUR NORTHERN WATERSHEDS:
Global Treasures We Must Protect

The entire front page of Minneapolis and Saint Paul's *River Cities Record* was devoted to a multi-article, investigative spread on copper-nickel mining "Up North" (as the paper's style sheet apparently instructed its reporters to call SB's part of Minnesota).

There was a straightforward, fact-based editorial on page one, too—a placement the *Record* almost never used for an opinion piece. Its writer concluded that the president had short circuited the environmental study ordered by his predecessor. She called on the Minnesota Environmental Safety Commission to complete the study on its own, and she wrote, "the state legislature should immediately begin the process of revising the MESC's charter, replacing the agency's so-called 'twin role' with a single role of protecting the environment for the health, safety, and well-being of the people."

"Looks like we've been scooped," SB said woefully to Lil, who blinked and looked away.

SB read every word on the front page and all of the copy carried over to the jump pages. An investigative reporter named Renard Bridges wrote:

> A company official who spoke on condition of anonymity affirmed that the international mining conglomerate, CUNIBelt, has, in fact, already secured a substantial interest in the locally founded mining company, BeneGeo. The source affirmed that CUNIBelt owner,

Garman Worsley, actively seeks to acquire a controlling interest and may be close to doing so.

A Zambian-born citizen of Britain, Worsley owns mining firms on five continents. All are held privately, exempting those incorporated in the U.S. from almost all financial reporting requirements. BeneGeo claims to have developed a novel and environmentally safe plan for storing the tailings from their proposed mine near Iron, but the company refuses to publicly share the details of their study methods and the findings.

Next to Bridges' four-column spread, a narrow sidebar appeared under a photo of the president's son and daughter-in-law in formal attire:

According to a source familiar with the matter, one week before the president tweeted his cancellation of the now famous Forest Service study, Worsley leased an Upper East Side condo to the couple at a price significantly below market value. When contacted by the *Record*, Worsley and the White House press office declined to comment.

SB reached into her pocket for her phone. She tapped out Gwen's number and felt her hand tremble as she waited for Gwen to answer.

"Did you see?" SB asked.

"The *Record*?" Gwen asked back.

"Yes."

"So much for local ownership."

"They beat us to the story," SB groused. "They outdid us and every other newspaper in the state."

"They dove deep," Gwen said,

"Gutsy," SB said. "The managing editor must have lined up the publisher and the editorial board before he dared go this far."

"It's brave stuff," Gwen said. "Good reporting. I'd rather be in his shoes than Latelle Washington's right now, wouldn't you?"

"Yes, but those are some pretty classy shoes," SB said. "I expect that she's up to the challenge."

"Still," Gwen said, "Wouldn't you love to have some kind of eavesdropping device in her kitchen this morning?"

"She's probably on the phone with her boss right now wondering how the *Record* found those highly placed, anonymous sources," SB said. "Makes me feel like a piker."

"Well, we ARE pikers," Gwen said. "Haven't you figured that out, yet?"

"I guess," SB muttered, reluctant to concede it.

"Think of it this way," Gwen told her. "The *Record* just gave us some really good cover. We're not the only ones asking questions. In a way, they've confirmed that we're on the right track. And don't forget that we're exploring some exciting sources of our own."

"You're right," SB said. "Keep talking, and I might even feel good about it by Monday."

On Monday morning, a familiar, metallic smell hit her nostrils as she entered the closed-up newsroom. Her grandparents had bought the steel alloy office furniture in the '60s. The heavy, gray desks, chairs, and filing cabinets predated the cheapening of everything, and so far they had proved indestructible and therefore worth keeping.

SB punched up Latelle Washington's extension at the MESC and wasn't surprised to find her call routed directly to voicemail. She had mentally rehearsed her message and managed to deliver it without tripping over her tongue.

"I'm looking for your take on some details we've come across in our reporting. Could you please give me a call back as soon as possible?"

Gwen came into the office restless with energy. She said, "Have you checked Twitter?"

"You know I don't," SB said.

"I mean have you heard what he's tweeted now?" Gwen asked.

"Clueless," SB said. "Why don't you fill me in?"

"He's fired the chief of the Forest Service. Says she was 'very disappointing. Sad. A weak chief. Couldn't lead a herd of mountain goats away from a cliff at a certain time of the month.'"

"What?" SB said. "That's so metaphorically inept. Did you make it up?"

"Not me," Gwen said. "I think mountain goats thrive on steep slopes, and as for the monthly thing—well, it's just flabbergasting. What can I say except the timing suggests that the chief must have balked at pulling the environmental study?"

"Almost for sure," SB allowed, "but try and prove it."

"Right," Gwen said. "I'm sure there'll be no consequences for him."

SB shook her head. "No. Only for the ones who speak up. Got any good news?"

"Well, yes," Gwen said. "Thanks for asking. I've made contact with two of our experts, and they're both eager to talk. Actually, it was one of them who cued me about today's tweet. She's dismayed about everything that's happened to the Forest Service recently. Their environmental research and compliance budget has been practically zeroed out."

"I don't suppose I have to tell you to set up the interviews," SB said.

Over the lunch hour, while SB was alone in the office, Mrs. Marilyn Bednar sailed through the front door dressed for teaching eighth grade social studies in skinny-legged slacks, a tunic-style blouse, and walking shoes. Her henna dyed hair looked slightly mussed by the exertion and whatever May breeze blew outside.

"I'd like to talk to you, Susan," Mrs. Bednar announced.

"Go right ahead," SB said. "As it happens, now is a good time."

"Well you might not think so after I've finished," Mrs. Bednar warned. "I've got a bone to pick with you."

Marilyn, as SB had known her since adolescence, grew up in Iron just a few years ahead of SB in school—close enough to become nodding acquaintances and occasional adversaries even back then.

"Why don't you just let fly, and we'll see?" SB asked, steeling herself.

"You misquoted me," Mrs. Bednar charged straight out, without any sort of qualifying or buffering banter.

SB heard it as unnecessarily heated—and on the risk-taking side of socially acceptable.

"You made me look bad," Mrs. B continued. "I never called the resort owners selfish. I wouldn't do that. They're our neighbors. And you got things other people said wrong, too. There's a lot of complaining online. They say you took things out of context and distorted their meanings or just plain made up whatever you thought might make us look bad."

"Those are some pretty strong accusations," SB said, choosing her words carefully. "I guess you don't really know me all that well, Marilyn, but I know you know that I grew up in this business. What you don't seem to understand is that I take my responsibility to the newspaper and to this town seriously. I would never set out to make anyone look bad, and I know exactly what you said at the meeting because I recorded the whole thing. I transcribed every quote that I used in the story, word for word, from the tape."

The rosacea on Mrs. B's cheeks had deepened as she listened, as had SB's sense that Mrs. B was barely managing to hold in powerful feelings. She blinked and looked set back for a moment, and then she launched into a series of cascading wonderments.

"You taped me? I never gave you permission. Did other people? Isn't taping people without their knowledge illegal? Don't you need us to sign some kind of permission form?"

"It's quite legal," SB said. "In fact I could be taping you right now if I wanted. In this state only one of the parties being taped needs to give their permission."

"Well, that's preposterous! It can't be right!" Mrs. Bednar sputtered. "It certainly is convenient for you, though, isn't it?" Her gaze traveled around the room as if looking for hidden microphones. "Are you taping me right now? Because if you are I'm not saying another word."

"Legally, I could be," SB said, "but I'm not."

"As if that's any consolation," Mrs. Bednar fumed. "I'll be seeing an attorney about this. You can be sure of that. And don't think you've won anything, Susan. I have thousands of friends online, and they will hear about this. The people you're messing with used to be your friends—and some of us used to be your customers. We're trying to save this community for our kids, you know—for the people you claim to care about."

"I appreciate that," SB said. "I have kids, too."

"Oh right," Mrs. Bednar said with a sarcastic roll of her eyes.

SB still felt aggrieved about the trouble Mrs. B had made for her and Ramona and the kids. She took a breath and searched for something positive to say.

She settled on offering, "You can always write a letter to the editor."

"As if you'd print it." The accusation came with a curled-lip snarl.

"Believe it or not, there's a good chance I would," SB said, "as long as it's signed, original, and not obscene, libelous, or threatening. If it's misleading, I might add an editorial comment."

"And who would decide if it's misleading? You, I suppose?"

"That's my job."

"Right," Mrs. Bednar snapped. "More like it's your prerogative. You're the snake biting its own tail."

"I think you'd better go before I bite yours," SB said. She puzzled over the metaphor.

"Is it about Eden or infinity?" she asked Gwen after lunch.

"Probably about desperation," Gwen laughed. "Marilyn must have thought she was still in her classroom. She probably didn't realize she was the one getting schooled."

"I don't know," SB said. "I don't think she learned anything from it."

When SB's phone chimed later, she announced to Gwen, "Latelle Washington."

"Thanks for getting back to me so fast under the circumstances," SB said.

"I imagine you're having a busy day."

"Ha!" Latelle huffed. "Are you planning to pile on with the rest of the crowd?"

"Could be," SB said. "Are they asking for your take on the president's announcement?"

"They are," Latelle replied. "And I'm telling them exactly the same thing that I'm going to tell you, which is that you should contact the Forest Service Office of Communications with that question. I think I'd also file a Freedom of Information Act request with them if I were you."

"What about the MESC?" SB asked. "Can you say anything about your agency's partnership with the Forest Service on the study?"

"I can't say much."

"Were you notified of the cancellation in advance?"

Latelle's voice turned cool. "As far as I know we had no notice. Of course, that has to stay off the record for now."

"Got it," SB followed up. "Is there any chance your agency will go ahead with the study on your own?"

"I don't make those decisions," Latelle said.

"Who does?" SB asked. "What will they take into consideration?"

"I'll have to get back to you on that, SB. Do you have any questions I might be able to answer?"

Latelle's exasperation must have carried with her voice because Gwen did a turn with raised eyebrows, and SB had to look away before she asked Latelle, "Have you received any permit requests from a company called CUNIBelt or from any other company doing business in partnership with CUNIBelt?"

"I'd have to check with the regulatory department, and then we will probably need you to submit a Minnesota Government Data Practices Act request."

"Just one more thing," SB pressed. "What does a hydrologist named Cheryl Solem do for the MESC? Was she working on the cancelled study?"

A sharp intake of breath told SB everything she needed to know before Latelle terminated the conversation. "If past experience is any guide," she said, "I imagine I'll be getting your Data Practices request this afternoon."

12. SOME ADVICE

In the afternoon the May sun promised summer, and Gwen came back to the office with a healthy-looking blush in her cheeks.

"Great news!" she said. "I talked to those two co-authors."

"On or off the record?" SB asked, hoping for the best.

"Some of each," Gwen said. "Neither of them has heard from Cheryl recently. She's definitely the principal investigator on the Forest Service study, and they vouched for her work and reputation. Off the record, they think she had some sort of dust-up with Garman Worsley's lawyers over research data from his mines in Ontario and the African Copper Belt. On the record, they confirmed what Chase Monahan said about the safety record of copper mining in sulfide rock."

"You have notes?" SB asked.

"Of course."

"Good. Start writing."

"Sure thing, Boss," Gwen chuckled, looking perfectly satisfied with herself.

Dave Maki came in later with a strained expression that looked like it signaled trouble. He got himself a cup of coffee and, on the way back to the advertising desk, stopped beside SB and said, "Got a minute?"

"Sure," she said. "What's going on?"

"Oh, this and that," he said. "I just want to share some of the feedback I've been getting from clients."

"What sort of feedback?" she asked.

"Oh, you know, none of it's really got any reality behind it."

"Like what?"

"Well," he paused and cleared his throat. "Some of them are asking about your stance on copper-nickel mining."

"What stance?" she asked. "We haven't taken one yet. What are they saying?"

"They're wondering if you're still an advocate for Iron." She heard reluctance in his voice as he went on cautiously, "They're questioning whether or not you're still pro-business and pro-worker in this community."

"Who exactly is saying these things?"

"Guys at Machinery Supply, the Tire Warehouse, Food Giant, and a couple of other shops. They're worried about economic spin-off if the BeneGeo deal falls through."

"How many have you heard from in all?"

"That's it right now," he said.

"Are they still placing ads?"

"So far yes," he said, "but a couple of them warned me flat out that they're considering dropping us if things don't improve."

"Well, I hope you assured them that we're the only source of local news and always working for community improvement," she said, "and so far, we haven't taken a stance for or against copper-nickel mining—just for getting the facts."

"I tell them that, SB," he said, "but people are getting each other riled up. With everything going digital, this thing could take a really bad turn if you're not careful."

"Thanks for bringing this to me, Dave," she said. "Keep me posted, would you?"

"Sure," he said. "It's a damn shame you have to worry about it at all."

"We'll muddle through," she told him.

When her phone chimed after supper, the letters WSLT flashed on her screen. "Oh god, it's Mom," she said to Lil before she touched the Accept icon.

"Congratulations on your work, My Girl," Artemisia cooed warmly, sounding a glass or two into her cups. SB pictured her on a chaise lounge in the communal lanai at WomanSpirit Land Trust, a cluster of patched-together, old Florida cottages tucked into a Gumbo-Limbo hammock on the coast of No Name Key, where Artemisia had taken a second chosen name, Shadow Crone. By early May the Florida summer was far enough along that SB imagined Artemisia would be dressed in shorts, sandals, and a T-shirt, red-cheeked from sun exposure, probably needing hydration, and opting for Pino Grigio.

"Thanks, I guess," SB replied. "What are you talking about?"

"Your coverage of the copper-nickel mining falderal," Artemisia said. "I follow you online all the time, you know. I'm practically a goddamn troll, though I don't usually say anything."

"I think they call that lurking," SB said.

"Do they? Well, I wonder if that's preferable to being called an interfering mother. It's just that this issue matters so much to all of us. I'm not exaggerating, Susan. Water. Earth. Fire. Everyone in the world is still under the sway of the elemental forces, even though we think we're the demi-gods in charge. It's bad around here, you know. Big Sugar has poisoned the Everglades. The manatees are dying again, and septic systems are going bad all over the Keys. You can't drive the Overseas Highway without smelling piss somewhere, and the only thing people seem to be able to agree on is that they don't like what's happening. Nobody wants to spend a dollar or change their own lives."

"Wait," SB interrupted. "I don't think they even agree on what's happening."

"That's where you come in, Susan. You've got to keep giving them the facts. I don't know if you understand how important your work is. For some reason, you're placed in a pivotal position at a critical turning point. The eyes of the world are on you."

"So, no pressure or anything?" SB asked.

"No, not at all," Artemisia said, chuckling. "By the way, I saw Alberta's picture in the *Miami Herald* yesterday. She was in Belle Glade meeting with the Seminoles and the sugar cane workers. They're making a big push to tie together social justice, Indigenous rights, and water quality down here. She's a force to be reckoned with."

"Between the two of you," SB said, "it's no wonder I struggle to get a thought in edgewise."

"Oh, come on, Susan, you disappoint me sometimes," her mother chided. "Envy of other women's powers doesn't become you, especially not while you're at the height of your own. You won't have them forever. Use them!"

The corrective advice didn't sit well with SB, especially since it seemed fairly true. She struggled to think of an appropriate response, but before she came up with one, her mother changed the subject.

"What do you hear from the kids?" she asked.

"Mostly the minimum," SB said, doing her best to switch gears. "I had to tell Skye that if he didn't check in at least weekly, I'd contact the Dean of Students, or Campus Life, or whatever they call that side of the staff these days. So now I get a tweet-sized text almost every day. He plans to spend the summer in St. Augustine."

"Is there someone to keep him there—some romantic interest?" Artemisia asked.

"You think just like Dad," SB told her. "Maybe it's just the romance of the new."

"Maybe, but I bet it's a girlfriend or boyfriend. Should I bring him down here and try to charm it out of him?"

"You'll have to get in line. Kjell's scheming to entice him with beer and a speedboat tour of the Intracoastal. He's probably already made the invitation."

"I don't suppose sunset at the Land Trust can compete with that," Artemisia said.

"In the company of a bunch of land-dyke crones with sea kayaks, vegan food, and bedtime at ten?" SB said. "I would venture to guess 'no.'"

"Hey, we're changing with the times," Artemisia told her. "It took us a year of study and discussion, but at our last steering committee meeting we renamed ourselves the Ineffable Spirit-x Land Trust. The young ones who flame us on our website are saying we need to be more open to queering gender identity."

"Arte would probably agree," SB said. "She's got a lot to teach us and not much to learn, she thinks."

"Sounds like you at her age."

"Point taken," SB acknowledged. "She does sound happy—finally."

"Still at that organic farm?"

"Yeah and planning a visit here sometime soon. She's bringing provisions for a barbeque. I think she's starting to feel grown-up and liking it."

"And what about you, daughter of mine?"

"Hanging in," SB said. "Work's exciting. How are you and Sam?"

"I'm fine. She's irascible as a bear."

SB heard Sam's voice shouting from some short distance, "Don't believe her!"

SB said, "Tell her I always take you with a grain of salt, Mom."

"I know, dear," Artemisia replied. "She does, too. You two keep me grounded. I can always count on that. Just remember that you got your steely spine from me."

"Did I?" SB bristled at the suggestion.

"Yes," Artemisia said with certainty. "If you don't know it now, you will someday."

13. GUESS WHO

O N A BALMY TUESDAY, Gwen came to work in a skirt and blouse of unmatched floral designs. SB never would have tried to pull off such an outfit. On her, she felt sure, it would have looked more like an overgrown garden than some trendy, Swedish designer's latest masterstroke. On Gwen it struck just the right notes of freshness and nonchalance.

Gwen was setting her lips like she wanted to say something—at least that's the feeling SB got, but SB jumped out ahead anyway and blurted, "Mom called last night."

"Oh," Gwen responded. She followed up warmheartedly, "How was it? Do you want to download?"

"I guess," SB said, wondering if it was a good idea. "I don't want to get too deep into the pity pool, but you know how my mother always manages to push my buttons. She just spews a stream of consciousness about whatever advice she thinks I need. She didn't even get around to asking about me or the kids until she hit a dead end and needed to change the subject."

"That sounds like the Artemisia I know," Gwen said. "She's nothing if not self-expressive. Where did you two leave it?"

"Unfinished," SB said, "as usual. We sort of patched things up—or at least patched them over—for now. We said our cheery goodbyes, and then she told me that I got my courage from her."

"And you don't agree?" Gwen asked.

"She wanted me to take it as a compliment," SB said, "but it was more like bragging about herself, wasn't it? How much courage does it take to leave your husband and daughter and retreat to some lesbian commune in the Keys?"

"Back when she did it, tons," Gwen said. "In the '70s, a lot of people were still living in the '40s around here, and Nikki was trying to come out while married to one of the most driven and powerful men in the state.

I'm sorry you ended up in the middle of it, but maybe you understand now that she didn't feel like she had much choice."

"I get that," SB said. "Things have changed, but not really that much."

"I know," Gwen said.

"I should try to lighten up on her. It's just hard."

"If it's any consolation," Gwen said, "I think you're doing great."

"You know what?" SB said ruefully. "I'm sorry. You're starting to sound like you're role-playing in some emotional support training exercise. That's my fault. Let's get on to something more productive."

Gwen scrutinized SB for what felt like a long time. Then—to SB's relief—her expression lightened, and she said, "Would this be a good time to tell you what else I've learned about the Cheryl Solem situation?"

"Definitely!" SB said with genuine relief and gratitude. "Please do."

"Okay," Gwen began. "I've talked to three more researchers who know her. They all think she's flat out disappeared. No emails, no Zoom invitations, no contributions to Google doc collaborations. They've tried to reach her, but she just dropped out of contact. No explanations."

SB asked, "Will they go public about that?"

"Yes," Gwen said. "The rest is complicated."

"What else?" SB said.

"They're concerned about BeneGeo's Mix and Separate plan. Off the record they think it's a sham and a looming disaster, but it's hard to show any proof because BeneGeo owns the design plans and test results and won't release them. The hydrologists are trying to do the right thing, but they want to protect themselves, too. The company—or Garman Worsley, if that's the one we're actually dealing with—could sue for damages and accuse them of ethical violations. Even if they could afford the legal fees, an accusation like that can be all it takes to ruin a professional career."

"So, these people aren't exactly profiles in courage material," SB noted dryly.

"Those are hard to come by these days," Gwen said. "They did all say on the record that they couldn't point to a single proven example of a safe storage method for copper-nickel mining waste in an environment and climate like ours. And damage from storage runoff has been documented at copper mines around the world. They say CUNIBelt has one of the worst records."

"And it looks more and more like we're dealing with CUNIBelt," SB said.

"Right," Gwen told her. "One of them said that BeneGeo's Mix and Separate plan looks like a knockoff of an old CUNIBelt technique that didn't work. She won't go on record about it because Worsley owns the data, and a researcher who worked with Cheryl on the study ended up dead in some accident near Worsley's mine in Ontario."

"What?" SB asked. "Did I hear that right?"

"Suspicious circumstances," Gwen confirmed. "They don't want to be quoted."

"But they're willing to say they have questions about the mine waste?" SB asked.

"Yes," Gwen said. "And they'll back up the things we've already documented, like the fact that CUNIBelt wouldn't let Cheryl complete her study of the system at Worsley's mine."

"Start putting the whole thing together," SB said. "We're going with it on page one."

Later that morning, the potter from Moose Horn came in, carrying a padded nine-by-twelve envelope and glancing nervously in Gwen's direction. SB jumped up to greet him.

"Good to see you again, Paul," she said, reaching out a hand and guiding him deeper into the office. "This is Gwen Groveland, our editor. She knows everything I do about the Cheryl situation. Gwen, Paul Mattson."

Paul worked his fingers nervously on the envelope and frowned. He looked to SB like he wondered if he should hold out for privacy but was too full of the news he'd brought to keep it inside any longer. He pulled an electronic tablet from the envelope.

"I followed your suggestion about the trail cam," he said. "You won't believe what showed up."

"You have photos?" SB asked.

She signaled for Gwen to come and join them while Paul powered up the tablet. With Gwen on one side of him and SB on his other, he scrolled through still images, showing them a whitetail deer, red and gray squirrels, a raven caught frozen in flight, and a dark SUV in Cheryl's driveway, parked in plain view of the camera. She saw two figures emerge in night vision mode, shadowy and greenish, looking like apparitions. She could hardly make out their physical features. One looked slight, the other larger. The slight one carried nested boxes that looked empty, judging from the casual way he carried them. The empty-handed one stood at the door to the house and opened it without seeming to resort to any kind of bar or screwdriver.

"Do they have a key?" SB wondered.

"Looks like it," Paul said.

When the figures came back out and passed in front of the camera, SB caught a full-face view.

"My God!" she said. "It's them!"

"The so-called security men," Gwen said.

Both men carried boxes, loaded this time, judging from the way they had adjusted their bodies to accommodate what must have been added weight.

"How long were they inside?" SB said.

"About fifteen minutes according to the time stamps," Paul said.

"Did this happen last night?" Gwen asked.

Paul pulled his mouth in a way that made him look displeased. He said, "We've got a show coming up, and we've been putting all our energy into building up our inventory. They're date-stamped three days ago."

"Oh," SB said, trying not to sound disappointed. "It's still invaluable evidence, Paul. Have you been inside the house since this happened?"

"Just to feed the cat," Paul said.

"Was the door locked?" she asked.

"Yes."

"Did the lock look jimmied?"

"No," he said. "And to save you the trouble of asking, I didn't notice anything that looked out of place."

SB said, "I'll make a copy of these to keep if it's okay with you."

Paul agreed, "That's why I came."

"And the Sheriff will want to talk to you," she told him.

"So?" Paul said. "He wasn't much help the last time."

"He had his reasons," she said. "Things should be different now. We're bringing him solid evidence."

"And you've got the evidence in your hands," Paul said. "Do what you have to do, but keep me out of it. I need to be at the show." His jaw was set hard, and she didn't see any sense in pushing him.

As soon as he left, she phoned Walker.

The one stoplight in downtown Iron turned red just as SB approached it on her way to his office. As she sat with her car in gear and her foot on the brake, she caught sight in her peripheral vision of someone who turned out to be Merle Byrne, waving from the sidewalk. She glanced quickly side-to-side, stepped down from the curb, and approached SB's front passenger window.

As SB rolled the window down, Merle said, "I just wanted to tell you I've got a bunch of new clients."

SB had to admit there was something about her. Something like life force overflowing, but that sounded like Shadow Crone talking, and SB had been born too late to buy into her mother's brand of mystic woo-woo.

Someone in a car behind them honked.

Merle stepped back and said in a sincere voice, "Thanks!"

"Any time," SB said before she drove on, disappointed and surprisingly addled about her part of the interaction. She couldn't fault Merle in any way.

She seemed nice and entirely unassuming. It was just that SB didn't need any new entanglements, and Merle felt like a potential entanglement, so the solution was obvious. If Merle texted, SB would reply with regrets and claim to be busy and unavailable. If Merle tried again, SB would mention her work on the BeneGeo situation and the kids—more busyness, and there always could be something to keep her unavailable—layer after layer of futility if Merle persisted.

Suddenly she found herself in the courthouse parking lot without a plan for handling Walker. She had meant to use the drive to prepare a checklist, but instead she had to wing her intro. She plugged a flash drive into her laptop and scrolled through copies of Paul's trail cam photos. She caught a glimmer of recognition on Walker's face when he looked at the SUV and the ghostly figures with their distinctively contrasting builds. By the time she got to the shot of their faces, Walker had seemingly prepared himself.

He kept his mouth shut until he heard her side of things and then he told her in a composed way, "Thank you for bringing this in, SB. I'll need a copy."

"I can give you the flash drive I brought," she said. "If you need the original memory card you'll have to talk to Paul Mattson. I think you have his number."

"I can take it from here," Walker said in an officious voice that he hardly ever used on her. He said, "I'll look into it and let you know if I need anything more."

"That's it?" she said.

He answered, "Did you want something more?"

"For starters," she said. "You recognize those burglars as the so-called 'security' men who work for Holton Skibo, don't you?"

"I don't know," he said. "I suppose there could be some resemblance."

"You know darn well there is," she told him. "Are you going to pick them up for questioning?"

Walker tried to stare her down, but she wouldn't look away.

He said, "SB, you and I have worked together on a lot of things over the years, haven't we?"

"Your point?" she said, still drilling into his obdurate gaze with her own.

"We've known each other even longer than that," he said.

"That goes without saying," she parried.

"My point is that you know damn well I can't discuss the details of an investigation."

"Oh," she said. "So, you've opened an investigation?"

"Christ," he practically spit back at her, "I can't confirm that. This whole thing is off the record, and I need to warn you that what you see in these pictures could spoil a lot of good detective work that's already been done. If Cheryl Solem is in any danger, as you say you think she might be, it could put her in an even more dangerous position. If you go public with these photos, you might guarantee that we'll never be able to find out what happened or hold anyone accountable for whatever that might be. That's all I can tell you, and I hope to hell you think long and hard about what you're going to do before you do it."

His argument set her back. She guessed he sensed it, too, because he looked away and said in a less pressing voice, "If you'll just hold your fire, there might be a heck of a story in it for you when I'm ready to release the details."

"You're promising me an exclusive if I hold off publishing for now?" she asked.

"Something like that," he said.

"That sounds like a mess that could blow up in both of our faces."

"I guess we're done for today then," he said, standing up.

"I'll think about it," SB answered on her way out.

Driving home along Mesabi she passed the Lucky Strike. The bar and cafe dated back to the 1920s and had changed hands twice since she and Ramona made it their special spot. Aging varnish on oak booths and wainscoting made the restaurant side of the operation as brown and shadowy as the bar. In the back corner booth two people could still explore the possibility of sitting side-by-side and leaving anyone else in the place to make of it what they would. If the two were as watchful and clever as she and Ramona had been, they could still steal a kiss and maybe even enjoy some lingering touch. No one would see a hand sliding across the Naugahyde bench, and even the most attentive busybody would need psychic powers to decode the blank faces the two of them presented to the world as their blood surged and nerve impulses exploded.

Back home, she got a text from Merle Byrne:

> Good to see you this afternoon. I've been meaning to ask about that horseback ride. This weekend? Or maybe next week?

SB replied:

> Good to see you, too. Glad you're settling in. Another time??? Work keeps me hopping right now.

Merle texted back a smiley face and this:

> No worries. I'll try you next week.

"She's game," SB thought to herself.

She also thought that she liked game. She liked game people who could muster the gumption to play against the odds. She decided to leave everything possible and let Merle have the last word for now. In the face of everything that worked against hope there was something admirable about holding onto it, wasn't there?

Saturday's *voice arrived from* the printer, and after the delivery-man unloaded the last stack of bundles and presented SB with the invoice, she and Jack found themselves temporarily alone in the office.

"Wow, kid," Jack said, peering over the bridge of his glasses at the headline she'd written to showcase Gwen's story.

Water Experts Question Cu-Ni Safety Record

"This looks like strong stuff," he said. "I can't wait to read it."

"Good to hear," she told him. "That's what we're in business for."

Beside Gwen's story, SB had put together a timeline of local sulfide mining proposals and setbacks across the past half century. She included letters from Marilyn Bednar, Chase Monahan, the union president Arno Toivola, and resort owner Jason Bjornstad. In an editorial she acknowledged the financial pressures on Iron and advocated for everyone to do no harm, take as much time as needed to gather evidence, and let the facts guide their decisions. She gave BeneGeo a chance to make their case for Mix and Separate on page two, printing the first six paragraphs of Cherise LeDoux's news release just the way she'd written them. She didn't mention Cheryl Solem's disappearance.

"Of course," Jack said in a cautionary tone, "one thing is that a lot of people won't read more than the headlines. And a lot of people have already made up their minds."

SB shrugged. "They'll read into it what they want," she said. She didn't know what more she could do about that.

"Or they won't read at all," he replied. "A lot of people know a lot of things that aren't so. Just keep that in mind when you start hearing from them. That's all I'm saying. You can't control what they think, but some of what they say might sting."

"I appreciate the advice," SB said.

"No you don't," he said. "I know you better than that. I just worry about you. Keep your eyes and ears open. Don't ever forget to watch your back."

"Because I'm playing with the big boys?" SB asked.

"That's part of it," Jack said.

"And what else?" she wondered.

"The mean little fuckers," he told her. "There's a lot more of them around, and they're everywhere—if you'll pardon my language, Boss."

"From your mouth to my virgin ears, Jack," she laughed.

Alberta stopped by around noon. The weather had taken another backward, wintery turn, and she shivered with her hands stuffed into the pockets of her jeans jacket. Like Ramona and Arte, SB's mother-in-law had a strong, broad-shouldered frame and a metabolism that burned every extra ounce of fat she produced.

She said, "Want to do lunch? I'm starving."

"We'd better get you fed then," SB replied.

"I'm buying," Alberta said, "just in case you get some other kind of crazy idea. Is the Lucky Strike okay?"

"Sure," SB said. "I'd be a fool to refuse."

On a weekday, the restaurant side of the Lucky Strike would have buzzed with the downtown lunch crowd, but since it was a Saturday, SB and Alberta had their choice of tables along the windows that overlooked Mesabi Street. Across the aisle a smattering of people sat on stools along the bar. One of them SB pegged from behind as Dave Maki. She recognized his dome shape and white comb-over and would have said "hello" except that Dave looked so deeply engaged in conversation with the man next to him that she chose not to break in. She recognized his conversation partner as a customer of theirs, the manager of Machine Supply, a parts and implement dealership out along the bypass.

A young waitress brought the water and menus. She looked about seventeen with a jaunty azure streak in her dark hair and a wild rose tattoo on her wrist. Alberta zeroed in on her and asked, "Aren't you one of the Martineau girls?"

"Yes," the young woman said. She sounded tentative, and SB wondered if she might have been a little put off by Alberta's directness. A lot of people were.

"I know your grandmother," Alberta said, holding the girl in her investigative gaze, "and I think I remember when you were born. You're Brianna, aren't you? And your mother's Shawna?"

The girl nodded, but to be known so precisely didn't seem to help at all to ease her discomfort. SB and Alberta had to give her their orders three times before she was able to recite back the correct drinks, entrees, and sides.

"Poor girl," Alberta said after Brianna left the table. "I wonder what she'll end up bringing us?"

"Hard telling," SB chuckled. "Is her grandmother one of your warrior women?"

"No," Alberta said, "a neighbor. Just one of those superwomen who hold everything together out there in the country."

"I know the type," SB said, feeling pleased afterward to see a hint of a grin as Alberta processed the compliment.

They talked about Arte and Skye, the grandmothers, the mining company, all the rest of the mining companies, the different kinds of afflictions different kinds of mines visited on Mother Nature, and where any hope might lie for the future.

"When the insects go, the birds are done," Alberta said with uncharacteristic pessimism. "When they go, we aren't going to be far behind."

SB felt guilty for letting the conversation lead them to the canary in the coalmine.

"Meanwhile," she said in a lighter voice. "I wonder when our food's going to come."

"Shh," Alberta told her. "You're making me hungrier."

At last, Brianna Martineau approached with a platter in each hand, thumb clamped tightly around the food side of each rim.

"Who ordered the walleye?" she asked.

"Me," Alberta snapped impatiently, "And you better give it to me before I take a bite out of your arm."

"Would you like onions on that?" the girl answered. Her half-lidded eyes told them she meant it flippantly.

"And ketchup," Alberta said, grabbing the squeeze bottle and pretending to get ready to lay a red line up Brianna's forearm.

SB gathered that Brianna's newfound aplomb really impressed Alberta. She tore into her walleye with gusto and didn't speak one more word of complaint until Brianna returned, asked whether she could get them anything else, and airdropped the check into the middle of the table.

"Mine! Remember?" Alberta asserted sharply.

"Hey," SB said. "I meant to ask. I hear you made the *Miami Herald.*" She was hatching a plan to distract her mother-in-law and grab the check for herself.

Alberta's eyes didn't stray from it. "Nikki?" she guessed. "It wouldn't have come from your dad, and I doubt Skye's reading the news right now. He must be too busy looking for love and weed or whatever the kids call those things these days."

"Basic human drives," SB said flatly. "You're right. It was Mom. Did she get up to see you? She said she might try."

'I wish," Alberta said, "but it would have been hard. I was staying with a family of Nicaraguan sugarcane workers out around Lake Okeechobee. Out there cell phone coverage is spotty as hell. As far as anybody who has the power to change anything cares, they're just a bunch of migrant farm workers who don't deserve anything but hard work and the cheapest possible pay and housing."

"She said you were helping them organize." SB eyed her hand's path around her water glass to the check.

"Did she?" Alberta smiled. "I suppose the *Herald* made it sound that way. I'd say the help was a give and take. The sugarcane workers and the Seminoles have been organizing out of Pahokee for years now. They've managed to tie it all together pretty well. Labor rights. Indigenous rights. Water protection. Environmental justice. But I suppose the paper made me out to be the expert because I came from way up north in the big woods. The land of Hiawatha. You know what they say about never being seen as an expert on your own home ground."

"Hah!" SB said with a scoff that was part acknowledgement and part irony. She knew all too well how it worked. She lived it. She said, "You could win the Nobel Prize, and it wouldn't necessarily get you appreciated around here."

"I'd just as soon fly under their radar," Alberta said. "It's easier that way. Of course, you don't have that luxury. Everything you do goes right out there in plain sight on Saturdays for everyone to see, like ta-da!"

SB felt honored to hear that her mother-in-law had seen to the heart of her challenge. Alberta's left hand slid across the table and covered SB's right with a squeeze that felt kindly and warm.

"Good work today," Alberta said. "I'm so proud to have you in my family, Daughter. You do know you've been my second daughter for a long time now, don't you?"

Then quick as a hawk strike she clamped down on SB's hand, grabbed the check with her own right, and jerked it out of SB's reach.

"You turkey," she hooted, louder than the buzz around the bar. "I told you this was on me!"

Toivo Niskanen, the Machine Supply manager cranked his neck to check out the commotion. Dave Maki swiveled just about enough to recognize the two of them, and SB flashed a smile that he returned more tepidly than she would have liked. She saw concern riding down the corners of his mouth and figured she'd hear about it soon enough.

Back at her apartment she received a text from Chase Monahan:

> Can we meet today?

She texted back:

> Is it urgent?

He replied:

> I think you'll want
> to know this.

She texted:

> Do you know Kettle Lake?

He replied:

> What time?

Later, when Artemisia's ringtone sounded, SB considered letting the call go to voicemail. Reluctantly she decided to pick up.

"I just finished today's online *Voice*," her mother said. "Kudos, kid. It's the most important spread I've ever seen in the old rag!"

SB drew a sharp breath and said, "Well, thanks. I guess. I'm just not sure how it's going to fly around here."

"I suppose you'll be experiencing some bumpy air," Artemisia told her. "That's not so unusual for you, is it?"

"You could say that," SB answered edgily. As often happened, she felt determined not to agree with her mother.

"Come on now," Artemisia cajoled, "What's the worst that could happen?"

"Really, Mom? Do you realize how pop psych-ish you sound right now?"

"I don't know," Artemisia answered. "In my experience it really helps to ask the question."

"Okay. Since you insist, here's what's could happen. Lost advertisers, lost subscribers, lost income, bankruptcy, foreclosure, assault and battery . . . Should I go on?"

"Susan, really."

"You asked!"

"I know you have real concerns and worries," Artemisia told her, "but you should ask yourself if there's any chance you might be catastrophizing."

"I genuinely hope so," SB answered sourly. She was not quite sure why she felt compelled to give her mother a hard time. Old hurts were definitely part of it. They were real, but with a grown daughter of her own, SB had enough experience to know it might be time to move on. She added, "I hear you. I'll try to think of it that way."

"You will?"

"Yeah."

"Oh. Wow."

"Let's leave it at that," SB said. "Don't say any more."

As evening settled in, she had Lil on leash heading toward Kettle Lake. Contending breezes stirred the green space, and they passed through streams of freshly sweet and sometimes shockingly cold air. The shadows of the woods spilled all the way to the shore as the two of them rounded the backside of the lake path. SB could barely make out the spare shape of the man waiting ahead in the trees.

Lil put on the brakes and barked with her hackles fully extended.

"It's me!" Chase Monahan's voice sounded across the space between them and set off an even more ferocious round of barking from Lil. As they drew nearer, he stuck out a hand, palm down. She gave him a good snuffling and reset her hackles to half-mast.

"What is this all about?" SB asked him.

"BeneGeo," Chase said with his ardent eyes fixed on hers, watching (it seemed to SB) to read her expression.

"What about them?" she asked.

"They may already be wholly owned by CUNIBelt," he said. "I'm in touch with someone in the organization—a whistleblower, you could say, a highly placed person who claims that Garman Worsley already owns the company as a secret subsidiary. They say he bought out the local partners' shares in a private transaction some time ago. You know BeneGeo has never gone public, so there's no public reporting requirement for a sale."

"Yeah, but reputation still matters," SB said. "They make a big deal of their local ownership."

"Exactly!" Chase agreed. "And being a good corporate citizen. This is bound to be a black eye for them when the truth comes out."

"You know I can't go to press over hearsay," SB told him. "Can you put me in touch with the whistleblower?"

His cold stare gave her the answer. "I'm just giving you a heads up. You might want to research the ownership issue yourself. I hear it's all going to come to a head very soon."

On the walk home, along the brushy backstretch of the trail, a scream erupted. A raccoon sprinted across the path, and Lil leapt after it. She pulled the extended leash to the end of its reach, jerking SB, as some other critter—a fox, judging from the pungent smell of it—scrambled deeper into the brush. In the beam of her phone's flashlight, SB saw blood on the grass. She inspected Lil as best she could. The dog didn't seem to have a scratch, but SB knew that the two of them had interrupted something primal.

Home in bed she heard her phone ding with a text from Kjell.

> It's late, so I imagine
> you're zzzz. Good work

today! Keep me posted
on responses. Don't
forget that your dad
and the family trust
have your back.

The family trust was another mixed bag, a source of relief and shame. As Kjell had explained it, a Florida Descendant's Trust was an entirely legal arrangement that gave people a way to pass assets to their survivors while deferring the inheritance taxes for 360 years. SB felt embarrassed to be a named beneficiary of such bald-faced self-interest and privilege, but she had to admit, with the *Voice* barely getting by financially, it felt good to know that the trust could catch her and the kids if she fell. When she was gone, the trust funds would go to Skye and Arte, and then everything the Ellingsons had made from their part in colonizing Red Stone County would be back in the hands of Ramona's people. It wasn't enough, of course. It wouldn't begin to make up for the wrongs done to the Anishinaabe, but it was some kind of start. At least her little slice of the circle would be closed.

15. WHOLLY OWNED

"I SEE THAT WALKER'S IN," SB informed the deputy as she strolled past his desk and into Sheriff Hayes' inner office.

"Hi ya, Walker," she chirped before he had time to even think about making excuses or closing the door in her face.

He covered his surprise fairly gracefully, she thought. The only thing that gave him away was a quite professional, almost imperceptible tightening of his lips.

He asked, "What's on your mind today?"

"Pretty much the same thing as last time," she said. "Cheryl Solem."

"For cripes sake," he told her. "Are you still chewing on that?"

"It's been almost a week, and I haven't heard a thing from you about those photos," she said.

He took off his glasses and made an elaborate project of breathing on each lens and wiping them on his shirttail while she stood there practicing patience until it ran out completely.

"You told me you weren't even sure that she was missing," SB reminded him. "I checked with the Mattsons, and they say she's still not home."

"I recall that I asked you to wait," he said, holding the glasses up to the light to inspect his work. "What happened to that?"

"We talked to some of her colleagues," she said, "and they're concerned."

He let out a long sigh. "We need to clarify something before we get started. This conversation is going to be off the record. Agreed?"

"Is that the only way you'll talk to me?"

"Yes," he said.

"Then okay."

"And you aren't recording me in any way?"

"No, I'm not," she said honestly, though she'd thought seriously about fitting herself with a wire.

Walker put his glasses on and studied her face in a way that she took to be an attempt to get the upper hand. She grinned and shook her head to let him know she would laugh off any such strategies.

"Like I told you before," he said, "not home is different from missing."

"This is more than that, though," SB argued. "Her colleagues told us they haven't been able to reach her for more than a couple of weeks."

"How many colleagues did you talk to?" he asked her.

"Three," SB answered. She knew the number didn't sound overwhelmingly convincing, but she didn't expect him to mock her.

"Three?" He said, "Dr. Solem travels all the time. She works with all kinds of people—hundreds of them, probably thousands if you count her students over the years."

"Sounds like you've done some research on her," SB said. "That's curious considering you say you have no interest in her situation. What about those photographs of the BeneGeo goons?"

"Those men are not goons," the sheriff replied in a stern and measured voice. "They're security professionals. I did talk to them, and they gave me a reasonable explanation."

"What was it?" she asked.

"I can't tell you that," he said. "And you might as well know that you're wasting your own time right now as well as mine. I'm not going to have anything else to say until some real evidence comes along to convince me that there's anything worth investigating."

"Really?" SB answered. "We have an unaccounted-for water scientist who was working on the Forest Service study that the president cancelled. The BeneGeo security professionals—as you call them—made a midnight visit to her house and took away boxes of stuff. It sure smells like there's a crime in there somewhere."

"You know, SB," the sheriff said. "You do good work, but you've got to learn when to push and when to let go. Right now, if you push too hard you could really mess up."

She asked, "Did you just admit in some backhanded way that there actually is something going on that you're investigating?"

"No," he said, "not at all. In fact, I'm not even sure that you and I are actually talking. If someone asks me later if I met with you, I doubt I'll be able to recall it."

"So that's how it is," she said.

"That's how it is," he repeated. "And if you don't take my advice, you're going to be responsible for the consequences of your actions. I hope to hell nobody gets hurt."

"I guess we've got very different ways of trying to ensure that," she said.

More stinging retorts came to mind, but she kept them to herself.

At the office Gwen took one look at her and said, "What happened?"

"Walker's trying to play some kind of Jedi mind trick on me," SB said. "He still won't even own that Cheryl Solem is missing, and he warned me that somebody could get hurt if we go with the story."

"What sense does that make if she's not missing?" Gwen asked.

"Right. It doesn't compute," SB said. "In fact, it sounds more like a way of admitting that we're right."

"Strange," Gwen said.

"Stranger still," SB told her, "Chase Monahan texted me to arrange another one of those clandestine meetings last night. He says he's got it on the authority of some CUNIBelt whistleblower that Garman Worsley has managed to get his hands on all of the BeneGeo shares."

"All of them?" Gwen asked.

"Chase says the company is now a wholly owned subsidiary of CUNIBelt."

"What? Aren't there some kind of regulations to stop that?"

SB shook her head. "They're both privately owned corporations. They don't have to report a stock sale to anyone except the IRS. According to Chase it's a done deal."

"Where's that leave us?" Gwen said. "How should we handle this?"

SB racked her brain and offered a couple of half-formed ideas: "CUNIBelt might have released some revenue numbers, and either company might have leaked some rumor of the sale if they thought it was in their best interest. Let's see what we can find. Chase thinks the news is going to break soon."

"And you believe him?" Gwen asked, looking doubtful.

"I don't know," SB said. "He was right about Cheryl Solem. At least I still think he was."

While they worked, Gwen broke the silence to announce, "CUNIBelt reported revenue of $256 billion last year, up 18 percent from the year before."

"They were trying to impress someone," SB said, "probably a bank or potential partner. I'm seeing only a few analysts' speculations about Worsley's interest in BeneGeo. I don't think we're going to find much that we can take to print."

Arte dinged in with a FaceTime request. SB touched the green icon on her phone's screen with some concern, hoping that she would not see an Arte who had reverted to the teary, red-eyed, exhausted-looking girl who'd returned from California to lick her wounds. But no. Her daughter stood against a black, turned field, bright-eyed, beaming with a face full of sun and shifting bronze highlights in her sable hair.

"The weather broke," she said, sounding relaxed and delighted. "We're getting the beans in! I'll be home in a couple of days!"

SB's own face in the inset box grinned like some love-besotted desperado. Catching a glimpse of herself, she turned her smile down a couple of notches to avoid scaring her daughter.

"That's great news," she said. "Come whenever you can. I can hardly wait to see you."

Before lunch, she noticed the BeneGeo security men leaning against the brick façade of the vacant building across the street. They had suited themselves in their business attire, accessorized with ties and holster bulges, and looked like they were staring at the *Voice*'s office windows.

"Take a peek across the street," she said to Gwen. "Are those goons looking at us, or is it just my imagination?"

Gwen got up and stood by the window. "Hard to tell from this distance," she said. "Sure seems like it, though."

They watched together as the men strolled toward the corner, moving at a casual, unhurried pace, and then turned and crossed Mesabi at the four-way stop. When they disappeared from view, SB and Gwen went back to their desks.

"Probably our imaginations," Gwen said.

"Paranoia strikes deep," SB said, and then she looked up and saw them staring through the window.

"Don't look now," she said to Gwen.

"I looked," Gwen answered. "That's creepy."

"Don't let them cow us then," SB said. "Stare right back!"

The big man took his time surveying the office. He gave the impression of lingering over details and getting the lay of the place. The smaller man's mirrored glasses, and the fact that SB couldn't see his eyes, made him feel even more menacing. The idea of two tiny reflections of her looking back at herself paralyzed her momentarily.

Gwen grabbed a reporter's notebook, carried it to the window, and slapped it repeatedly against the glass. The men stood fast.

"Shoot some pictures!" she called to SB.

SB pulled out her phone and hit the video button. The men seemed to take forever to decide to move on. Maybe it was only a minute. Time gets so distorted by alarm that it was hard to say, but they did move on.

Gwen hurried to the door and hollered after them, "What did you think you were doing?"

SB grabbed her arm and pulled her back inside.

She said. "Let's not give them any reason to come back."

She transferred a copy of the video file to the hard drive of her laptop and felt annoyed to find that her hands were trembling again.

Gwen looked uncharacteristically shaken. She told SB, "I keep wondering about that conversation you had with Walker Hayes. Could he have tipped BeneGeo off, or am I way off base?"

"If he did," SB said, "it must have been by mistake. Walker can be a pain, but I think he's honorable."

"But if Garman Worsley's billions are in play," Gwen speculated, "who knows how wide and deep any kind of payoff scheme might go?"

"Let's not start spinning conspiracy theories," SB said.

"Why not?" Gwen answered. "Isn't that what people do these days?"

The landline rang, and caller ID displayed, "BENEGEO CORP."

"Looks like the circuit is about to be completed," SB said.

Cherise LeDoux hurried through the opening pleasantries while SB waited for her to get to the point.

"What I called about," Cherise said, "is our afternoon press conference. It came up kind of suddenly, and I wanted to be sure that you'd seen my email."

"I've been too engaged to check my inbox recently," SB said.

Cherise seemed happy enough to explain and said with her usual exuberance, "Chairman Skibo will make an important announcement about the company's future. Congressman Lubovich and Commissioner Karlsrud will join us at four o'clock this afternoon in the plaza next to our headquarters."

"Does it have anything to do with a change of ownership?" SB asked, listening for any noticeable intake of breath.

She thought she heard one before Cherise replied, "Why do you ask?"

"Just a shot in the dark," SB said.

"The news will be big and positive for the Range," Cherise assured her. "That's all I can tell you right now."

SB thought the communications director had made a fairly agile recovery. When they disconnected she pulled up Cherise's email message, posted the company's news release to the *Union Voice* website, and forwarded a screenshot attachment of it to her email alert list, which included the whole range of stakeholders who'd shown up for the meeting at the Carnegie Library.

The afternoon turned warm and sunny, and BeneGeo's plaza felt like a carnival in motion. The usual barkers, roustabouts, and rubes buzzed and circulated in anticipation of the main event. A floor microphone and amplifiers had been set up on the concrete. By fifteen minutes to four, SB had recorded short interviews with Arno Toivola, Cherise LeDoux, two of the resort owners, and Marilyn Bednar, who seemed to have recovered her confidence after her earlier dustup with SB. Arno was still spouting his pro-family, pro-company line, and Marilyn kept the dream of big school budgets alive. Cherise refused to be drawn further into the ownership question and only repeated her earlier anodyne that "the news will be big and positive."

The grandmothers circulated through the crowd in their outfits, handing out bottles of water decorated with the skull and crossbones papered over the original labels. SB overheard Alberta offering a bottle to Chastain Nguyen, the stringer who covered northeastern Minnesota for the *River Cities Record.*

"What flavor do you prefer," Alberta asked her, "lead, arsenic, or mercury?"

"Hmm, that's a hard choice," Nguyen replied. "Would you mind if I take your photo with the bottle?"

Chastain was in her late twenties and good looking in a gothic, brooding way. When she approached SB, she made eye contact and asked, "What do you think the story is?"

"Tell you for sure after it's announced," SB answered with a double-edged grin. Despite the age difference she thought Chastain had friendship potential. She was definitely ambitious and intelligent. For the present SB thought it most prudent to stick to respecting her as a rival.

At the last minute, Gwen arrived, and SB watched as people stepped apart to let her pass through the crowd. Gwen was magic like that. Wherever she went, people seemed aware of her presence, and SB looked forward to the running commentary that would begin when Gwen settled into the space beside her.

At four o'clock the side door of the headquarters building opened, and Holton Skibo came out followed by Casper Karlsrud, the lanky, brown-haired congressman from a neighboring district, Dan Lubovitz, and Cherise LeDoux.

Cherise stepped to the microphone, welcomed the crowd, and introduced "the man you all know as our Minnesota-born Chief Executive Officer."

Skibo's pale, Nordic face looked flushed. He came to the mic and started in a rush, "I'll get right to the good news. BeneGeo is ready to move forward in our quest to bring renewed prosperity to Giants Range. We've formalized our partnership with the internationally respected mining corporation CUNIBelt. This partnership will supply us with the capital and expertise we need to put our local plans in action. CUNIBelt brings vast experience and resources to the table. With their help we'll complete the required reviews of our innovative Mix and Separate disposal plan, and with approvals in place, we hope to break ground within the year on the mine that we've named the 'Twenty-first Century'—a safe, clean, and profitable copper-nickel mine that will provide needed resources for a green economy and jobs in Red Stone County for generations to come. Please help us welcome the Twenty-first Century!"

"Well, I guess that beats the Skibo, if that was their alternative," Gwen whispered as the clapping and shouting started.

"Or the Worsley," SB said in full voice so that Gwen could hear her over the noise. "It sure does lay claim to a whole lot of future time."

The congressman came next. "I'm always happy to work with BeneGeo and the mining families of the Range," Representative Lubovitz said. "As you know I serve on the House Committees on Natural Resources and on Mines and Mining, assignments I requested because that's where I can do the most good for the people of my district and this one. I'm proud to say I've helped move this project along, and I'm ready to do whatever I can to cut through all the Washington red tape and get this project started."

When the applause came mixed with booing, he added, "We aren't forgetting the environment. We know water and tourism are just as important as mining around here. We're going to make sure the Twenty-first Century mine is the safest and our water remains the most pristine in the world. We can do it all. We're Rangers!"

Karlsrud followed him and mugged for the crowd, applauding and extending a hand toward Skibo and then toward the congressman.

"What they said!" he quipped, looking as if he'd coined the phrase and was entitled to feel proud about it.

The crowd's response ran the familiar gamut from celebration to grousing. The noise level didn't drop until the CEO and congressman shifted their body posture and made it clear they were moving toward the headquarters building.

SB figured she needed to seize the opportunity. She shouted in two loud bursts, "What does your partnership look like? Any change in ownership?"

Skibo flashed a photogenic smile and signaled to Cherise with a point of his finger and jerk of his thumb that she should connect with SB.

By then the audience had started to shift and talk among themselves.

Gwen leaned into SB and said, "We'd better get going before Cherise hands you another informational packet."

16. BS ERLINGSEN

S B WOKE FEELING Lil push off against her stomach. The dog flew from the bed, sounded a fierce alarm, and raced toward the back stairs, barking. While SB swung her legs over the edge of the mattress, she caught a glimpse of the clock. A little after two, and Lil clamored down the back stairs, barking all the way.

On her feet SB felt the chill of the hardwood floor and the stairs, but she was already on her way and didn't want to reverse course and look for her slippers. She heard Lil scratching and snarling at the back door, but when SB got there everything looked okay. The deadbolt was still fastened just as she'd left it. She wanted to check the newsroom, and looked for something she could use as a defensive weapon just in case she needed one. As it turned out, she fell entirely short of handy knives, baseball bats, and tire irons. Lil's dog brush lay on the floor by the boot tray. It was a ridiculous choice. There wasn't much heft to it, but at least it was wooden, and she had something in her hand. She was holding it when she heard glass breaking and a thud from the newsroom.

"Wait now," she said, grabbing Lil's collar. She did her best to turn the knob and ease the door open with the hand that held the brush while she kept a death grip on Lil. The dog yipped and thrashed from side to side, but SB managed to hang on. Once she'd wrestled the knob and managed to push the door open, she took a firmer grip on the brush and yelled, "Who's there?"

The office was dark, but the streetlamps threw enough light inside for her to see that the front window had been shattered. Jagged glass framed her view of Mesabi as she and Lil ventured deeper. Lil continued to sound off.

"Shush," SB whispered. She wanted to listen for anyone who might have been breathing or moving around in there.

She left the overhead light off, figuring that the low light from the street gave her some kind of advantage over any stranger in her familiar space. Once she'd had a chance to look around and see that she and Lil were the only ones there, she turned her attention to the good-sized projectile that lay on the floor up front. It was flat and wide, wrapped in something, and resting amid chunks and shards of glass. Getting to it for a closer look would be no job for the bare-footed, so she pulled Lil back upstairs.

SB dressed in the dark and called 911 from her bedroom. The city police dispatcher said an officer would be with her soon, so she shut Lil in upstairs and went back down alone. She'd covered enough crime scenes to know that she shouldn't disturb the evidence, so she turned on the lights and shot some photos. She could see from its wide, oval shape that the projectile most likely was a rock wrapped in paper and duct tape. She could make out the letters "BS."

The police parked their cruiser in front and came to the door in their blue uniforms, setting off another round of hysterical barking from upstairs. The officers turned out to be the same ones she'd seen talking to Walker Hayes at the Carnegie Library—Angela DeMarco, the grown daughter of a local miner, and Luke St. Jean, a shirttail cousin of Ramona's on the Desjardin side of the family. People of mixed Native and European ancestry, the Desjardins had traveled the country that we now call the international borderlands. Some of them identified as Métis and were recognized as Indigenous in Canada. Some went with Anishinaabe, Cree, Ojibwe, Chippewa, or white. Luke, a slender, youthful, modest man, went to high school with Arte. He had never talked about identity in SB's presence. She didn't know how he saw himself. Angela looked to be at least fifteen years younger than SB. She had sharp, dark eyes, stripes on her sleeve and a full head of wavy, brunette hair.

"Sorry to bother you two at this time of night," SB said.

"Don't worry about that," Angela told her. "It beats driving around in the squad making conversation with this bonehead—not that I mean to make light of your trouble, Ms. Ellingson."

"She just means to make light of me," Luke interjected with a restrained chuckle. "If it's okay with you, Sarge, I think I'll go have a look around the perimeter, and you two can say whatever you like about me while I'm gone."

"As if we'd talk about him at all!" Angela said loudly enough for him to hear as he walked away.

"We are talking about him, though, aren't we?" SB said.

The sergeant raised her eyebrows in acknowledgement before she got out her phone and started shooting photos.

"Are you going to dust that thing for prints?" SB asked, "Or don't you get into that kind of detail for this level of offense?"

Angela flashed SB what looked like an indulgent smile. "We'll hold it as evidence at least," she said. "Shall we have a better look?" She pulled on a glove and rotated the object until they could see the entirety of the message:

BS
Erlingsen
Watch your
self

"Dyslexic?" Angela said.

"I doubt it," SB replied. "It's a lame joke I've heard before. Not since junior high, though. The last name's just a misspelling I'd guess."

Angela shrugged. She had a sweet looking face at times, thanks to heart-shaped lips and a generous smile that occasionally broke through her practiced reserve. SB concluded that Angela cultivated kindness as a survival strategy.

"How does it work for you being so nice and being a cop?" SB asked her.

"I don't know how nice I am," Angela shrugged. "I keep getting promoted, and I haven't had to shoot anybody. Maybe that tells you something."

"Maybe it does," SB said.

"Or maybe I've just been lucky," Angela shrugged. "I'd shoot without a second thought if I had to."

Luke's flashlight beam lit up the surviving window. He opened the front door and said, "Sarge, you might want to take a look at something in back."

"That sounds ominous," SB said.

"Looks like somebody tried to jimmy the door," he clarified.

As SB followed Luke around the building and looked where he pointed his flashlight beam at the scraped and chipped doorjamb, she felt her stomach clench and cinch tight.

"Someone has used some kind of screwdriver or pry bar to try and force the lock," Angela said. "Pretty good catch, rookie!"

"They might have been using too light a bar," he said, and then, under Angela's corrective gaze, he added, "Good thing."

They checked all the way around the building before they took SB's story.

"I don't see any security cameras," Angela said at one point. "Am I missing something?"

"No," SB said. "We've never needed one."

"I see," Angela said. Her mouth turned down disapprovingly. "You might want to reconsider that. We're going to sit in the car and fill out the report, and then we'll need you to read and sign it, and you can have a copy when we're done, okay?"

"Whatever you say," SB agreed.

She still needed to deal with the window. That meant going down into the basement to get supplies. She had no intention of waiting until after the police had left, so she went to the top of the basement stairs and turned on the light. On the way down, she stopped every couple of steps and looked around. Each time she saw nothing but the same old basement with the same old hulking, decommissioned linotype machines taking up one whole end of the space and the same old coal furnace converted to natural gas, extending its tentacles to every quadrant of the building. She walked around and looked into the shadowy places, and when she'd satisfied herself that she was alone, she got the duct tape and the plastic drop cloths she'd tucked away after her last painting project. Upstairs she put them aside and started picking up the bigger pieces of glass by hand. She worked carefully and drew blood only once before she switched to the dustpan and broom. When she thought she had swept up all of the smaller shards, she backed up and looked at the floor from different angles—a seemingly endless task. She kept seeing little glints that meant she'd missed a fragment and had to go sweep it up. Even the smallest shard wouldn't do—not in a lobby open to the public and to Lil's vulnerable paws.

When Angela came back with the police report on a clipboard, SB was standing on a chair in front of the window. She had run a line of duct tape along one edge of the drop cloth and was stretched nearly to the limit of her reach, trying to secure the plastic along the top of the window frame.

Angela said, "Luke can help you with that."

"I don't want to trouble him," SB said reluctantly. She didn't want to appear ungrateful, either, but at that point she really wanted nothing more than to be left alone.

"No trouble at all," Angela said, "I need your signature over here."

By the time SB had read and signed the paperwork, Luke had the drop cloth pulled tight, taped around the edges, and trimmed neatly around with his jackknife.

SB signed where Angela pointed, and listened while she explained, "We'll do our best, but no guarantees. Call me if you think of anything important that we haven't already covered."

Once they'd gone, the loveseat in the lobby looked like the best seat in town. SB went upstairs, got Lil and a blanket, and then flopped down on the seat, upright with the back of her head against the windowsill and her legs splayed on the floor. The hour was some time after four. First light would arrive around five, and SB felt sure that she wouldn't be able to drop off to sleep—not the way her brain was racing under the influence of whatever mix of bio-chemicals her fear and stress had stirred up.

Her mind drifted to the time she jolted awake from an anxiety dream and heard Ramona sleepily ask, "What happened? You cried out. You sounded so pitiful."

SB didn't think she should answer honestly. She thought fast and told Ramona, "I dreamed you'd left me." Ramona was eight-and-a-half months pregnant with Arte at the time, and SB had been going through the terrors and misgivings of expecting a first child. In truth, she had dreamed that Ramona died in childbirth. She felt guilty about the lying and didn't know if she had done wrong or right. Everything felt so intense back then. She felt so jumbled up inside.

By all rights, SB should have been the one comforting Ramona, but instead it was her immense-bellied wife stroking SB's face and whispering, "Don't you know I'd have to be crazy to leave you? Where would I find anyone else like you? You're perfect for me. You must know you're the love of my life. Who else would put up with me?"

Twenty-three years later, SB still felt ashamed. She couldn't let her younger self off the hook. How foolish she'd been to feel fearful when she'd had Ramona beside her, Arte in the womb, and their precious, finite lives together stretching ahead. Then again, as the predawn chill leaked through the plastic patch behind her head, she thought maybe she'd been wiser than her years. In a universe where stars eat other stars and whole solar systems slide into black holes, what chance did love have?

17. OH, MOM!

S B DID FALL ASLEEP, as it turned out, and she woke on the loveseat, chilled and shivering with Lil beside her and a jabbing pain in her lower back. The morning was fully bright. She could see to every corner of the newsroom even though the sun hadn't appeared over the roofs of the downtown buildings. She washed her face in the employees' bathroom, put on a pot of coffee, and checked the local glass company's listing online. They didn't open until eight-thirty, so she took Lil out back to the grassy fringe around the parking lot and told the disgruntled dog to make do. They weren't going to the park.

Dave Maki came in before eight, looked around with surprise, and said, "What the hell happened here?" As he listened to SB tell the story, she watched his pug-like jaw tighten. He said, "You've got enough on your hands as it is. Let me take care of this."

He called the direct line of the glass company's owner and schmoozed about wives, kids and fishing before getting around to business. Overhearing Dave's side of the conversation, SB gathered there was some complication.

After disconnecting Dave explained, "He'll send someone over right away to measure it, but they'll probably have to order the plate glass from Duluth. They might not be able to replace it until tomorrow."

"I hope that doesn't mean another night of sleeping in the lobby," SB said.

"No, not at all," Dave assured her. "We'll secure it with plywood if it comes to that. I'll get Jack to help me."

It was most likely too early to call Arte. The twenty-one-year-old who'd left home for California would most definitely have been sleeping at 8:45, but the twenty-three-year-old Farmer Arte might be a whole different person. Who knew what she might be doing, maybe getting up with the sun to dance to Chris and Ashley Sunberry's supervisory rhythms? SB sent a text in the hope of hearing back in an hour or so. 'Sad' did not begin to describe how heartsick she felt to write what she did.

> Good morning, Sunshine! I hope you slept well. I've been sooo looking forward to seeing you, but there's been a complication. :(I'm swamped right now. So sorry but this isn't the best time to visit. Can we postpone?

Of course, what she said was true and then again not. She did feel swamped, but she had felt swamped for decades. The real problem was the situation—the rock thrower, the cranks, the thugs, the know-it-alls, and the chill that Cheryl Solem's disappearance had thrown into everything. SB felt the visit wasn't wise—temporarily, she was sure, but for the time being she didn't feel safe, she didn't feel generous, and she didn't want to put Arte in danger. Two minutes later the piano riff that was Arte's ringtone sounded.

"What's going on?" SB heard the tense and elevated pitch that signaled Arte was feeling wronged and ruffled.

"Things are just a little crazy around here," SB minimized, trying to keep her own angst under wraps. "I didn't get much sleep last night, and I'm running kind of ragged. I'm hoping we can . . ."

"Things are always a little crazy in your life!" Arte interrupted.

SB recognized the whiny, irritated tone all too well.

"I didn't sleep much either," Artie groused, "and I'm already most of the way home! What am I supposed to do? I thought you wanted to see me, and I thought we had a plan! Now I'm really confused. The pork's in the back, thawing more and more as I sit here talking, and I've got no place else to go with it!"

SB asked, "Are you driving right now?"

"I'm pulled over."

"That's a relief," SB said.

"Is it? Honestly, Mother, you seem to think I have no sense sometimes." Arte sounded more and more peeved with each outpouring. "I'd rather be driving. I'd rather be getting closer. I really want to get there, Mom. I really want to see you!"

"I want to see you, too, Honey," SB assured her.

"You do?"

"Yes."

"You know what?" Arte began to sound slightly calmer and more appealing. "Why don't you let me cook for you tonight, Mom? Seriously, let's just go ahead with this. You won't have to lift a finger. I got a recipe from Ashley, and I'm bringing the juiciest, most delicious ribs and chops you've ever tasted."

"Oh, Arte, I don't know," SB sighed. She knew she might as well capitulate. She found her daughter impossible to resist.

"And greens from our cold frames," Arte offered. "They're so fresh you can just feel the vitamins and minerals going into your system when you eat them. It'll be so good, and just what the doctor ordered for your stress. I've got stories for you, Mom. I've got news. We need to talk."

"We do?" SB said. "Do tell."

"Not now," Arte answered. "After I get there."

Somehow the little vagabond had learned to tease.

"Should I brace myself?" SB asked.

"I wouldn't bother. I think you'll be happy. And relieved."

"OK then," SB said with a sigh of capitulation. "Drive carefully. Watch for deer."

"Always," Arte asserted before her caller ID blinked off.

After lunch Dave Maki and Jack Bono came in through the back in worn pants and T-shirts. They got to work measuring the perimeter of the window.

"The replacement glass is coming from Duluth," Dave told her. "They'll install it as soon as it gets here tomorrow. Meanwhile we're closing it up so you can sleep tonight."

SB leaned against the tailgate of Jack's pickup and watched as he and Dave marked and measured a sheet of plywood with a pencil, tape measure, and square. When Arte pulled into the parking lot the guys had the sheet arranged across two sawhorses. SB heard her daughter's car motor and looked up to see Arte pulling into an empty parking space. Her window was rolled down. Her hair looked wild and windblown. Probably no AC in the little, old hatchback.

Arte announced in a strong, cheerful voice, "I'm here!"

Lil barked from inside.

"Hurray!" SB cheered and hurried over for a hug.

"Hey, who's that happy looking kid?" Jack grinned when Arte approached looking suntanned and curious. "What happened to the black eye shadow and nail polish?"

"I figured you old hippie would be all over my natural, indigenous look," Arte winked, eliciting an even bigger smile from Jack.

"Whatever you're doing, keep doing it," Dave said, thumping her on the back, "You look great, kiddo!"

"You guys, too," Arte said distractedly. SB noticed a dawning look of concern cross her face, and then Arte asked, "What's going on?"

"We had a little accident with a window," SB interjected before the men could spill the beans about the vandalism.

"Oh," Arte said. "That sucks."

"Doesn't it?" Jack said. "But we got it covered. Nothing to worry about."

The hatchback was caked with road dust. SB tried not to brush against the exterior as she helped Arte unload her things—a backpack, a grocery bag full of laundry to be done in SB's machines, and a cardboard box lined with a blanket and piled on the bottom with packages of pork, folded towels for insulation, and greens on top, keeping fresh from the cooling effect of the thawing meat.

When the guys tried to help, SB waved them off, insisting, "We've got it! You're doing enough."

On the stairs, Arte said, "I hope the ribs are thawed. I've got to get them into the oven."

"It's only three o'clock," SB said.

"They're supposed to cook for three hours," Arte answered.

"Oh," her mother said.

"Slowly."

"I see."

"You do have a roasting pan, don't you, Mom?"

The ribs looked beautiful when Arte unwrapped them, more brightly colored and leaner than any you could find at the grocery store on the bypass. Arte had brought the spices she needed, and SB watched her mix up a dry rub, apply it to the ribs, and arrange them in the pan, blanketed in aluminum foil from SB's cupboard.

"By the way," Arte said casually as she slid the pan into the oven, "I invited Grandma Al."

"You did?" SB asked, trying not to let too much disappointment color her voice. She had wanted Arte all to herself.

"I really wanted to see her," Arte said, "Did I mess up?"

"No, no, not at all," SB told her. "I'm always happy to see Alberta. I was just hoping for an early bedtime."

Arte said, "Are you still having trouble sleeping?"

"Not really," SB answered.

"Huh," Arte said skeptically while her sensitive, discerning eyes made a close appraisal of SB's face.

Alberta arrived right at six and hugged them both, saying, "Boozhoo. So good to be with both of you!"

"Boozhoo, Grand-mère," Arte said, mixing languages with a clever grin that made Alberta light up.

SB herself relished every word and feature of her daughter. With glee, she watched Arte's efforts to uncork the bottle of wine she'd brought.

"Be sure you get the corkscrew all the way to the bottom of the cork, or it might break off," SB instructed.

"I know," Arte said. "Don't hover. I can get it." And she did. She told SB, "Why don't you sit while I get the glasses?"

Arte placed a round, wide-bodied piece of stemware in front of her mother and poured it half full. She did the same for Alberta. Clearly, she had learned to manage this particular, useful social grace.

"It's an organic red blend from Wisconsin," she said. "I picked it up at the Madison farmer's market."

SB lifted her glass, and said, "To the return of the prodigal!"

Arte laughed, "Only I'm the one who's provided the fatted calf, so to speak."

"To the sacred sow," Alberta said, glass still in the air. "Thank you for feeding us! You sure do smell good!"

The scent of garlic, oregano, and salty, caramelized flesh filled the air when Arte pulled the ribs from the oven. While she rested them on top of the stove, she dumped a bag of spring greens into a bowl. When she had brought everything to the table, Alberta looked impressed and expectant, and SB felt her own face flush with pride.

Over a heaping plate Arte asked, "How was California, Grandma?"

"Oh! Did you hear about that?" Alberta said. "They're organizing around water there, too, only a lot of the fight is over who has the right to get some."

"Have you ever met Dolores Huerta?" Arte asked.

"A few times," Alberta said as modestly as if she had been talking about her next-door neighbor. "I was in Florida with the Seminoles and the sugarcane workers last month. It's all about the water there, too, and environmental justice, like everywhere."

"It gets pretty basic, doesn't it?" Arte said.

"Yeah," Alberta answered. "We've got to keep the Earth and the water for everybody. It's going to be up to you kids soon. Your mom's in the fight."

"You are, Mom?" Arte said. "I thought you never took sides."

"Think again," Alberta said. "Your mother just got a rock through her front window for telling the truth about what the mining company is trying to push through around here."

"Is that what happened?" Arte asked.

SB shrugged it off. "Some crank got his nose out of joint."

Arte looked dumfounded.

"Hey," Alberta said to her, "why don't you tell us about your farming adventures? You look so good. It must suit you fine."

"It does," Arte said. "I love everything about it—the land, the work, the animals . . ."

"The people?" Alberta queried.

"The people are the best," Arte said, letting loose a mysterious smile.

"Anyone in particular?" Alberta asked.

"Oh!" Arte said, blushing. "I love 'em all in one way or another."

She got up and poured what was left of the wine, distributing it in roughly three equal portions.

"Surprise!" she said. "Skye wants to come to our party! I'm going to FaceTime him. Scrunch together over there. Take your wineglasses. I'll come over to your side of the table."

When Skye accepted her invitation, she propped her phone against the salad bowl and adjusted it to take them all in. It was good to see his face, sun tanned and circled by his mop of sun-bleached blond hair. He was outdoors somewhere with other people, but the screen was too small and zeroed in on him to make sense of the setting.

"Thanks for inviting me," he said, lifting a beer bottle while they returned the salute with their wine glasses. "How's everybody?"

"Good!" Alberta declared. "Your sister just fed us a delicious feast. Your mother and I continue to battle on in our own ways. How about you?"

"Can't compete with any of that," he said. "I'm just trying to have a good time." He could have practically patented the disarming, trickster grin that he flashed. His mother knew it well. His mask. He never wanted anyone to think he was too serious, though in truth he ran about as deep and unpredictable as Lake Superior. He said, "I'm going to spend a week with Grandpa on his boat. He wants to show me the Intracoastal."

"Just you and him?" Alberta asked.

"Just him, me, and the porpoises," Skye said. "And maybe a manatee if any of them have survived the algae blooms."

"Well, tell him Skol, whatever the hell that means," Alberta said. "I think it's supposed to be a good thing."

"Don't let Dad talk you into drinking too much," SB added. "Don't do anything I wouldn't do."

"I don't think that'll be a problem," Skye grinned. "We pretty much like the same temptations."

"There you have it," Arte said. "Thanks for joining the party, Bro!"

"Love you all," he said, flashing a set of healthy-looking teeth, orthodontic work sponsored by SB.

"Love you, too," SB called back before he blinked out of sight.

She was enjoying the soft, gauzy cushion that Arte's dinner and the wine had wrapped around everything.

"Arte," Alberta threw in, "I wasn't sure what you were telling us about love earlier. Are you seeing anyone special?"

"Maybe," Arte said.

"Maybe what?" Alberta asked her.

Arte downed the last gulp of her wine before answering.

"I'm seeing someone," she said, "and maybe it's special. It's like having a friend who might end up being something more."

SB felt quite a bit more awake and alert then.

"Boy or girl?" Alberta asked.

"Genderqueer," Arte said.

"Is that like Two Spirit?" Alberta said.

"Maybe sort of, only I don't think they're Native, so I don't know," Arte said.

"Do they have a name?" SB asked.

"Cayenne."

"You know," Alberta said, "when Ramona told me she was Two Spirit, she never hid it after that. One day our neighbor came over and told me she asked her priest about it, and he told her that was sinful. He said nobody can have two spirits. What do you think about that?" Alberta laughed. "They might not know what it means, but they know it's wrong."

"Is Cayenne male to female or female to male?" SB asked.

"Oh, Mom," Arte said. "It's so beyond that. Nobody thinks in those old binaries anymore. Think gender fluid. Think flow."

"If you like them," SB said, "that's all that matters to me. How's that for flow?"

"Not bad," Arte said with a nervous chuckle, "only I don't know how to tell if I like them or love them. I mean I love them, but how do I know if I love/love them—you know what I mean?"

"I think I do," SB allowed. "That's a hard one."

18. WILD THING

SATURDAY'S FRONT PAGE FEATURED SB's photos of the rock, the jimmied doorframe, and the broken front window, along with a three-column story and a boxed announcement offering a thousand-dollar reward for information about the rock thrower and the attempted break-in.

After Jack and his paper deliverers had come and taken away their bundles, SB said to Arte, "Let's close down and do something fun."

Arte looked surprised. "I'm in if you are," she said. "Sounds kind of wild for you, though, Mom. Are you sure?"

"You just never know about me," SB razzed, relishing a chance to complicate her daughter's notions of her. "What are in you in the mood for?"

Arte's smooth, elastic face pulled lopsided, making her appear to put a major effort into thinking before she said, "I'd like to drive out to Rocky's and spend some time with you and Mara."

"You would?" SB asked. "You used to diss me something fierce when I wanted to take you to Rocky's. You accused me of dragging you there."

"I know," Arte said, looking a little abashed. "I called you Annie Oakley."

"And you called her Rocky Balboa," SB said.

"I guess I've got a new appreciation of some things," Arte said.

When they pulled into Rocky's barnyard, SB saw Merle Byrne's green car parked near the barn. What was going on? Running into the woman again seemed to defy the odds of coincidence. Had Arte told Rocky they were coming? SB pulled her SUV into the remaining space and hesitated in the driver's seat after she turned off the engine.

Arte shot out of the car and stood in the open-door space on the passenger side, then stuck her head back in and asked impatiently, "Are you coming?"

"I will," SB said. "I'm just feeling a little uncomfortable."

"About what?" Arte asked.

"Did you arrange this whole thing?"

"Arrange what whole thing?" Arte cocked her head, looking concerned.

"Never mind," SB backpedaled. "I just had a little momentary thing. It's nothing."

"Are you sure?" Arte said. "If you're sick . . ."

SB waved her off and got out of the car.

"Look at the nice buckskin!" Arte exclaimed when they approached the open barn door and saw Merle inside, currying her sleek gelding.

Merle turned her head to see who was coming. Her face broke into an off-guard expression of surprise.

SB said, "Merle Byrne and Dillon, this is Arte, my daughter, and vice versa."

Merle reached her right hand toward Arte and asked, "Is Arte short for something?"

"That's the way it is on my birth certificate," Arte said, looking roused with curiosity and a chance to hold forth about her personal history. "It was inspired by my Grandma Artemisia, but it was my other mom's idea."

"Definitely not mine," SB interjected. "There was only room in the world for one Artemisia as far as I was concerned."

"Gram can be kind of overwhelming," Arte added, "in a well-meaning way."

"I think I know the type," Merle said. "Did you two come to ride?"

"Yes," Arte answered before SB had time to concoct a more ambivalent answer.

"Why don't we ride together then?" Merle said.

"We could," Arte enthused. "We could double up, couldn't we, Mom? We haven't done that in a long time."

"There's a reason for that," SB grumbled.

"Come on, don't be Susie-So-Sad," Arte argued. "It'll be fun!"

"We're not out to set any speed records," Merle said. "I don't mind sticking to a walking gait if that would work for you two."

What else could SB say?

She relented, "I'm game if you two are. I'll have to catch Mara, though."

"Is that a problem?" Merle asked.

"Sometimes," SB answered.

"I'll go with you," Arte said.

On the way to the pasture, they talked and bumped against each other, joking about whatever crossed their minds—the greening plants, the horses, the early pollinators, the rasping slide of whole oats against the sides of the bucket, the catching rope that SB had tucked where Mara wouldn't see it, and the mare's habit of toying with SB for sport.

"Makes you wonder who's catching who," Arte teased.

As usual, once they were inside the pasture, Mara's rules applied. She got her mouthful of oats and consented to let SB catch her. When SB snapped the lead rope onto the halter ring, Arte jumped on Mara's back, and SB led them back to the barn. Merle waited outside with Dillon saddled, bridled, and standing quietly. He nickered and pointed his ears in Mara's direction as they approached.

"Sorry for holding you up," SB apologized.

"You're not," Merle said brightly. "We're soaking in the atmosphere."

SB had Mara saddled and bridled before Rocky appeared in the doorway.

"Hey," Rocky said, striding toward Arte, "who is this stranger?" Rocky clamped her hands on Arte's biceps and held her at arms' length with muscles that looked rock hard inside their crepe-skinned sheathing. "You've got some meat in there, Girl! You must be doing some serious work these days!"

"Slopping hogs and digging in the dirt," Arte said, sounding proud about it.

"Around here?" Rocky asked, and then answered herself, "No. Must not be. Not many raise hogs around here anymore."

"Wisconsin," Arte answered. "South of Madison."

"Ah, they do things like that down there I guess," Rocky said. "How about you, SB? I see hell's breakin' loose at that newspaper of yours."

"I stay busy enough," SB said, purposely keeping it tepid. She didn't want Arte to gather that there was any reason to worry.

"Me, too," Rocky laughed. "I had four foals born this spring. Real spark-plugs. Now I'm working on gentling them to the halter."

"Could I help you with that?" Arte said. "I love babies."

"I was just about to go and work with them now," Rocky said. "Come along if you want."

"What about the ride?" SB asked.

"You two go ahead," Arte answered.

SB looked at Merle and shrugged a complaint, "Kids."

"I know," Merle said. "I was one once."

SB was still chuckling when Merle lifted her left foot and inserted it into the stirrup. SB hurried then and mounted Mara in a rush so that her launch would be close to simultaneous. She didn't want Merle to watch her looking as rusty and awkward as she thought she might be, but her upward thrust unto the seat felt fairly smooth, and once she was aboard, she relaxed a little.

"Ready?" Merle asked, waiting for SB's confirming nod before she urged Dillon ahead.

SB squeezed Mara with her calves. The mare overreacted and jumped into a faster walk than SB expected, leaving her a little behind the balance point, but she recovered.

Down the driveway and onto the township road, the horses matched their paces and lengthened into smooth, efficient walking strokes. SB's back loosened, and she was able to rock more deeply into the seat of the saddle.

"Did you grow up with horses?" she asked Merle.

"No. With wolves," Merle said.

SB laughed abruptly. She had to give the woman points for being quick on the uptake.

"Seriously," Merle said, "I didn't grow up with horses at home, but I used to ride at my grandparents' farm. I spent a lot of time with them."

"Where was that?" SB asked.

"Not far from my place now," Merle said. "It was a little dairy out in Willow Township. Grandpa worked at the IronTac mine before the company shut it down. Grandma took care of the cows."

"I hear that a lot of people divided up chores that way back then," SB said. "Do you still have family around here?"

"Shirttail cousins somewhere, I guess," Merle told her. "The ones I know have gone to the Cities or one of the coasts. It looks like I'm the only one foolish or stubborn enough to come back."

"Now that you've got a portable job," SB said.

"Yeah, and a lot of big ideas," Merle said. "Mind if we trot awhile?"

Behind Merle and Dillon, SB clucked and nudged Mara into the bumpy, two-beat trot that let a horse cover a lot of ground. She posted from the stirrups as Rocky had taught her forty years earlier, legs lifting her seat above the saddle and returning in cadence with Mara's strides. She heard Merle and Dillon beating a similar rhythm a horse length or so behind them, and SB felt that she'd like to look sharp. It helped that she knew Rocky's trail. Groomed through woods and brush, it led to a logging road that branched for miles through a mix of logged-over and standing woodlots. Berry bushes, poplar shoots and scrub growth alternated haphazardly with towering hardwoods and evergreens. Riding through the older growth, she watched for low hanging branches and tried to stay balanced and ready to dodge on short notice. When they came to a wide, open stretch Merle pulled beside them with Dillon at a canter. She whooped teasingly as she passed, and when SB rocked back to give Mara the signal, the mare jumped into the faster, smoother pace. The brush and branches flashed past. The damp, fecund smell of the woods and Mara's tremendous breathing and exertion felt familiar and intoxicating. SB wondered why she hadn't gone riding in such a long time.

A mile or so from the barn, Merle slowed Dillon to a walk, and SB urged Mara up beside them.

"What about you?" Merle asked.

"What about what?" SB sidestepped.

Merle flashed an inquisitive look, her mouth in a slight, curious skew. "Where are you coming from? Why the newspaper? Why all the work all the time? Why the jibs and jabs you take, and the broken windows?"

"So far there's only been the one broken window," SB corrected.

Merle looked entirely unimpressed with her answer.

"Seriously," SB added, "Flak comes with the territory, but the Ellingsons have learned to blow it off. It's family stuff. It's complicated. It's intergenerational. It's a responsibility I took on willingly. It's about truth telling and the blowback that goes with being the voice and the ears of the people—or trying to."

"Sounds noble," Merle said without a note of cynicism as far as SB could tell. Those blue-green eyes fixed on her in a way that made her feel scrutinized.

SB shrugged, "I don't know. It's freaking fascinating. I mean, we all know objectivity is impossible. We're all self-interested, and yet I've got to believe there's a trail of truth that can be ferreted out if we work at it. What about you? What drives you? Besides massage I mean."

"So, you think massage drives me?" Merle said, "Maybe it did once, but now it's only my work. I would have said good, available food."

SB wouldn't have guessed that. She found herself echoing, "Food?"

"Yeah," Merle said. "Ever heard of an edible landscape?"

"What is it? Like things to forage?"

"That's part of it," Merle said. "You know that park around the little lake in town?"

"As a matter of fact, I do know it."

"Then you know how the green space leads to that senior citizens' high rise on one side and the elementary school beyond?"

"Yes," SB said, finding herself surprisingly intrigued.

"I'd like to get the school kids and the elders working together on a project to landscape those green spaces with apples, berries, and edible native plants and maybe a community garden with raised beds. And then we could get all sorts of people involved in teaching and learning about foraging, gardening, and food as medicine."

"Impressive," SB said. "You're going to run into some interesting local politics."

"Interesting in the Midwestern, pejorative sense, you mean?" Merle asked as if she already knew the answer.

"If you like," SB said, "I'd be glad to fill you in on what I know about who decides what and who plays well together around here."

"I'd definitely take you up on that," Merle said.

"Of course, I should remind you," SB said. "I just got a rock thrown through my window, so you'd have to consider whether or not I'm really the right person to ask."

"Isn't that always the danger with everyone?" Merle said.

SB thought her cheek muscles might be starting to hurt from smiling.

19. ROUND THE BEND

ON SUNDAY NIGHT, Arte did laundry. She topped off her load with a few things of her mother's, and when she finished, she left them folded on SB's dresser. On Monday morning she appeared in the kitchen with her bags stuffed full of clean clothes. SB got up from her chair and opened her arms, and Arte slipped into them.

SB said, "Thanks for all the food and the cooking. My god! I ate so much I can hardly close my pants! Look!" She stuck out her belly and patted it with such a sad look on her face that she managed to make Arte laugh. One thing SB knew for sure: There would be no clinging goodbyes from her, no regrets voiced, no pressure to stay longer.

When someone knocked on the back door, she said, "That'll be your fairy godmother."

Gwen glided into the kitchen in a loose-fitting, cotton pants suit, carrying a yellow gift bag that she handed to Arte.

"Just a little care package," she said.

"Wow, nice," Arte declared as she sorted through Moose Track cookies from the bakery on Mesabi, whole grain bread and peanut butter from the Iron Food Co-op, and two jars of home-canned, wild berry jam.

"It's all local stuff," Gwen said. "I made the jam. I put in a couple of plastic knives, too, just in case you experience a food emergency. Chuck and I have found that PB and J sometimes hits the spot on the road."

"It wouldn't be the first time," Arte said, looking genuinely pleased and reaching out to initiate a hug with Gwen.

SB felt proud watching her daughter interact as a grownup among grownups. Remembering her own mixed feelings about her parents and their friends, she often wondered just how much Arte really liked spending time with her. She was relieved to see Arte growing into a self-determined person who, more and more, could see through other people's faults and fictions and still take them as they were. SB thought that, with luck, she herself might achieve that goal if she lived to be about a hundred and ten.

Gwen patted Arte on the back and said, "You're doing so wonderfully!"

"Thanks," Arte smiled. "I try. And if it's any help, I think you are, too."

Then Arte picked up her pack. SB thought she saw a glisten of water in her eyes.

"It's been great," Arte said cheerfully. "Thanks for everything."

SB picked up the paper bag and said, "I'll walk you down."

Arte put her pack on and reached for the bag, saying, "Would you mind just saying goodbye here? I think it'll just be easier for both of us that way. And no waving from the window, either, okay?"

SB saw one tear start to roll down the valley between Arte's cheek and nose.

"Okay," SB said, putting on an agreeable smile. "A hug here then?"

While they squeezed each other, Arte said, "Stay strong. Remember I love you."

"Those were going to be my lines to you," SB told her.

Going out the door Arte turned and said, "See ya 'round the bend."

It was something they used to say all the time but had stopped when Arte decided it sounded too corny and embarrassing.

"After you've driven me there," SB responded with their old standard reply.

When the door closed, Gwen said ruefully, "Wow, it's hard to let them go, isn't it?"

SB nodded and said in a flattened voice, "If you don't mind, I'll be down in a few minutes."

"Right," Gwen answered. "You know where to find me."

SB watched from the back window as Arte steered her Toyota out of the parking space and disappeared down the alley. Afterward she went to the bathroom sink and splashed her face with cold water until most of the redness disappeared from her eyes.

In the newsroom, Gwen greeted her with an encouraging smile.

SB asked, "Have you ever heard of 'genderqueer'?"

"Did you just do a search?" Gwen said.

"Last night," SB told her. "The term has been around since 1995. Did you know that?"

"I've heard of it," Gwen said.

"That's more than Arte's whole life," SB lamented. "God, I'm so out of touch!"

"Is Arte doing okay?" Gwen asked.

"I think so," SB said. "In fact, she's probably outstripping me."

"Maybe someday," Gwen said. "That will still take some doing."

"I don't know," SB said, exuding a cloud of stress. "What's new around here today?"

"Big stuff," Gwen said. "The governor's office sent out a press release. He's ordered the attorney general to look into suing the feds over canceling the Forest Service study."

"He did?" SB asked. "I didn't know he had the balls for that."

"That's pretty much what the president said on Twitter," Gwen replied.

"This might lead somewhere worth following," SB said. "Let's do some calling and get started on a story."

"Will do," Gwen said. "I also got an email address for Cecilia Baez at the University of Chile in Santiago."

SB couldn't quite retrieve that name from the sorrowful fog that enveloped her memory bank.

Gwen must have read the confusion on her face. She clarified, "The hydrologist who worked with Cheryl Solem."

"Hmm," SB responded, "Great! Let me know what you find out."

Mid-morning, Arno Toivola walked in carrying a bouquet of mums and daisies in a vase. His timing suggested that he'd come on a break from work. He was still in his high-visibility vest and heavy canvas pants, and SB noticed a ring of clean, pale skin across his forehead where the adjustable band of his hard hat had protected him from the clinging, red Taconite dust.

"Ladies," the union president said, addressing both Gwen and SB with his usual congeniality, "I was sorry to read about what happened to your window."

SB met him at the counter and felt impressed when she saw the vase and the tag that meant he had bought the flowers from the florist down the street and not from the big box store on the highway. Such a touch showed a level of taste and care that had become exceedingly rare.

"Nice of you to stop by," she said, withholding more enthusiasm until she knew more about his intentions.

"A little peace offering," Arno said, "even though it wasn't any of our people who did it. I'm pretty sure of that."

"No," SB said ironically, "the miners' union would never resort to violence against property—even when it's richly deserved, which in this case it wasn't."

"You're right," he said. "The Ellingsons and the union go way back. Our families have been allies too long for that kind of petty crap."

"Thank you for knowing your history, Arno," she said, feeling a little more inclined to give him the benefit of the doubt.

"I probably know my history about as well as you know yours," he said. "The thing I'm having trouble understanding is what you're doing around this copper-nickel mining thing. Honestly, SB, some people think you don't understand how tough times are right now. The kids have been leaving for generations, and the companies have us pressed just about completely against the wall. As it is right now, twelve people do the work of twenty."

"How does it help to give the owners a free hand then?" she asked him.

"It keeps them here," he said. "I wish it hadn't come to that, but that's about it. It's like paying for protection. It lets some of us keep working— and maybe some of our kids."

"My kids come first with me, too," she said, "but I can't keep them here against their will, and I'm not sure how it helps to let the companies do whatever they want with the water."

"I don't see how we've got the power to change that," he said. "You don't seem to get that we need the mines, and Big Tech's going to make sure they get the copper one way or another."

"You don't seem to get that things need to change," she told him. "We're on a death trip now."

He nodded, looking glum, and said, "Enjoy the flowers. They won't last, either."

After he'd gone, she looked across Mesabi and saw that thick, gray clouds had pushed in, layered low and heavy enough to completely block the sun. As she watched, the BeneGeo security men walked slowly in front of the windows.

The big man turned his head and frowned when he saw her. He said something to the smaller partner who turned his head and aimed his mirrored glasses in SB's direction, and then the two of them moved on.

"If that's not harassment I don't know what is," she said to Gwen.

"Probably not illegal, though," Gwen responded.

"No," SB said, "probably not. It's about time for me to check in with Walker again, though. Maybe I'll ask him."

This time the deputy on duty intercepted her before she reached the sheriff's inner office.

She argued back and forth with him until Walker hollered from inside, "For god's sakes! I'll see her! Send her in!"

"Thanks for the rescue," SB said when she stood in front of him.

He had his feet on top of his desk with his ankles crossed, and he didn't bother to remove them for her sake.

"Rescue's my line of work, but I don't know if that was one," he said after he'd made her stand a while looking at the scuffed soles of his Wellingtons. "What can I do for you?"

"Those BeneGeo thugs just strolled by our windows again," she said. "They walked really slowly and let us know they were looking inside."

"And?" he asked.

"And it's clearly harassment," she answered. "Is it illegal?"

"Doesn't sound like a prosecutable offense," he said, "and jurisdictionally speaking, it's city police business—not ours."

"You know why I'm concerned about these two guys," she said.

"I haven't started having that kind of memory problem yet," he muttered.

"Have you questioned them?" she asked.

"If I had I couldn't tell you."

"Can you tell me if you have any news about Cheryl Solem?"

"The Cheryl Solem matter is still not really a matter," he said.

"So, you're sticking with the same old, evasive BS?"

"I'm sticking with I've got nothing to say to you," he growled, "and you need to get out of my face—no offense or harassment intended." He moderated his voice some at the end, though it was too late to smooth over the insult. His irascibility offended her quite a bit.

She threw up her hands and told him, "I'm so disappointed in you, Walker Hayes. I really thought you were a better man than this."

"Well, it's a good thing I don't live for your approval," he said. "I really don't care what kind of man you think I am. Now can you see yourself out? Or should I call for an escort?"

On the way back to the newspaper office she stopped by the City Hall complex and followed the arrows pointing down a long hall to the Police Department. Sergeant Angela DeMarco was in, and SB asked her for an update.

The sergeant said, "We don't know much, but we've got some pretty sketchy surveillance images from across the street. We can't even tell if it's a man or a woman."

"It's not always easy," SB said, "or relevant."

"Looks more like a ghost," Angela said, missing the humor in SB's comment entirely.

"One person or two?" SB asked.

"Just one is all we see," Angela said.

"Can I view the tape?"

"I'm not set up for that right now," Angela said.

The answer felt evasive to SB, so she pressed on. "Can I get a still image for the *Voice*? We could feature one of those 'Do you know this person?' stories."

"I'll check into it," Angela said. "I have to run it by my captain."

SB decided not to mention the unwanted attention from the BeneGeo goons.

That evening, when she went to strip Arte's bed, she found an envelope on the pillow. Made of thick, grocery-bag-brown paper, it was addressed in silver ink to "Mom." Inside she found a card and a gift certificate for an hour-long therapeutic massage by Merle Byrne.

The note from Arte read, "Enjoy this! You deserve to take care of yourself."

20. KISMET?

S B HAD A MAJOR case of nerves when she pulled into Rocky's driveway and parked in the empty space where Merle had parked on Saturday. The barn loomed behind her, big and dark and inviting. Inside she got her rubber bucket, scooped some oats into it, and tucked her horse-catching gear into the back of her waistband. Through the open doorway, she saw Merle arrive and park her little hatchback in the space beside SB's car. She watched Merle emerge, unfold her body into the warm May air, and spread her arms into an enormous stretch.

When she spotted SB, Merle called over, "Thanks for the invite. Sorry if I kept you waiting. My last session ran a little long."

"I just got here myself," SB said.

"Should we go get the horses together?"

"I should probably go first," SB said. "If my mare sees your rope and halter, she might spook and not let me catch her."

Merle looked at the bulge in the back of SB's pants and grinned. "So that's why you do the tuck-in thing."

"That's why," SB said with her mouth screwed into a lopsided line that she hoped came across as entertaining.

Along the pasture path she had walked just four days earlier, more blossoms had appeared. She saw anemone, columbine, vetch, and a scattered bouquet of spring wildflowers that she'd seen other years but hadn't yet taken the time to learn to identify. The early pollinators had hatched and were flying sorties—big, looping flight paths from blossom to blossom. Up ahead by the gate Mara stood shoulder-to-shoulder with Merle's gelding and watched SB's approach. The horses had shed nearly all of their long, winter coats and looked sleek and shiny in the sun. When SB slipped through the gate, Mara whirled and turned, acting out her usual drama of false alarm. She high stepped with her tail and nose in the air, pretending to run away, but SB stood still, cradling the bucket and waiting until Mara came for the oats.

When the mare surrendered, SB said, "Methinks thou dost protest too much, my lady."

Merle teased from behind, "I'd say you're right about that!"

SB felt a flush of embarrassment that nearly knocked her to the ground. "You made me jump," she yipped. "I thought you were waiting at the barn."

"Sorry," Merle said. Her wide-eyed expression made her look contrite and keen to put everything right. "I kept a distance, but I did see it all unfold as I came up the path."

"Ah well," SB sighed. "Mara's a pill, but at least she's predictable."

"There's a lot to be said for predictability," Merle told her.

"You know this from experience?" SB asked.

"Oh yes," Merle said, "more experiences than I should probably get into right now."

She walked straight up to Dillon with the halter in her hand, and SB watched with envy as he waited, eyes and ears aimed in Merle's direction. He stood while she slid the halter over his muzzle and buckled the crownpiece behind his ears. Along the path toward the barn, Mara jerked her rope to grab a mouthful of the fresh, sweet meadow. SB felt some empathy but gathered the rope up short and held fast.

While they saddled and bridled the horses, Rocky appeared outside the barn door, shading her eyes with a leathery hand so that she could peer into the shady interior.

"What a day," she said. "You two sure picked a good one!"

"I know," Merle said. "It's a great day to be alive and conscious!"

"Conscious?" Rocky laughed. "Well, I guess it's better than unconscious."

Merle grinned and allowed, "You're right about that."

They started down the driveway side by side at a gentle walk. When they turned onto the logging road, Merle said, "These two should be warmed up enough, don't you think?"

"I'd say so," SB agreed.

"Want to trot?" Merle asked. "Should I take the lead?"

"Go ahead," SB said.

Merle urged Dillon into a trot, and SB followed suit on Mara. She noticed Dillon's even, two-beat cadence and the fluid way that Merle sat it. A half-mile or so into the forest she popped him into a canter, and SB saw Merle look back over her shoulder to make sure that she and Mara were right there. Her mare felt relaxed and happy to stretch out and let off some steam.

After Mara slowed Dillon to a walk, she called back to SB, "Ready to go back?"

"I guess so," SB said.

The horses were breathing heavily, and all around, the leaves had filled out and changed to their later spring, deepening greens. Gems of dappled sun appeared through the not quite mature canopy. In a week or two the leaves would fully shade the trail, but even as it was SB couldn't see very far into the woods.

"I feel like I'm riding through a green tunnel," she said.

"I know what you mean," Merle answered. "It's kind of mesmerizing."

"I expect some magical creature to appear any time now," SB said.

"Here I am," Merle said, teasing with her eyes. "Just call me Epona."

"A goddess, huh?" SB parried. "I was thinking of a munchkin or a wood nymph."

"Either would work for me," Merle answered. She fell silent for a little while before she added, "How's Arte? I sure did like her."

"She's fine," SB told her. "She got home safely. We had so much fun. She's really coming into her own."

"She likes Hog Heaven Farm then?"

"Raves about it," SB said.

"And your son?"

"Skye? He's fine. He's exercising his independence at the moment."

"That must smart a little," Merle said.

"It isn't easy," SB said, "but what am I supposed to do? Right now, I just know that I'll push him away if I try to pull him closer."

"Must be hard to watch your kids grow up."

"Harder still to live with them," SB said. "It's downright humbling—and horrifying at times. Just when you think you've learned how to handle something, they change, and then you realize you've changed, too, and so has the rest of the world. Like the GPS lady says, time to recalibrate. You start out thinking you're going to raise perfect children, and you wind up feeling lucky if you can just keep them fed and housed and relatively safe."

"Wow," Merle said.

"Do you have kids?"

"No,"

SB looked closely at her, hoping for more information.

"I like kids," Merle said, "but having them never really quite worked out. My ex said absolutely no. My girlfriend before her did, too. And I don't think I have much of a maternal drive. Otherwise, I suppose I would have found a way."

"Ramona and I were lucky," SB said. "We both wanted a family."

"Sounds like it was Kismet," Merle told her.

"I suppose it does," SB replied, "only I don't believe in romantic ideas about fated love."

"What do you believe?" Those aqua eyes were fixed on SB's in a way that didn't feel demanding so much as open to imagination and possibility.

"I don't know," SB said. "I guess work. Communication. Care."

Up ahead, the logging road opened into a sun-drenched meadow. At the intersection with the gravel road, they turned toward Rocky's.

Merle said, "My poor mom wanted grandchildren so badly. She practically begged me to have them. She said, 'Lots of women are single parents these days. Couldn't you just have an accident, Honey?'"

"That's a big stretch for a woman of her generation," SB said.

"Right," Merle said. "But accidents like those are impossible to come by for women like us."

SB said, "Oh." She felt herself looking at Merle in a bemused way.

"You were still wondering?" Merle asked with surprise. "You didn't know about me?"

"Well, I suspected," SB said. "I had the feeling, but I tried not to suppose."

"You thought right," Merle told her. "Feel free to suppose. I guess it was easier for me to find out about you. You're kind of a legend around here."

"A legend, huh?" SB said. "More like the subject of gossip and speculation. Ramona and I stayed closeted for a while, but keeping up appearances got too complicated. We weren't the first ones to come out around here—just the most visible."

Far ahead on the road a vehicle approached, followed by a cloud of dust. To make room the riders hugged the edge of a drainage ditch. There was a ditch on the other side of the gravel as well, and beyond the ditches there was the green, the sweetness, and the singing birds.

"I don't want you to get the wrong impression of me because of what I said about my mom," Merle told SB. "I did think she was clueless back then, but now I understand that she was doing the best she could. In those days a queer kid was a big embarrassment."

"And a knock against the parents," SB said.

"It's been hard for her," Merle said, "and she's managed to love me through it. Some of my friends got much worse. My ex got beat up by her sisters."

SB made out the shape of a pickup at the head of the dust trail.

"I'm going to drop back to single file," she said.

She kept a tension on Mara's reins until Dillon had moved ahead enough for her to steer Mara closer to the ditch. As the truck neared, she heard its body rattling and banging on its chassis. In the last few seconds of its approach, she recognized Kent Nowak's rust bucket and saw the man himself at the wheel. He goosed the engine and crowded them. Mara spooked and plunged into the ditch, and SB felt herself lose her balance and leave the saddle. She hit bottom on her downside arm, trying to brace herself against the fall.

Nowak bellowed as he sped past, "Too bad we can't all ride around like princesses!"

And then Merle screamed after him, "Try using your fucking brakes, you jerk!"

SB got herself up and tried the arm. Her elbow, wrist, and collarbone stung when she moved them, but everything moved. Nothing seemed broken. Mara looked okay, too. She stood square on four legs, grabbing mouthfuls of grass from the ditchbank.

Astride Dillon, Merle came back and looked at SB appraisingly.

"Think you're okay?" she asked.

"I think so," SB said, rotating her arm to check the shoulder. "It could have been worse."

"Well, yeah," Merle scowled. "He could have killed all four of us. What an asshole!"

"That he is," SB told her. "Probably drunk or high on something else."

"You know him?"

"Local hothead and ne're-do-well," SB said.

Mara allowed SB to walk up to her and take the reins without a fuss. SB checked the saddle's cinch.

She said, "Nowak has it in for me."

"Why?" Merle said, "If you don't mind answering."

"The copper-nickel mining thing," SB told her. "He doesn't think I'm supporting the miners."

"Like he could hold down a job anyway," Merle scowled. "Do people always play such nasty games around here?"

"Don't they everywhere?" SB asked.

"Not like that," Merle said. "Or maybe I lead a sheltered life. We should probably get back to the barn before he comes around again. Do you need help mounting?"

"He won't come back," SB said with certainty. "He's too much of a weinie to try a stunt like that without surprise on his side." When she pulled herself into the saddle, her arm smarted from wrist to shoulder, but she thought she managed the mount without a noticeable, outward hitch.

In the tack room, she thought Merle's hands looked a bit shaky undoing Dillon's gear.

SB said, "I feel like what happened just now was my fault."

"Not at all," Merle answered without hesitating.

"No, it's on me, and I'm sorry for putting you at risk. The truth is nobody around me is safe right now. I'm in the middle of a firestorm."

"I've noticed that," Merle said, "and I appreciate your honesty. Another truth is that none of us is ever safe. It's a lifelong condition."

"Yes, but we have some obligation," SB said.

"I need to tell you that I haven't been completely open with you," Merle said, "about the situation with my ex."

"Isn't she your ex?" SB felt more discomforted about it than she would have expected.

"No, she's definitely my ex," Merle clarified.

"What then?" SB asked. "Is she dangerous?"

"Not that way," Merle said, "not violently—at least not physically. She's just making me crazy, which is actually the worst. For a while she was kind of like stalking me. That's why I left Duluth. She's still having trouble letting go."

"After how long?" SB asked.

"Two years."

"And you?" SB asked.

"I am so done," Merle said. "I needed time to be alone and sort things out, and I've done all that. I'm ready to move on."

"Good," SB said.

"I'm looking to make new friends," Merle said.

"I am, too," SB said. "I think I'm open to that."

"Good," Merle said, smiling nervously. "Good!"

"Shall we ride again?" SB asked.

"Definitely," Merle said. "We'll just keep an eye out for that jerk."

"Nowak," SB said, taking care to emphasize the consonants in a way that made his name crack like an obscenity.

When they stood beside their cars before leaving, Merle said, "Looks like your arm and shoulder could use some work. Let me know when you want to collect on that gift certificate." She didn't wait for a reply.

On the way into town, SB stopped by Walker Hayes' office and found him hunched over his desk.

She opened the conversation by announcing, "I just got physically harassed by Kent Nowak."

"What happened?" Walker said. "Are you hurt?"

"Scuffed a little," she said. "I could have been killed, though. A friend and I were horseback riding, and Nowak came along and swerved as if to hit us. My horse spooked, and I got dumped in the ditch."

"Are you saying he did this deliberately?" Walker asked.

"What else?" She didn't even try to keep the annoyance out of her voice. Her wrist was shooting pains through her elbow into her collarbone and vice versa.

"I could talk to the man," Walker said, "and if what you say checks out, I can consider charging him with something."

"You mean if he confirms it? How likely is that?"

Walker looked down at the paperwork on his desk. "The prosecutor hates these things. They're hard to prove."

"Damn considerate," she said.

"Is that it then?" he asked in a clipped voice.

"Apparently," she said. "For now."

21. TALK TO THE SALAMANDER

THE NEXT MORNING Gwen blew into the office wearing a dress with a full, swirly skirt that she had trouble keeping under control in the breeze that hurried her along. Her hair stood in wild, disordered corkscrews. At her desk she smoothed and tamped them into a rough order, using her hands without benefit of a mirror.

"Thursday already," she said, eyebrows half-cocked in what seemed like an acknowledgement that she must have appeared a comic figure at the moment. "What do we need to wrap up?"

SB frowned. Her wrist, elbow, shoulder, and collarbone ached, and she felt all in, stuck, and stymied. Walker's pigheadedness really ticked her off.

"The story should be Cheryl Solem," she groused, "if only we'd managed to come up with some answers."

"Couldn't we just ask the questions?" Gwen offered in the brainstorming, no wrong ideas mode that the two of them turned to when nothing else seemed to be working.

"Maybe," SB said. "There's the BeneGeo ownership question, too, where we also have dug up very few actual facts. What kind of reporters are we, anyway?" One glance at Gwen told SB she wasn't going to get anywhere with the self-doubt and negativity.

"What about Paul Mattson's trail cam photos?" Gwen asked brightly.

"Right," SB said, drawing out the vowel in a way that conveyed some seriously mixed feelings. "Walker's got me convinced to hold back on those, I guess. His rationale was freaking convoluted, but the last thing we want to do is put Cheryl in greater danger, if she really is in any danger. Not to mention us. Any mistake we make could be used against us in this funhouse we call our local political climate."

"What if we just call attention to her studies?" Gwen said, "She's a local expert. We could mention her findings and the fact that we tried to contact her. You know, she's currently unavailable for comment. Yada. Yada. Some of her colleagues are wondering why, etcetera."

"That might work," SB said. "If nothing else, it might shake loose more information from someone we haven't reached out to. Have you heard back from that hydrologist you're waiting on?"

"Cecilia Baez?" Gwen said, "Not yet."

"Let's go with what we've got," SB said. "See how it feels when you get it on paper." She toyed with ignoring Walker's warnings altogether. He'd talked in such circular evasions, she wasn't even sure she'd understood him. She could always claim she hadn't if she found herself needing to beg forgiveness.

A little before noon, Alberta opened the door and leaned in from the sidewalk.

"Hey!" she announced, sounding out of breath, roused and eager. "I just thought you might want to know that some of us grandmothers are hosting a flash mob demonstration down at the old BeneGeo headquarters in a few minutes." She had on her appliquéd grandmothers' vest with a traditional Anishinaabe design of intertwined vines and flowers trailing from the shoulder seams to the bottom hems on both sides.

"What's going to happen?" SB asked.

"Drumming, speakers, a little local color. Stuff like that," Alberta said.

"And it's happening now?" SB asked, looking for her notebook somewhere in the piles of paper on her desk.

"In a few minutes," Alberta said. "You should come, too, Gwen, if you can."

"Sounds like a blast," Gwen said.

"See you two there then," Alberta said. "I gotta split."

When the door closed SB caught Gwen's eye, and Gwen threw up her hands as if to say, "Really?"

"I know," SB said. "Are flash mobs even still a thing?"

"And would this even qualify as one?" Gwen said. "Mind if we lock up so I can go, too? I wouldn't want to miss whatever happens."

"Sure, come," SB said. She unearthed her notebook and stuffed it into her canvas bag with the recorder and camera.

Outside, she felt the drumbeat pound against her ribcage. The bass drone of it reverberated through her like a second pulse.

"The heartbeat of Mother Earth," Ramona had called it. When SB complimented her on the metaphor, she responded with a blunt correction.

"It's not mine," she said. "It's what the people have called it for who knows how long. It comes through the old stories and from the Creator. That is, if you believe in the traditional ways."

"Which you don't exactly," SB said.

"I take what I need from what I gather," Ramona said.

At the time, she'd been studying about the drum with a two-spirited healer she met at a powwow up north in the Red Lake Nation. He went by the name of Rick Wind.

"Desjardins have been crossing borders and bloodlines since before the French paddled into Lake Superior," Ramona told SB. "We have relatives from Winnipeg to Sault Sainte Marie. We call ourselves Métis, Indigenous, Anishinaabe, Cree, Ojibwe, First Nations, First People—even white, French Canadian, and Quebecois, for those who want to pass. I don't know what else, but you can be sure I left out something."

"This whole thing makes no sense," SB said. "Are our kids entitled to call themselves Indigenous or not?"

Ramona snarled back, "Sorry if you feel uncomfortable, but we're the ones post trauma, not you. The kids will be who they think they are."

Not long after that Ramona started dreaming of drums.

In the small, grassy plaza that surrounded BeneGeo's corporate head-quarters, the American flag flew high and stiffly horizontal in the wind. The glassy cubes of the headquarters building squatted like stacked crates on the far side of the property. A wide, concrete walkway led from the public sidewalk to the stainless-steel front door. The singers sat in a tight circle with a big drum at the center. All men by the looks of them, they pounded a traditional rhythm and sang an honor song that SB recognized from ceremonies she had attended with Ramona.

"Feels like another carnival," Gwen waxed excitedly.

Some people stood around tables unfolded here and there in the plaza. A few sat on blankets arranged on the grass. Some appeared to be selling things. Others handed out flyers. Many just talked and circulated. SB spotted Alberta standing with a bullhorn in one hand and her other hand punctuating the conversation she was having with two people SB thought she recognized. One, all long bones and sun-tanned skin, looked like the resort owner Jason Bjornson. The other, seen in partial profile, resembled a fifty-something woman SB had met a few times at get-togethers like this, a willowy, gray-haired volunteer from the local community radio station called KORE.

The wind whipped Gwen's skirt again. She gathered it with one hand and grabbed SB with the other. "Look!" she said. "Mojigangas!"

Three giants loomed over everyone—sizable people carrying on their shoulders colossal, brightly painted, papier-mâché heads. SB thought they must have been recruited for their physical strength. The heads made them look mythical, larger than life, and hilarious at the same time. She shot pictures of the fish, the frog, and the salamander.

The last of them spoke to her in a morose, self-pitying baritone, "I don't like arsenic, lead, or mercury in my water."

"Can I quote you on that?" she asked, thinking there was a good chance she might elicit something fresh and interesting from an actor playing an amphibian.

"Of course," he said, "what I've said goes for the fish and frog, too, in case they don't have a chance to tell you. We're all in crisis right now, you know. Some of us are growing extra body parts. Not because we want to. It's the chemicals in our water."

The drum fell silent, and SB heard Alberta's voice crackle through the bullhorn. "That was the Sea Smoke Circle Drum Group out of Red Cliff, Wisconsin."

It took a minute for the crowd to pick her words apart from the static and start clapping. Once they did, Alberta waited for the applause to die down before she introduced an unassuming-looking person with long, glossy, black braids and a soft, kind-looking face. Rick Wind spoke quietly in what some still called Ojibwa and others Anishinaabemowin. SB had signed up for a year of night classes to study it. In her busyness she had managed to attend just enough sessions to recognize a prayer of blessing when Rick Wind starting saying one. The crowd quieted, and he gestured to the directions, lifted and lowered the pipe, and prayed until, at the end, SB felt people around her let out a collective breath.

Alberta repeated Rick Wind's full name and thanked him before she introduced Chase Monahan as "an ally in this fight to protect our Earth and water."

Monahan talked directly into the bullhorn's built-in microphone, enunciating so carefully that his words rang surprisingly clear.

The thing he said that SB thought she'd end up using was, "They talk about safety, but what does it mean? They talk about money coming in, but what does that mean? We know that we can't afford to lose the water. We can't replace it at any cost. We can't afford to kill the fish. They're already so full of mercury that we can only eat one of them a month from most of our lakes and rivers. Why don't we do the right thing for a change?"

The fish and the frog joined arms and danced some kind of impromptu jig while the Salamander clapped a rhythm. The crowd clapped, too, when they caught on, and some of them cheered approval.

Alberta introduced the lanky Bjornstad, who said, "Now that the fishing season has started again, the tourists are back. We see them all around town and the countryside, spending their money. They show up as predictably as the migrating flocks, and what do they want? The same things we do. Unspoiled woods and safe, clean water."

When Bjornstad handed the bullhorn back to Alberta, she aimed it at the BeneGeo headquarters.

Accompanied by squawking feedback, she said, "Now we invite the BeneGeo people to come outside and talk. Come out and meet the people. We want to hear from you. We want you to tell us a lot of things. Like who really owns your company? Who is the boss? Who answers for what you do? We want to know how you're going to keep the water clean for our children and grandchildren. We want to know how you're going to protect Shkaakaamikwe, our Mother Earth, and the water that is life."

She paused then and continued in a more strident voice, "Let's hear you people!" She started the crowd chanting, "Come out and talk! Come walk the walk!"

The people were having fun and kept the chant going a long time. Some in the crowd lifted their fists, and some pointed fingers toward the BeneGeo headquarters. The City of Iron Police cruisers came without sirens but with their rotating roof lights flashing. After they stopped and parked beside the curb, SB watched about a dozen people peel out of the crowd and saunter casually away in separate directions. The ones who stayed grew quiet and watched with uneasy, adrenalized eyes as the two officers who had been first to arrive climbed out of their cruiser and stood beside their open doors, facing the crowd in body armor and helmets. One of them, judging from his fine-boned, youthful build, looked to be Ramona's cousin, the rookie Luke St. Jean. The other was a more senior man with rounded shoulders and a pregnant-looking belly—a sergeant named Petersen, she thought, or Jensen. He looked imposing and red faced enough to be possibly explosive. He had six inches of height and at least fifty pounds on SB, but she felt pretty sure she could outrun him if it came to that. It wouldn't come to that, though, would it? She started shooting pictures.

Cherise emerged from the main door of the BeneGeo building. Her meticulously performed femininity was flanked on each side by the hyper-masculinity of a suited-up hunk of a BenGeo security man. The three of them marched straight to the first patrol car, wind lifting Cherise's hair and bangs, revealing a strained and put-upon face. As SB closed in on them with her telephoto lens, she felt a little tickle of sympathy.

That stopped when she heard Cherise tell the ranking officer, "You need to clear all of these people out of here! They're trespassers. None of them has permission to be here."

Alberta came and stood on the sidewalk to the rear of the BeneGeo contingent. Three of the grandmothers followed and implored people from the plaza to join them on the sidewalk. A chunk of the crowd came and took up positions around the elders.

Alberta put down the bullhorn.

"You're standing on Anishinaabe land," she shrieked in a voice full of portent and anger. "Why don't you talk to the people? We want to ask you some questions about how you're managing our land for our grandchildren. We want to ask why you can't seem to hear us. We just want to help you do better."

SB watched people carting boxes, folded tables and blankets from the plaza. Two of the singers went past with the drum and put it in the back seat of an old sedan across the street. The *River Cities Record* stringer, Chastain Nguyen, arrived from somewhere, notebook in hand. The frog, salamander, and fish took up a position behind Alberta where they made a telegenic backdrop for SB's photos. The senior policeman lifted his visor and watched.

"The thing is," he began. He started out looking at Cherise but projected his voice loudly enough to be heard by the crowd. "I can't disperse people who are peacefully assembled on a public sidewalk."

"They only just got on the sidewalk now," Cherise argued. "You saw it with your own eyes. They were on our plaza until just a few minutes ago. That's land we own. That's trespassing! You're a witness!"

"Looks like they've exited voluntarily," Petersen said.

"What about the city noise ordinance?" Cherise countered. "Listen to how loud they are. They must be violating that."

Petersen said, "The ordinance only applies between 10 p.m. and 7 a.m."

"You're kidding me."

"No."

"So now what?"

The sergeant shrugged.

"Can you at least stick around until they clear out?" Cherise said. "I shouldn't have to worry about them coming back later and maybe doing some damage."

Alberta stuck the bullhorn in the air and mocked, "She doesn't want to worry about us doing some damage!" A screech of feedback made SB flinch. Alberta went on as if it hadn't happened. "CUNIBelt doesn't want us to do any damage. They don't want us to hurt anything."

A lot of people laughed, but not Luke St. Jean—and it was clear when he took off his helmet that the second officer was, indeed, Luke, with his fine, expressive face transformed into a stoic, noncommittal mask—the kind of look SB had seen Ramona put on when things happened that shouldn't be accepted but couldn't be fixed or forgiven or escaped. Only his eyes seemed to telegraph to Alberta, "Be careful, Auntie."

SB got shots of it all.

The sergeant looked at Alberta and said, "What do you think? Are you and your people done here?"

"The man wants to know if we're done here," Alberta yelled through the bullhorn. "Are we done?"

"No!" people shouted back. "Are you kidding?"

"We'll never be done here," Alberta said, striking a chin-up pose with her hair fanned across her shoulders. "I think we could go home now, though," she added. "We got our points across. We'll fight another day."

The crowd cheered and came entirely apart, everyone heading in their own direction. SB noticed that Luke let out a huge breath, and Chastain Nguyen sidled next to Cherise.

Nguyen asked, "What's going to change now with CUNIBelt's new relationship to BeneGeo?"

Cherise gave her a frosty stare and said, "Not one thing. Nothing needs to change."

Nguyen's dark eyeliner and augmented lashes emphasized the skeptical way that her eyes constricted as she followed up, "What about the owner-ship question? What about the rumors that CUNIBelt has bought out all of the shareholders?"

"I'm not even going to dignify those fallacies by trying to address them," Cherise said. "We're still as committed as ever to the safety and prosperity of this community, this state, and this nation."

"They've got no real answer," Gwen whispered to SB.

"Obviously not, or she wouldn't have to sound so dismissive," SB said. "Want to grab some grub and head back to the office? We've got to remake the front page."

22. BLAME IT ON THE LAVENDER
AND BERGAMOT

THE OFFICE FELT UNNATURALLY quiet on Friday morning. A stringer from Red Clover township brought in a wedding announcement, and a subscriber from the senior citizens' center bought six copies of the previous week's paper so that she could send originals of her cousin's obituary to relatives out of town. The rain had returned with skies so thick that the streetlights stayed on, and all of the occupied storefronts that SB could see from her desk spilled light onto Mesabi from the inside out. She sat at her computer hunched, thinking, remaking the week's layout to accommodate her photos from the demonstration. Keyboarding aggravated the dull ache that ran from the base of her left thumb all the way to her collarbone.

When Gwen arrived she stopped just inside the door, turned around, and shook the rain from her umbrella outside before she brought it in.

"Morning," she said with a toothy smile. Her cheer seemed out of place under such a dismal sky, but SB returned the greeting. Gwen hung her raincoat on the rack in the lobby before she disappeared into the back and returned with her fingers laced around a steaming cup of coffee.

"Did you get the Cheryl Solem story I emailed you?" she asked.

"I did. Thanks," SB said. "I was going to run it as our banner until Alberta's thing came up."

"Ah well, the paths of glory," Gwen said. "How can I help with the remake?"

"I hate to ask," SB told her, "but would you mind cutting out a couple of your paragraphs about the research studies? And then take a hatchet to the school news, the track meet preview, and Bjornstad's fishing update."

"Sure thing," Gwen said.

"And would you mind calling the smooth-talking Cherise LeDoux and asking if she's got anything more to add about CUNIBelt's possible ownership of BeneGeo? Find a way to imply without saying it that we know her answer yesterday was total BS."

"Sure," Gwen said in a chipper voice that gave SB the impression she looked forward to soliciting whatever version of alternative reality Ms. LeDoux might choose to dish out next.

"It's not easy being on the receiving end of the bullhorn," SB said. "We owe her a chance to tell her side. Those big-headed what-do-you-call'ems are going to look pretty splashy on page one."

"Mojigangas," Gwen said. "It's like mummery."

"But our readers . . ." SB rested her fingers above the keyboard, thinking.

"Why don't you just call them bigheads?" Gwen said. "Without a hyphen."

"Works for me," SB said, resuming her keyboarding. "And I wanted to ask you, too. Could you cover the office for an hour or so today?"

"Of course," Gwen said. "When?"

"I don't know yet," SB said. "I've got to see if I can make an appointment."

"Not a problem," Gwen assured her, though SB got the impression that she'd left Gwen wondering if there might be a serious problem.

"My arm hurts a little," SB explained, "from the fall off Mara."

"So you're going to the doctor?"

"No," SB said, lifting the arm to demonstrate that her range of motion was still more or less intact. "Just a massage if I can get in."

"Good," Gwen said. "You're going to use your gift certificate."

"You know about that?" SB asked.

"Arte told me," Gwen said. "She was pretty impressed with Merle."

"She was?" SB said. "She didn't mention anything about it to me."

"Maybe she did if you stop to think about it," Gwen said.

"Oh. You mean the gift certificate?"

"Bingo!" Gwen nodded.

SB kept her text exchange with Merle terse. Merle had an opening.

SB replied:

Book it.

After lunch she walked down Mesabi to the old, remodeled Woolworth's building where Merle had rented an office on the second floor. SB did not entirely trust massage. Up to this point in her life, she had tried exactly two of them, and neither had gone well. One therapist commented judgmentally about spots she found that needed work, saying things like "Your neck is stiff as a board" and "Do you ever do any stretching?" The other one served up advice from a mash-up of spiritual practices that SB dismissed as whacky woo-woo. She didn't know how a successful relationship between a client and a therapist was supposed to work or whether she should expect to experience anything better from Merle, but to get inside the old five-and-dime was almost a good enough reason to go all on its own.

Woolworth's had been one of her hangouts as a kid. She bought her favorite chocolates and gummies by the ounce at the candy counter up front and communed with canaries, parakeets, and goldfish in the pet section along the back wall. After the store closed a local developer bought the building, lowered the ceilings to save on heating, and remodeled the second story into a cloister of depressing, closed-in apartments. In 2018 a developer from the Twin Cities bought the building and remodeled it into office space. SB had missed the grand opening.

Inside she saw that the developer had brought back some of the old, airy expansiveness by restoring the original ceilings and excavating the escalator from behind a wall. Stationary now, it served as a flight of retro, steel-toothed stairs. At the top, a lobby opened along a line of windows opposite a wing of offices. On one of the closed doors, she saw Merle Byrne's nameplate. The others announced an acupuncturist, a chiropractor, and a life coach. The seats in the lobby consisted of mismatched, comfortable looking chairs and couches arranged in casual configurations such as she might have expected to find in an independent coffeehouse or the home of young people starting domestic life with hand-me-downs from their parents. She chose an overstuffed chair that looked reasonably upright. When she sat, she sank a little, and her shoulder sent a twinge that reminded her why she had come.

A tall man she knew as a downtown businessman came out of Merle's office and nodded as he passed. Not long after, Merle appeared, looking comfortable in yoga pants and some sort of loose pullover top. She had tied her hair back into a short ponytail that SB thought looked jaunty. A single curl escaped across her temple.

"Hi, how are you?" she said in a welcoming way.

"Good," SB said, "and you?"

"Good," Merle said. "Can I get you a glass of water?"

"I don't think so," SB said.

"You need to stay hydrated when you have body work done," Merle told her. "Massage causes the muscles to release toxins, and you need to flush them away."

"Then yes," SB said, trying not to let her nervousness show. "I'm kind of a novice at this." Taking off her clothes and putting herself into someone else's hands wasn't something she did any more.

Merle went to her office and came back with a bottle of water. She handed it to SB and said, "The washroom's down the hall if you need it."

"I think I'm okay," SB said.

"If that changes, just let me know. Happens all the time."

The massage room was small and warmer than the lobby. A high, narrow table occupied the center, covered with a shallow mattress wrapped in indigo-colored sheets. Merle directed SB to a chair with a side table covered by a swathe of India-print fabric. The walls were busy with hangings, a large print of a long-haired dog, a weaving by an Anishinaabe artist related to the Desjardins somehow, and a poster of women working with hand tools in a field. That one had a slogan on it, but SB didn't recognize the language.

"Gaelic?" she guessed aloud.

"Right," Merle said, looking mildly pleased. "It translates roughly to 'Home, Work, Sisterhood.'"

"Good old sisterhood," SB said, and then wondered if Merle would understand that she meant it sardonically. She could tell stories about the political kind of sisters turning on each other. Those kinds of damages ran deep, but this wasn't the time to bring it up. She asked, "You've been to Ireland then?"

"An internship," Merle said. "With an NGO. During the troubles."

"That must have been scary," SB said.

"Not as much as you'd think. Sad mostly and damp and dreary."

"Your dad was Irish?"

"His dad was," Merle said. "Despite the name, I'm only about a quarter old sod. I supposedly have cousins of some degree there, but I wasn't able to find them. Genetic testing wasn't a thing then like it is now."

"Weird stuff, DNA," SB said.

"Wyrd meant destiny in Old English," Merle replied. "Did you know that?"

"No," SB said. "Interesting, though." She was starting to feel anxious about the time the preliminaries were taking, and more and more apprehensive over exactly what would happen when they finally moved on to the massage. Merle must have picked up on her body language.

"Do you have any questions?" she asked.

"What's the protocol?" SB asked back.

"What do you mean?"

"How does it work? What happens exactly?" SB didn't want to sound stupid or prudish, but she felt fairly certain that she did.

"Is this your first massage?" Merle asked. The corners of her mouth took a small upward turn, giving her an air of surprise that didn't feel like judgment.

"My third actually," SB said. "The first two weren't what I would call successes." She had a thought that she could still bolt down the escalator and retreat to the *Union Voice*.

"I can go as deep into your muscles as you want," Merle said in a gentling voice. "It's up to you. We can figure it out as we go. Most people get completely undressed, but you can keep your underwear on if that makes you feel more comfortable. When we're ready to start, I'll step out. You'll undress and climb on the table, under the covers, face down. Before I come in, I'll knock on the door and ask if you're ready."

"Okay," SB said. The procedures sounded reassuring enough.

"Anything else?" Merle asked.

"I don't think so."

"All right," Merle said, rising from her chair. "I'll leave you to it. You can hang your clothes on the hooks there or leave them on the chair."

The massage table looked inviting with its thick, blue sheets folded into a dog-eared corner awaiting SB's entry. She could see herself crawling in there and resting, lying still while Merle worked out her pains and stiffness. Why not open to a little bit of luxury? She took off all of her clothes, folded some neatly, hung the rest, and slipped between the covers. They were warm. She hadn't expected a heated table and felt entirely comfortable when Merle knocked on the door.

"Are you ready?" Merle asked.

"Close enough," SB said.

"Would music be okay?"

"I guess."

From her prone position, SB looked through the oval opening of the table's headrest. She saw only the legs of the table, a laminate floor, and the clean, dust-free, right angles where it met the baseboards.

The music struck her as odd. It had no discernable melody, rhythm, or harmony. Now and then a note overlapped another one in a seemingly random way. When Merle came closer SB saw that her feet were bare.

Merle asked. "Is the table warm enough?"

"It's great," SB said. "It feels welcoming."

"That's the idea," Merle said. "Let me know if you need any adjustments."

"Okay."

To lie waiting on the warm table was beginning to feel promising and something SB could afford to give herself in the future if everything continued to work out.

"How about an aroma?" Merle asked. "I've got a nice lavender-bergamot blend that helps with stress."

"Sounds like I could use it," SB answered.

Merle folded back the covers on one side and tucked them around SB in such a way that only her sore arm and half of her upper back and shoulders were exposed. When Merle touched her, SB felt oily warmth. She felt strong hands slide across her skin, finding and kneading her stuck and aching places. Merle's hands pushed and slid into just the right spots, the ones that SB hadn't realized needed attention until she felt them resist and then loosen and relax. Merle honed SB's messed up arm until she had worked a path to the tips of her fingers. She then stretched and released each one before she pulled the covers back across SB's shoulder and moved around to SB's right side. In SB's field of vision again, Merle's bare feet, her anklebones, and the cords that ran down to her toes looked strong and supple and able—maybe even fetching in some way. SB let the thought flit away with the peculiar and unpredictable music. Somehow the warmth, the touch, the music, and the fragrance opened spaces where SB couldn't have gone on her own. They took her places, and sometimes she wasn't sure whether she was dreaming or awake.

Merle lifted the covers from the center and held them so that they enclosed SB like a tent. She said, "Flip onto your back."

The maneuver proved harder than SB expected on the narrow table. When Merle started work on her collarbone, SB felt an electric charge that made her flinch. Then something she didn't expect happened. The sting passed quickly and took the underlying ache with it. The relief almost made SB cry. She hadn't been so deeply and physically touched in a long time. Merle's touch felt ministering. It felt like a healing touch, and only in that way a loving act. There was nothing sexual about it.

When she returned to the office, Gwen asked, "How did the massage go?"

"Okay," SB said. "Better than I expected."

JACK BONO SAT ON the edge of Gwen's desk with his legs sprawled and the bridge of his reading glasses barely gripping the wings of his nose. He was studying Saturday's front page. SB had put the photo of the police approaching her mother-in-law front and center. A determined Alberta addressed the crowd through her bullhorn, backed by the picturesque bigheads. SB had made sure to include a conflict-of-interest disclosure informing readers about her relationship to Alberta. All the same, the headline jumped out in a bold, postmodern font.

CUNIBELT PROTEST AT BENEGEO PLAZA

Jack Bono looked at SB over his glasses and said with a certain amount of glee, "You just can't keep out of trouble, can you?"

"Trouble's our business," SB answered. "You should know that as well as anyone, Jack."

He laughed and looked like he was searching for a better comeback but had to settle for saying, "Can't wait to read the story." Just then one of the city carriers came in to pick up his bundles, and Jack jumped up to help.

SB thought that this week's paper had substance as well as flash. Gwen's story about Cheryl's research findings, with its buried paragraph about the mystery of her possible disappearance, went deep into the waste disposal problem and gave its own pizzazz to the space below the fold. SB had included a snapshot of Cheryl that Gwen charmed Paul and Jessi Mattson into letting her use. As she saw how it looked in print, she realized that the portrait of the hydrologist in her close-fitting cargo pants and waffle knit Henley presented a more complicated vision than she'd first thought. In the full-color original, she had noticed Cheryl's upright posture, the bronze and silver highlights in her brown hair, and the fact that she stood gazing into the distance beside a sparkling stream amid what must have been the peak of autumn colors. In black and white what struck SB was Cheryl's face with its round cheeks and heart-shaped mouth set in an uneven line on the troubled side of serious.

The bundles had all gone out, and Jack had gone home before Skye texted to let SB know that he was with Kjell on the Intracoastal:

> kicking back soaking up
> atmosphere

Whatever that meant he left up to her to decipher. Beer, sun, fishing, she imagined—and some kind of company, if she knew her father.

She replied with a sun emoji and a message:

> Have fun. Be safe.

Skye answered with a thumbs-up.

Lil came, wagged, and rolled her eyes toward the door.

"Wait a minute," SB said.

She was just about ready to close up and lock the front door when it popped open, and Merle Byrne came in. She wasn't smiling. Her whole bearing seemed to have taken a solemn turn. She looked around and found the office empty except for the two of them.

"Would you have time to talk?"

"I was just about to walk my dog," SB said.

"I could go along. Would you mind?"

Earlier, there would have been no question. SB would have delighted in Merle's company, only now it seemed complicated and potentially hazardous in some way.

Lil went over the top with excitement. She performed so many variations of the canine greeting ritual that SB apologized to Merle.

"It's okay," Merle said, rubbing Lil's ears with both hands. "I'm a dog person."

"Funny we haven't really talked much about that," SB said.

"We haven't really talked about much at all," Merle told her. "I'm sure it would have come up eventually."

"Yeah," SB said. "It did come up." Her brain got stuck on Merle's use of the word 'eventually.' It seemed to imply some inevitable process, but all sorts of things come out of people's mouths. She told herself not to overthink it. Warming into the walk she noticed that her stride seemed easier and longer than it had the day before. Her whole body seemed to move more smoothly with less effort.

She told Merle, "You know that massage really made a difference."

"Good," Merle said. "That's the idea."

"I didn't realize how much better every part of me works when it's happy," SB said.

"Really?" Merle took her in appraisingly. There was no smile, no charming gap between the teeth, just observant attention that SB found unnerving.

It was the Saturday of Memorial Day weekend, and more people than usual were at the park. Kids ran, played and shouted, and groups of various sizes picnicked in the shelters and on the grass around the lakeshore.

"God, we brought Skye and Arte here so many times," SB said. "They loved this place."

"Did you ever forage here?" Merle asked.

"Oh sure," SB said. "Wild strawberries and raspberries when they were in season and the kids were a certain age."

"I see a lot of edibles here," Merle said. "Juneberries. Apples. Chokecherries. Some domestic rhubarb has gone wild over by the senior center. Ramps. Hazelnuts."

"I guess they're here all right," SB said. "I don't always notice."

"Most people don't," Merle said, " but with a little planting, pruning, culling of invasive species, people could pitch in. We could have workshops."

"I see what you mean," SB said.

Merle's smile was back. Around the far side of the lake, Lil slowed to a poke. No one else was in sight when they stopped beside the far shore and looked back.

"I need to tell you something," Merle said.

SB braced herself. Whatever might be coming, she didn't want it to be anything that needed any kind of working out.

"You're going to have to find yourself a new massage therapist," Merle told her. "I can't be that person anymore."

That definitely wasn't anything that SB wanted to hear.

"Why not?"

"Because it wouldn't be ethical."

SB checked Merle's face to see if she was kidding. Her jaw was set. There was no softness to her eyes.

"Why?" SB asked. "What are you saying? We haven't done anything wrong, have we?"

"No, of course not," Merle sighed. "I didn't mean that."

"What then?"

Merle looked her straight in the eyes. "It wouldn't be ethical because I'm attracted to you."

SB had a hard time responding. The first thing that came to her mind was that she wasn't ready to start a new relationship. She was still too fragile, too freshly posttraumatic even after five years of mourning, which was really hardly any time at all from her perspective, not compared to the endlessness of her loss. She couldn't bear to offer herself up to the chaos of a fresh start right then, and that's how she saw the possibility: a slippery, chaotic ride, starting with the touch of a hand and rapidly progressing, desires floating to the surface, opening up and being opened on every level, the fingers, tongue, thighs, however creatively applied, however gentle, brusque, skilled, or hapless. She wasn't ready for whatever would come from opening that door. She needed her wits about her. She had the kids and the newspaper.

"I . . . I don't know what to say," she told Merle. "What does one thing have to do with the other?"

"We'd just be crossing too many boundaries," Merle said. "I try to keep my studio a safe, spiritually pure space for healing."

"I see. That's how I experienced it." SB got it, and she knew she ought to own up to her part of the truth, but she didn't want to.

Merle hesitated and finally said impatiently, "This is where someone might say whether or not it's mutual."

SB took a deep breath before she allowed, "I'm not ready. I mean, I've had an inkling, but I wasn't sure how to handle it."

"I get that," Merle said. "I thought I could compartmentalize it so that it wouldn't matter."

"And now?"

"Now I know I can't." Merle looked like a school kid who'd just dived in for a first peck on the cheek and got by without getting smacked—somewhat hopeful and encouraged but still very much up in the air.

"I don't know," SB said. "I might be a little too needy right now."

"I'm not going to push you," Merle answered. "You can be as careful as you need to be."

"Sorry it's so complicated," SB said.

"How about if we just try not to have too many expectations for a while?"

The sunlight reflected a dazzling beam from the far end of the lake to the edge of the shore in front of them. Lil had tired of standing still and whined to get going.

"How long is a while?" SB asked.

"I don't know. However long we need, I guess."

"And in the meantime?"

"Would it be okay if I kissed you?"

SB wanted to say yes, but she wasn't able to speak. She answered by shifting closer and delivering a firm press against Merle's lips.

"Now that's the kind of leaning in I think women should be doing," Merle said.

SB admitted to herself that she liked it before she said, "I've got to go."

24. MEMORIAL DAY

SB DRESSED IN CARGO pants and a long-sleeved shirt while Lil watched, eyes lit with expectation. When SB put on her hiking boots, Lil started trembling.

"Wait!" SB said in a no-nonsense voice before she straightened her back and walked into the living room.

Near the top of the built-in bookcase, she put her hands around a lidded birch-bark box and lifted it down with tender care. Inside, wrapped in a silk scarf and woven into a slender braid tied with ribbons, she'd secured a lock of Ramona's hair. She carried the box and its contents to the kitchen and tucked them into a khaki pack she'd owned so long that she'd forgotten whether she got it at the army surplus store on Mesabi or the one she frequented in her twenties on Franklin Avenue in Minneapolis. She slipped her arms into the straps of the pack and pulled it snug against her shoulders.

"Come," she said in an encouraging way that sent Lil into a scurry out the back door and down to the back entry where she sat expectantly until SB caught up. In the parking lot SB opened the hatchback, and Lil jumped in.

SB settled the pack on the passenger seat. She thought about strapping it down with the seatbelt and decided that would be going too far. The morning was beautiful, sunny and fresh—a good day for what she liked to think of as her annual Memorial Day ritual trek to the places she and Ramona loved. This was the fourth year she'd done it. Last year she'd hiked through fog and fifty-degree rain. She felt lucky to have it so easy this year and started with her usual creeping drive uphill to the courthouse and back down along the other side of Mesabi, passing the Lucky Strike in both directions, and ending with a stop at the Kettle Lake parking lot, where she got out of the car and opened the tailgate for Lil.

The dew was still on the grass, and by the looks of things, the trail, the time, and the surroundings were all hers. She strapped on the backpack and got Lil on leash, setting a brisk pace around the lake. She planned to circumnavigate it—hopefully encountering no one, and she succeeded. The only sounds that came to her were the branches brushing one another in the breeze, Lil's snuffling explorations in the undergrowth, and the singing of the nesting birds. Afterward, she loaded up her dog and backpack and drove northwest on the state highway to the empty, four-space parking lot at the head of the Giants Range mixed-use trail. She left Lil unleashed for the climb, and carried her pack up the rocky, steep, and sometimes tricky terrain to an overlook identified by its signage as Devil's Slide. At the edge of the overlook, beyond a welded steel railing, the side of the ancient, eroded mountain fell away in a long, steep tumble through granite outcroppings to a tortured-looking landscape below. Stone cliffs resembled canyon walls that a traveler might expect to see in the southwest—striped horizontally with red chert, glittering hematite, and bands of iron-bearing rock stained dark gray, purple, yellow, and, less surprisingly, rust. The exposed Precambrian rock looked like it had been carved by running water across its two billion years of existence, but most of the carving had been accomplished in just a few decades by explosives and machines. At the very bottom, blue water sliced through the heart of the canyon. At first glance it looked like a flowage of interconnected glacial lakes, but SB knew that it was, in reality, the remnants of a water-filled, open pit mine.

"It would have been so awful to have known this place a hundred and fifty years ago and to see it as it is today," she said to Ramona on one of their trips to the overlook.

Ramona had wasted no time pouncing, "You think I've never imagined that? As an Anishinaabe-identifying person? Really? Are you trying to earn empathy points?"

"Oh," SB had replied in a rush, "I mean no! I mean, you should be the one telling me."

"I see survival here," Ramona said, looking out across the colorful vista. "I see this place got named for the Devils, and I think I know who they are. They're the ones who keep trying to take everything from this place, but it won't be defeated. Look how it manages to give beauty even from its ruins."

Ramona spit into a tube one day and mailed it away for genetic testing. She didn't act surprised to learn that she had almost as much DNA from French and Scandinavian ancestors as from the ones who called themselves Anishinaabe and Cree.

"There might be a little Dakota in there, too," she said. "My people have been crossing bloodlines since a long time before there were borders."

In a way, the Dakota named the state. They called their homeland at the convergence of the Minnesota and Mississippi Rivers Mni Sota Makoce. In English, it means something like "land of tinted waters" or "land where the waters reflect the clouds." SB liked the second version. She understood that translations, like memories, were fluid things, subject to interpretation, shift, and change. What she grappled with and hadn't yet managed to entirely grasp was what it meant to benefit from taking other people's homes and words and using them in your own ways for your own purposes. What responsibilities came with such behavior? What repairs were required?

"Don't expect me to tell you," Ramona told her. "You're on your own with that."

Arte was four years old when Ramona announced that she would need to spend some time apart from her wife and daughter. SB fought the whole idea until she realized it really wasn't up to her. One way or another, their increasing discomforts and disagreements made clear, Ramona would claim her freedom. She started traveling to powwows, camping with friends on Indigenous lands, meeting new people, and pulling together a circle of women who, like her, identified as Native and mixed-blood Métis and believed that their destiny was to drum and sing to help the people. "Renegades" was the name they took for their group after it came to Ramona in a daydream.

"It's a power-over word," Ramona explained to SB and anyone else who asked. "We're making it a power-to word. We know the drumbeat heals."

When the Renegades drummed and sang at their first powwow, no one danced. The rebuke stung Ramona deeply. Afterward the argument played out online. Only men could play the big drum some said on the website *Native News Hotline*. They said they were protecting the traditional teaching. They said women's reproductive powers were spiritually strong, and their potency could interfere with the big drum's spirit.

One asked, "What is wrong with our girls?"

Another said women should accept their place and wait patiently for people to learn from them while they used the small hand drums to accompany their singing.

Ramona said, "My choice was spirit-driven, so how could it be wrong?" She told SB, "They're just afraid of women's power."

SB knew enough to know that she didn't know enough, and then Ramona came home pregnant again.

"This little one's going to look like you," she told SB. "Some of you north woods Norwegians are practically Indigenous."

Little Skye in Ramona's belly could have been the end of them. The upheaval, feeling of betrayal, and resentment almost made SB say things that couldn't be said and loved through to a lasting finish, but now, looking back on it from the remove of time, acceptance felt like her inevitable choice. In retrospect, Skye felt inevitable, too. They were a family, and he looked like an Ellingson.

Back at the trailhead SB loaded Lil and the backpack into her Subaru. She drove past Rocky's farm and spotted Mara in the pasture, standing with the rest of the horses near the tree line. She didn't see Dillon, which made her worry that she might meet Merle coming or going on the road. She felt a little stir about the possibility, too. The cheeky kiss she'd landed on Merle's lips had meant something, but she couldn't say exactly what. She would have felt awkward if their paths had crossed right then. She counted herself lucky when they didn't.

Back home she felt sorry for herself and peeved at fate or whatever it was that drove human doings to their logical and illogical conclusions. She imagined that right about then people all over the country were enjoying the company of their wives and husbands, lolling around their living rooms and patios with full bellies and feet up, or stretching out on boats, cocktails in hand, watching sunbeams zigzag on water.

The young woman who drove the other car had passed through Ramona's shelter as a girl. That was the strangest twist of all. By the time of the accident, she had a child of her own. In the interval, Ramona had worked her way up from a sexual assault victim's advocate to intervention coordinator and then director of the regional anti-violence shelter for First Nations women. She was always trying to heal the world, but trauma set in motion had a way of continuing to reverberate. The child hadn't been in the car that night. SB didn't know what happened to her. She wasn't sure what sense anyone was supposed to make of any of it.

When her phone chimed, she was surprised to see Gwen's name appear on the caller ID. They tried to spend their holidays apart since they saw so much of each other at work.

"I just heard from Cecilia Baez!" Gwen said excitedly.

"Oh, nice," SB said, struggling to find where in her brain she'd stored the bit of information that would remind her who Cecilia Baez was.

"She's that Chilean hydrologist," Gwen filled in. "One of the researchers who worked with Cheryl."

"Oh, right. Her credentials checked out then?" SB asked.

"Yes," Gwen reminded her. "She's a for-real PhD hydrologist at the University of Santiago, a bona fide expert in mining hydrology. Turns out she's got a lot to say, too."

"Like what?" SB asked, feeling herself perk up.

"First of all," Gwen said, "she hasn't heard from Cheryl since right after the president cancelled the study, and she thinks we're on the right track about that and everything else."

"Meaning exactly what?"

"For one thing, she thinks we're right to be concerned about BeneGeo's ownership change. She says that everywhere CUNIBelt goes they leave behind broken agreements, hostile buyouts, and polluted water, and that's the least of it."

"Wait a minute," SB said. "Is she willing to go on record with any of this?"

"I think she's justifiably afraid of being identified," Gwen said, "but she's wondering if we would allow her to send us some stuff."

"What kind of stuff?"

"Documents," Gwen dropped her volume nearly to a whisper. "Get this, SB. When she saw that the feds were stalling the Forest Service study, Cheryl sent Cecilia a trove of documents for safekeeping. Cheryl said they were her insurance policy, and if anything happened to her, Cecilia should get them to the press right away. Cheryl wanted them out in the open."

"And this Dr. Baez is choosing to go through us?" SB asked incredulously.

"I know," Gwen said, "improbable, but she explained that she got my email inquiry and decided to check us out before she answered. She read Saturday's paper online and was blown away. She didn't know anyone else thought that Cheryl might be in trouble, and she felt like she had better do something fast. Also, she said she knows Alberta, and she saw your conflict-of-interest disclosure about the two of you being related."

"What?" SB asked.

"Dr. Baez met Alberta at an Indigenous women's water conference in Sao Paolo years ago. She said to be sure and greet her. Dr. Baez admires her work. Your relationship to Alberta sealed the deal!"

"For god's sake? The power of the Desjardins! How many documents are we talking about?"

"A lot," Gwen said.

"Hundreds?"

"Thousands I think."

"Has she offered them to anybody else?"

"She says no."

"Is she looking to get paid?"

"Absolutely not!" Gwen sounded surprised that SB would even go there. "She just wants anonymity. She says her life and other people's lives could be at stake and Cheryl is definitely in danger. She says people who've watched Garman Worsley know how rough he can get. People who cross him tend to suffer all sorts of unfortunate accidents and unexplained disappearances."

"What kind of people are we talking about?"

"Reporters for one." Gwen left an ominous pause before going on. "Also researchers, business competitors, government inspectors, labor organizers, politicians who don't cooperate, cronies who want to get out of arrangements. Dr. Baez can cite a long list. Basically, Worsley goes after anyone he thinks is getting in his way. She says—and I quote, 'These international plutocrats have long reaches.'"

"And she's saying there's evidence of all that in these documents?" SB asked.

"Far as I can tell, yes," Gwen said. "Sounds like it's company emails, drafts of suppressed studies, criminal complaints, death certificates, testimonies from union organizers, whistleblower statements—no way to know how much there is or what it might be worth until we get a look at it."

"Can I call her?"

"She said not. She said she bought a prepaid phone for the one-time use of calling us, and she's probably already disposed of it. She specifically said not to call her at the university. If we're willing to take the risk of publishing the documents, she wants us to send her a coded email text that she dictated to me. If not, we send nothing. In that case, she'll look for someone else."

"Holy cow!" SB said. "Garman Worsley! Talk about your big boys! Chase Monahan knew what he was talking about, and Cheryl really is connected! Or was."

"So do you want to think about it for a while?" Gwen asked.

"No! If I do, I'll never agree to take the stuff. Send the message."

"I told her to look for the email from you," Gwen said.

The thick tension felt like it needed to be transformed into some kind of action. SB said, "I guess the stuff should come to my office computer in case I have to smash the hard drive later or some such espionage-type thing. It's pretty much a hunk of junk anyway."

"And you'll get a nice tax deduction for the replacement cost."

"Right. We've always got our priorities in order at the *Union Voice*."

Gwen was still smiling when she said, "We don't have to do this, you know."

"I know," SB answered. "Tell me what I'm supposed to write before I chicken out."

Later she had trouble slowing her thinking. The trek had taken more out of her legs and energy level than she'd expected, but she felt like she needed to spark more endorphins. She strapped the rucksack on again, whistled up Lil, and took a meander on foot through downtown, past the courthouse, out to the edge of Iron. She sat cross-legged on a hill there, below a little copse of birch and poplar, and watched a stream of traffic swell with RVs and boat-pulling SUVs, snaking along Highway 53 toward the Twin Cities.

She said, "Mona, I hope I'm doing the right thing."

Back home she took Lil into the office, put the pack on the floor by the stairs, and switched on the computer. She found her inbox choked with messages from Cheryl Solem forwarded by someone using the name Moji Ganga. When she opened the first one, an icon of an attaché case labeled Archive.zip appeared. The rest contained .zip attachments, too. It looked like she and Gwen would have a lot of reading to do.

When she doubled clicked the first archive, a file labeled "Forest Service Final Draft" appeared. She opened it and read the executive summary:

> The Minnesota Environmental Safety Commission was charged by the state legislature's Natural Resources Oversight Committee with 1) analyzing the suitability of the proposed BeneGeo mining site and 2) investigating BeneGeo's strategy for mitigating the leaching of heavy metals from the mining waste. After a thorough review of BeneGeo's plan and existing research on waste site design plans and outcomes at comparable mining sites, a preponderance of evidence leads to the conclusion that BeneGeo's plan is not currently adequate to ensure against degradation of the surrounding watershed and ecosystem. Therefore, our recommendation is that no permit should be issued until further studies have been completed.

The racing feeling started up in her head. A document called "CUNIBelt Zambia Study" appeared to outline the failure of waste containment systems in Garman Worsley's mines along the Zambian Copper Belt. In a folder labeled "White Collar," she saw financial statements, tax documents, invoices, and receipts. There was a Zip portfolio of records from Worsley's nonprofit foundation, Green Futures. She found folders of internal CUNIBelt email conversations and external exchanges between government officials and a wide range of recipients around the world. She found a subfolder labeled "Karlsrud" and another labeled "Lubovitz." And there was a portfolio labeled "Red Hands" that contained pdfs of death certificates, court records, and newspaper accounts of murders, disappearances, and assaults.

She read long past dinnertime and into the night. She saw enough to know that someone needed to look through every folder and read every word. Threads had to be identified, connections made, and stories teased out to explain how the details fit together. She didn't see how she and Gwen could possibly manage it. The reading alone would take them years, and she would need a libel lawyer and probably a criminal lawyer, too. And lots of money—more than she had, anyway—for a team of researchers, writers, security personnel, lawyers . . .

It was beyond their scope. They needed help.

She hoped Kjell wasn't lollygagging in a cellular dead spot on some brackish Intracoastal backwater. She opened her contacts list and selected him.

"Happy Memorial Day, Susie," he said when he picked up the call. "Did you forget about the time difference?"

"Good to talk to you, too, Dad," she said.

"I suppose you want to speak to your son."

"That's not why I called. Is he still there?"

Kjell sounded genuinely regretful. "I said goodbye to him this afternoon. We had a great time on the boat. He's a little sunburned now, but he's fundamentally okay. School's going well. Two of his paintings got selected for the end-of-year show. He's girl crazy, but there's no particular girl. He's having fun playing the field."

"Ouch," she said. "I suppose you know how sexist that sounds."

"Well, you know me. Hopelessly dated patriarch. Am I supposed to change now? At eighty?"

"It would be nice."

"Well, don't hold your breath. I don't want to have to worry about you keeling over from lack of oxygen while we're talking," Kjell said. "Your son just wants to experience life. He wants to make friends, make art, make love. He wants to do it all, you know. Like you did at his age."

"I only remember that vaguely," she said.

"Probably the fault of the marijuana," he told her. "I wrote him a check."

"I guess I should thank you, only I wanted him to get a job for the summer. Take some responsibility."

"Well, he wants to paint, and I thought his future was worth supporting. He's ambitious and talented."

"He's a good kid," she said. "And lucky."

"Yeah," her father agreed, "whether he knows it or not."

She left a long pause, thinking about how to word the request she wanted to make. "Skye's not actually the reason I called," she said. "The thing is, Dad, I could use some advice."

"What?" Kjell thundered. "I never thought I'd hear that from you! Did a meteor land on Mesabi or something?"

"In a manner of speaking."

She didn't know exactly why she and her father were so hard on each other after all these years. She just knew that she couldn't bear for him to feel like she was dependent on him for anything, and maybe the reverse was true from his perspective, too.

She said, "I got a data dump of some pretty explosive stuff on copper-nickel mining. Tons of documents. It's hot stuff. High impact. BeneGeo and CUNIBelt records, emails—all kinds of related papers, like a draft of the cancelled Forest Service study. Turns out it recommends against the mining permit."

"Jesus!" Kjell yelped. "Did this stuff come from a trusted source?"

"From two topnotch hydrologists who've been working on copper-nickel mining studies around the world. They've gathered all kinds of supporting documents. It's a freaking treasure trove."

"Are they going on the record?" he asked.

"Anonymous," she said.

"You need a team to pick this stuff apart," he said. "You need to partner with a big media organization. Someplace with resources and lawyers. I could call my friend Mel Levine at the *River Cities Record* and feel him out about it if you'd like."

"I don't see how we can handle it any other way," she said. "Don't tell him too much."

"How could I?" he said. "I don't know too much."

"Just enough to make it interesting, right?" she said.

"Damn right," he said.

"I'll be grateful," she told him.

"All right," he said. "I'll call him in the morning and get back to you, my girl."

The excitement in his voice let her know that she had made him feel like the old Kjell again. She decided to take a glass of wine to bed and call it supper.

25. A PROMISING IDEA

THE SUN HAD BEEN up for two and a half hours when SB heard a key turning in the front door lock. Gwen came inside wearing a light sweater over her cotton dress. Her eyeglasses swept in shallow swoops to pointed ends that made her look like she was viewing the world through cat's eyes.

"Kjell thinks we ought to partner with the *Record*," SB told her. "He'll put out some feelers with one of the editors."

"I'm surprised you didn't tell him you'd do the feeling-out," Gwen said. She put her purse on the desk and stood beside it, facing SB full on with her brow furrowed disapprovingly.

"I need him on the team," SB explained. "This way he's got a part to play, but it's just to make the introductions. He can feel good about his status and his connections, and I'll be the one who negotiates the deal."

"Who's he going to talk to?" Gwen asked dubiously.

"Mel Levine."

"Should I know that name? I think I might have some vague memory of it as a byline, but I don't recall seeing it for quite a while."

"He's managing editor now. Has been for a decade or more. You probably knew him as an investigative reporter. When he was starting out, the *Record* sent him up here to cover the Rust Tec Mine disaster."

"Oh god, I remember that!" Gwen grimaced. "A tailings dam full of mining sludge washed out and buried a couple of low-lying farms and a stretch of highway. When was that?"

"Late eighties," SB said. "It was Mel's first big story. He came north and dug up a lot of mistakes and downright violations—safety regs ignored, false statements on permit applications, shoddy inspections, and stuff like that. He made a lot of enemies around here, and he won a Pulitzer Prize. Dad always likes to tell people how he mentored Mel back then."

"Are you saying that he didn't?"

"When he tells the story he frames Mel as some sort of protégé," SB explained with a shrug. "Maybe it's earned. Maybe not. They did work together some. Dad opened our clipping library to him and introduced him to the local players."

"That sounds like help to me," Gwen said.

"Yeah. It's just that Dad has a way of taking up a lot of credit. That's how I see what happened with him and Mom. Bit by bit he squeezed out all her credit."

"Hmmm," Gwen said. "And you?"

"I squeeze back."

"Have you thought about how you're going to handle Levine?"

"I've got some ideas."

"Such as?"

"We need to spell out a lot of details, like how we'll structure our work together, what kind of recognition we'll get for our contributions, when we'll go to print . . ."

The horn fanfare that was Kjell's ringtone interrupted.

SB caught Gwen's eye and hit the speaker icon.

"Good news, kiddo," her father said while Gwen got settled at her desk.

"Gwen's here, too," SB told him.

"Have you got me on that goddamned speaker phone again?"

"Yeah, Dad. I want Gwen to hear this."

"Christ! I wish they'd never invented that thing! Just because you have the ability to do something doesn't mean you should do it, you know."

"You were saying?" SB asked him.

"Levine's interested. You should call him."

"Good!" SB flashed Gwen a thumbs-up.

"Okay," Kjell said. "That's it I guess. Go get 'em, kid."

"Really?" SB said.

"Yeah."

"You're not going to offer any unsolicited advice?"

"I wasn't going to, though it does surprise me that a competent investigative reporter like you hasn't asked for Levine's direct line or his cell number."

SB sighed, more annoyed than chastened. "Would you please give them to me if you have them?"

She watched Gwen write the numbers on a legal pad as her father recited them.

"Don't let Levine take all the credit," he added before signing off. "Make sure you stipulate that you need to be on the reporting and editing team, you get a shared byline on any story the team produces, and the *Voice* gets full credit for discovering the documents. You should also insist that they supply a legal team and a research team."

"Thanks, Dad. We've pretty much got that figured out on this end. Can I call you back if I have any questions?"

"Don't sign anything if you have any doubts."

She wished he could have resisted shoehorning in that one additional piece of advice, but she assured him in a good-humored voice, "Don't worry. I've got it." After she disconnected, she sat back in her chair and said to Gwen, "I'm phoning Levine right now. Might as well dive in."

Levine answered in an effusive voice, "SB, my god! How long has it been?"

"Decades I think," she said.

"Can't be," he schmoozed. "We're both so young."

His voice had the same warm, smooth cadence that she remembered, and she pictured him as he'd appeared in his late twenties, a broad-chested, soft-skinned, not particularly athletic man with thick, sandy hair and eyebrows like wooly caterpillars.

She answered with a small chuckle. She would have preferred to skip the small talk but didn't want to give him the impression that she was too impatient to observe the niceties. She waited for Levine to make the transition to business.

"I spoke to your dad," he said. "It was good to reconnect."

"He was excited about it, too," she said.

"Good," Levine paused and cleared his throat. "He says you've got something interesting that you might want to work on with us."

"We do indeed. Ready to hear more?"

"Can't wait."

She started with the story of encountering Chase Monahan on the dark street near the Carnegie Library almost a month earlier.

When she arrived at the document drop from Cecilia Baez, Levine asked, "You're in possession of these papers now?"

"Yes."

"Are you working with any other media organization on this?"

"It's all in-house so far."

"We're definitely interested." She could hear the appetite in his voice. He added, "Of course, we'll have to see the documents before we go any further."

"Understood," she said. "That's reasonable. We could provide some samples right away, but we'll need some assurances in writing first."

A man she didn't know came into the lobby and walked up to the counter, smiling and looking around in a way that bothered SB. He let his languorous gaze travel the newsroom, taking in everything in a probing way and distracting her from her negotiations with Levine.

Thankfully, Gwen got up and asked, "How can I help?"

"What kind of assurances?" Levine wanted to know.

SB refocused as best she could. "For one thing, anonymity for our primary sources. Their names can't come into it at all."

"That should be doable," Levine assured her. "Anything else?"

"We need full credit as named partners in all the work that follows from what we're bringing you. I also want to partner on the writing with whatever team you put together. I want bylines for any writing I contribute, and I want credit in print for my research partner."

"I'll run those by upstairs," he said.

"I thought you *were* upstairs," she told him.

"You must know I don't own the paper. Legal and the publisher's office have the last word on almost everything around here."

"Wouldn't you know?" The man at the counter exclaimed in a volume that seemed out of proportion to the problem, "I've forgotten my wallet!" He patted his pockets dramatically and said, "I'll have to come back later."

"That's fine," Gwen said. "No problem."

The door opened. SB looked up and saw him on his way out, unaccountably still smiling.

She told Levine, "This is a big one. We need assurance that your lawyers will address our legal concerns. We'll need them to advise and defend us along with your team."

"I'll talk to the powers," he replied.

"We'll need to see it all spelled out in writing," she said. "I also want the right to publish our co-written stories concurrently with the *Record*."

As Gwen returned to her desk, she flashed SB a smile of encouragement.

"I don't think we've ever given that kind of right," Levine said.

"Keep in mind what I'm bringing to the table." She tried to project much more assurance than she felt she possessed.

"I'll take it up the chain of command. It would help if you'd send those samples."

"As soon as I get something in writing," she said. "Everything that follows can be contingent on the documents being what I say they are."

"I'll get back to you as soon as I can," he said.

Gwen squealed when SB ended the call. She said, "You did great!"

In the aftermath, SB felt a shiver of apprehension.

"You know," she said, "this is downright terrifying. It's one thing to struggle after a story. It's another thing to get one as big as this handed to you."

"I know," Gwen said. "We've got work ahead of us."

"We sure do. We need to figure out how we're going to confirm these documents, starting with the Forest Service study draft. If it's real, it's page one all the way."

"I don't suppose we can run it by Latelle Washington?"

"Ha! Maybe try some of the researchers. Offer anonymity. They're probably feeling pretty aggrieved right now. If they confirm it's real, we can reach out to Latelle from a stronger position. What are we going to do about the BeneGeo and CUNIBelt documents? We've got to confirm those somehow."

Gwen brainstormed. "Maybe we should work from the bottom up. I mean office managers and clerks. We should see if we can find out who's been let go recently. Somebody might have spoken up and got canned for it, or somebody might know somebody who knows something."

"Sounds good," SB said. "Let's see what we can find out."

Gwen got busy on the phone, and SB browsed the Karlsrud file. She clicked through emails and financial documents and started to get the picture that someone—Cheryl Solem, she guessed—had arranged them by subject and chronological order, making it as easy as it could be to match money and requests coming in against money and confirmations going out.

"Where did Cheryl get all this stuff?" she said to Gwen. "It looks like inside informants have been feeding her material for years. I'd better start making notes."

Less than an hour later, Gwen looked up and said, "I've found our first corroborating source."

"Already?" SB asked. "Who?"

"A hydrologist who worked on the study team. I sent him a copy of the executive summary, and he confirmed that it's an exact copy of the one they submitted to the Forest Service. He'll go on record. He's outraged by what's happened."

"That was quick," SB said.

"It pays to ask," Gwen told her. "Sometimes that's all it takes. He suggested some other people to call."

"What the heck," SB said, "I'm reaching out to Latelle." On voicemail, she asked for a call back.

Before the end of the day, her phone sounded its standard ringtone.

"Mel Levine!" she crowed to Gwen.

While Gwen listened, he told SB, "Check your email for the preliminary agreement. We'll do everything you asked, providing the papers prove to be what you've described."

26. PARTNERSHIPS ABOUND

The next morning Gwen came in and announced in a chipper voice, "I had an eye-opening phone call last evening."

"Really?" SB asked out of a fog. "Who?" She had been awake since five reading BeneGeo documents.

"A woman named Rebecca Lyon," Gwen said. "Know her?"

"I know the family name," SB said, "but I don't think I know the person."

"She was Holton Skibo's office manager. She says she's got some company papers we might like to see."

"Huh," SB said. "This sounds too easy. Could she be some kind of Trojan horse? Maybe still working for Skibo?"

"I don't know," Gwen told her, "but I don't think so. She said she was shocked to get the sack. She thinks she asked too many questions when the stock buy-out was happening. Things about it struck her as not quite the usual way transactions are handled."

"Sounds like it's worth following up," SB said. "Can I sit in on the interview?"

A few minutes later the Alpine horn sounded, and SB touched the speakerphone icon.

Kjell's voice echoed across the newsroom, "I see you've got your agreement with Mel."

"What do you think?" SB asked.

"I think my daughter's a pretty sharp operator," he told her. "Of course, I taught her most of what she knows."

"Not true," she contradicted with a chuckle. "If you only knew."

"About the business of journalism," he amended.

"Levine and me both I guess," she said with a wink to Gwen.

"Look, kiddo, I may have exaggerated from time to time about my role with Levine. We were both much younger then, but he was even greener than I was. I think I did help him."

"And it looks like he's returning the favor." She was feeling more generous about her dad than usual.

He surprised her with his gruff response, "Don't be so sure! Haven't I taught you anything after all? The *Record* will act in its own best interest, and so will you. That's the only assurance any of us can rely on, so keep your eyes and ears open and your brain activated. That goes for you, too, Gwen, if you're listening!"

"We're on it, Mr. E," Gwen sang out.

Rebecca Lyon arrived on time, dressed neatly in office-casual slacks, a woman in her early-to-mid sixties with her hair colored a stark, plum brown and arranged in a nineteen-eighties, working girl perm. She carried a bulging portfolio in slender arms that made it look like a heavy burden.

Gwen stood up and introduced herself. She said, "Let's go into the publisher's office. You can put your things down in there, and, if you don't mind, our publisher will join us."

Ms. Lyon looked SB over and said hesitantly, "I guess that's okay."

"Could I help you with that?" SB asked her. "I'm really very interested in what you have to say."

In the inner office, SB set the portfolio on the desk beside their informant.

Rebecca Lyon needed no prompting. She said, "Something wasn't right. I could see that. I had my suspicions when they brought in a new bookkeeping system. There were a lot of strange ways of shifting money in and out. I'd never seen anything like it before. I've been a bookkeeper for thirty years, but I'm no accountant. I just made entries on a spreadsheet where I was told to, and I handled a lot of in-house communications for our files."

"And you kept copies for yourself?" Gwen asked.

"I did, when I felt like I should," Ms. Lyon said. "As much as I dared to." She opened the portfolio to show a large collection of papers sorted into file folders. "I needed the job," she said, "but I didn't want to go to jail for those people."

"Understandably," SB said. "Would you be able to verify whether or not a BeneGeo document that we received from someone else was authentic?"

"Probably," Mrs. Lyon said. She perked up and offered more confidently, "I might even have a copy of it in there."

"About those payments you mentioned," Gwen asked, "are they recorded in some kind of coded language?"

"No," Ms. Lyon said. "I don't suppose they thought anyone who mattered would ever see them. Here's one bunch." She pulled out a file marked "Karlsrud."

SB felt her blood pressure rise. She said, "Can you leave them with us?"

"Sure," Ms. Lyon said. "You'll need to send someone if you want the rest. It's more than I can carry."

"Roughly how much more?" Gwen asked.

"Boxes."

"We'll send someone," SB said. "I may even come myself."

Around eleven she took a call from Mel Levine.

"I'm blown away!" he said. "Am I understanding correctly? Do we have THE Forest Service study results?

"We're sure of it," SB said. "We've managed to get one of the co-authors to corroborate it."

"Impressive," Levine said. "We'll get a team on it, too, once we firm everything up. And we'll get Legal involved. I'll email you an updated partnership agreement. If you could sign it and FedEx the signed copy back to us overnight, that would be great. And what about the rest of the documents?"

She wanted to sound a victory yap across the room to Gwen but reminded herself to attend to details and try to sound opaque and businesslike.

"Let me look at the agreement and get back to you," she told Levine. "If it looks good, I'll email the documents. Do you want them to go directly to you?"

"Yes," Levine answered. "And we'll want you down here to meet with us in person, too. How soon can you make it?"

"Monday morning?" she said.

"We'll make it work," he said. "We're in our new building on University between Midway and Prospect Park now."

"I know the neighborhood," she told him. "Or I did once."

"Are you an alum?" he asked.

"Of the U?" she said with only minimal enthusiasm. "Go Gophers."

"J-school?"

"You know it."

"We'll have to compare notes," he told her.

"I think I forgot to take any," she said.

His snigger sounded appreciative, an encouraging sign since not everyone got her attempts to break out of workaholic sobriety and take a flyer at irony. He said, "I'll have my assistant email you a parking permit and directions."

27. THURSDAY, STARTING WAY TOO EARLY

THAT NIGHT SB HAD trouble sleeping. She woke from one anxiety dream after another. Or half-woke. She was never sure which. One of those times she found herself running until she was near exhaustion, chased by the two suited-up, BeneGeo security men through a half-lit, shadowy downtown Iron, and then the goons morphed into some kind of even more threatening forms—hulking creatures or supernatural beings. Their breathing filled the soundscape and burned the back of her neck, and they seemed about to overtake her when she forced herself awake and found herself panting in her cushy bed.

Sometime after that, Ramona stood, alive, in front of her, luminous, her dark hair tumbling across her milk-filled breasts. Those uncompromising, bullshit defying eyes flashed anger.

"I can't believe you thought I was dead," she complained with bitterness so sharp it woke SB.

Thus accused, she tossed and repositioned herself until Lil jumped down from the bed and flopped onto the floor with a reproachful groan.

And then again SB felt Ramona beside her, breath heavy and hair tousled. In the semi-darkness their bodies smelled of yeast and sweat. SB pulled her closer, wanting to bask in the heat of having just made love.

Ramona pushed her away.

"You can't keep me hanging around here," she complained.

"I . . . I'm not," SB stuttered. "Am I?"

"You do know that I'm dead, right?"

"No!" SB denied. It couldn't be.

"It's the same old story," Ramona said. "You don't listen. And you don't see what's right in front of your eyes!"

After that SB sat up and felt the disappointment settle into her stomach again. It was always this way when she dreamed of Ramona alive and then woke up to face the grief that never went away but just kept changing shape, forcing her to look at it from different directions. In the beginning she had stared into the void, the incomprehensible absence of light and breath. Now it looked to her more like the mark on your permanent record, the one that her teachers had warned about, the stain, the unresolvable misstep, the handicap that limited your options forever more. She turned on her bedside lamp and fixed her pillows so that she could sit up against the headboard and read. She was an old-style reader, a paper and ink woman all the way, and she had given up caring what this researcher or that said about light interrupting her sleep cycle. In the middle of the night, reading was her only hope of finding her way back to sleep. She needed a story powerful enough to carry her into someone else's facts and lull her to the rest that came from standing as an observer, outside the drama, but this time it wasn't working. The lines kept falling apart in her head, making room for the rerun of the accident to take up more and more space. There was no use trying to stop it.

It was Skye's birthday. SB and the kids waited for Ramona to get home from work so the whole family could go out to dinner together. They had booked reservations at a supper club on Lac Cadotte, half an hour closer to Canada. Adelle Snow, an Anishinaabe chef, was making a big splash there, filling the place every night. People drove from Duluth and the Twin Cities to taste her updated versions of traditional indigenous foods. SB looked forward to whitetail roulettes stuffed with wild rice and mushroom sauce and a chopped salad of rattlesnake beans and three kinds of squash. They had waited two months for their reservation and were running way too late.

Arte paced back and forth between the living room and the back stairway window, watching for Ramona's car and complaining, "Where is she? She can't be hung up with some client again, can she?"

"Of course she could," Skye said with the disappointed sarcasm of someone who had just turned thirteen. His cake sat in the middle of the dining room table, dressed with unlighted candles and piped icing, surrounded by wrapped presents. There was more than one kind of hunger in his eyes as SB watched him roll them from one to another of the good things waiting for him. The cake was from Delgado's Sweets on Mesabi. Giselle, the decorator, had outdone herself with food dye and sugary images of an artist's brushes and paint box. Their reservation was for six o'clock, and Ramona was supposed to have been home by five. Why wasn't she answering her phone? When the clock across the street on the Miners and Merchants Bank struck six, SB felt wronged, mistreated, outraged on Arte's and Skye's behalf. She was planning the case she would make for Ramona's putting her own family ahead of the struggling ones who walked through her door. The possibility of an accident kept floating into her mind, and she kept pushing it away until she heard Artie trumpet from the back.

"It's Walker Hayes!"

Her daughter's words brought SB's dread crashing through her defenses. Skye followed her at double time toward the back. Before she could make her way to the window where Arte was standing, to see for herself, she heard the knocking on the lower door. Heavy. As if someone were beating on it with a baton.

"Stay put!" she ordered the kids.

She opened the outside door to Walker Hayes, standing on the porch in all his bulk and diligence, avoiding her eyes and looking afraid to open his mouth. One glance at him told her the news wasn't good.

He asked, "Is there somewhere private we can talk?"

"Go inside, kids!" she yelled up the stairs. She expected resistance, but when they complied without complaining it was clear that they knew, too. Something was coming that none of them wanted to hear.

"In the newsroom," she said to Walker. She fumbled to find the light switch she used every day.

Under the cool fluorescent lights Walker said solemnly, "There's been an accident." He let it hang there while she searched his face for more information. He looked pale and exhausted. He said, "I'm really sorry to have to tell you. It's bad news." He paused for what seemed like hours. "Ramona's dead."

SB didn't scream or cry—not then anyway. She stood there trying to get her brain working as she felt her world and everything she knew folding in on itself, collapsing like a tent in a tornado. How would she live now? How would she breathe?

"The other car crossed the centerline," Walker said. He seemed to be trying to lessen the impact by keeping his voice flat and his delivery ploddingly careful. "It was a head-on."

"Where is she?" SB said. That's what she remembered saying, anyway.

"At the hospital in town," he told her.

There had been a hospital and a clinic in town then, before the overgrown medical system from Duluth bought them out and replaced them with an urgent care center closed nights and Sundays.

SB wanted to know, "Was she alive when they brought her in?"

He shook his head. "I don't think she felt any pain."

"When can I see her?"

"In a while," he said. "We might need you to identify her at some point. I'll try and spare you that, but there'll be papers to sign."

"Don't tell me you'll spare me," SB said. "I want to see her!"

"Sure," he said in a voice that she had never heard him use before, a flat and genuine, if ultimately inept, attempt at soothing. He laid a hand on her forearm and said, "I'll take you when you're ready."

She didn't know what to say. When would she ever be ready? She asked, "How did this happen?"

"We'll know more later," he said, "after the State Patrol does their investigation."

"Investigation?" she repeated. "What are they going to look for?"

"Speeds, skid marks, placement of vehicles, driver impairment. Stuff like that," he said, looking embarrassed to have taken a moment's refuge in what for him must have been the anesthetizing details of professional procedure. "Can we get you somebody to help out here?" he asked. "Maybe somebody to stay with the kids?"

"Could you call Gwen and ask her to come?" SB said. "I've got to call Alberta."

"I can inform Mrs. Desjardin," he offered. There was something courtly about the way he put it.

"Thank you but no," SB said. "It's got to be me."

Alberta took the news with a primal moan. She cried and said through her sobs, "Hug the kids and hang on tight. I'll be right there."

"Get someone to drive you," SB said, though she doubted Alberta would wait for anyone when she could get herself to Iron in the time it would take one of her relatives to drive to her house in the boonies between Iron and the Res.

Gwen arrived first, mouth pulled tight, eyes wild, shocked, questioning. She went directly to SB and threw her arms around her.

Walker said, "Take your time, Ladies. I'll wait in the car."

SB wondered how she herself must appear. She didn't want to add to the kids' trauma, but as soon as the thought crossed her mind, she doubted she could make them any more afraid than they already must have felt at that point, left to their own devices and imaginations. When death struck, people's faces and body language gave it away—evasiveness in the eyes, a pall of shock covering the face. She didn't like knowing that Arte and Skye would surely read it on her even before she could say a word. She climbed the stairs as if moving through a heavy sludge and found the kids in the living room. Skye sat on the couch, tears running down drained-looking cheeks. Arte paced, wild-eyed and angry. SB gestured toward the couch. She sat next to Skye and held out an arm that Arte avoided slipping into. She stood out of reach, rigid and on edge.

SB said, "There's been an accident."

"How bad?" Arte asked.

"Bad," SB said, searching for words that wouldn't come. Only euphemisms occurred to her. She felt humiliated. At a time when aid was most needed, the family's wordsmith could think of nothing helpful to say.

"Is she dead?" Arte demanded to know.

"Yes," SB answered plainly. "Your mom was hurt so badly. She never would have left us, but she didn't have a choice."

Skye heaved and sobbed. He threw himself against her, and suddenly SB understood what the old phrase "drowning in your own tears" literally meant. She pulled him closer, and he buried his face in her shirt. Arte worried her just as much but in the opposite way, as she stood dry-eyed and silent, holding everything in.

SB said, "It's okay to feel however you feel."

Arte stared. Her eyes looked afire, almost hateful.

SB gave it another shot. "We're not the first ones to go through something like this. It's horrible, and we didn't do anything to deserve it. It's not fair, and it's not our fault. It makes me mad at the universe. It makes me want to scream and break things, but it's something that happens to people, and now it's happened to us."

"It happened to my mom," Arte snapped, "not to you!"

Her words struck deep. Ramona had carried the babies. She had the touch, the way of knowing that some called maternal, the warmth that made people feel loved and connected, and SB had always fought a feeling that, as a mother, she was incompetent if not a total fraud. The depth of her inadequacy opened under her like a yawning pit.

"I don't know how we're going to get along without her," she said. "We're going to have to dig deep and do our best to get through it."

"I'm never going to get over it!" Arte wailed.

"None of us is ever going to get over it," SB said, reaching out a hand to pull Arte closer. "I didn't mean to say that at all. We just need to try to help each other get through it."

Arte swatted SB away. She was seventeen and strong enough to cause some pain. "You're not in charge of how we feel!" she screamed. "I don't have to do anything you tell me!" She whirled, ran down the hall, and slammed her bedroom door.

SB's instinct was to follow, but everything felt so futile as Skye's tears soaked her shirt. Everything she wanted seemed to have already dissolved in saltwater and sorrow.

Gwen touched her cheek and said, "I'll stay with the kids. I'll plan to spend the night, too, if that's okay with you."

"Yes thanks," SB responded. She patted Skye with gentle tip-taps, the way she had done when he was a much littler boy. She told Gwen apologetically, "Walker has things he needs me to do. I've got to go. I'll be home as soon as I can."

She would have changed out of her wet shirt, but what did it matter? If people didn't like the way she looked, they could stuff it.

She stood up and watched Gwen slide into her place beside Skye. On the back stairs, she met Alberta coming up. They grabbed each other and held on a long time.

"I can go with you," Alberta offered, and SB felt tears well in her eyes. She was forty-nine years old, and now that a real mother had arrived, she could cry.

She said, "I think Arte needs you more than I do."

In bed, remembering, she cried again.

Around six in the morning she woke to her phone clanging like an old Ma Bell. Caller ID said "Latelle Washington."

"This is off the record," Latelle told her. "The study draft you've got is the real thing."

28. AGAINST HER BETTER JUDGMENT

ON SATURDAY, THE SUN looked glorious through the windows. After the *Union Voice* bundles had gone out, Merle phoned, and SB accepted the call.

"What would you think about a horseback ride?" Merle asked. "It's not a bad day for one, is it?"

According to the forecast SB had heard on KORE-FM Community Radio, the temperature was likely to rise all the way into the sixties. She sat at her kitchen table eating toast and flipping the occasional nibble to Lil.

"I don't know," she said. "I'm awfully busy."

"Maybe a dog walk then? I could come to town."

SB hesitated before saying, "Okay."

She wasn't at all sure what she was doing. She thought she needed to take more time, but she liked Merle. In fact, being entirely honest with herself (if any of us really can be that, she mused) she had to admit that she wanted Merle's company.

"I guess a dog walk could work," she added. "Sounds fun."

Merle showed up in muddy hiking shoes, an old pair of jeans, and a cotton Henley with the sleeves pushed above her elbows. Her forearms had a nice, plump-looking muscularity, covered as they were with sun-browned skin and downy hair that SB found hard not to look at. Now that they had kissed, she wondered what the protocol should be between them. Obviously the kiss changed things, even though it had only happened the one time. They hadn't come anywhere close to the perfunctory stage where every hello and goodbye has to be marked with a smooch. She didn't offer one when Merle knocked at the back door with Bernie on a leash, but she accepted a hug and gave a soft one back.

Merle said a little awkwardly, "Are you ready?"

"Yeah," SB answered. "Should we get going?"

They took the alley paralleling Mesabi all the way to the avenue that ran along the edge of the park. Bernie lifted his leg and marked two garbage cans, a spot in the gravel, and a patch of grass. Lil had to sniff each spot and leave a calling card of her own.

"Dogs," SB said, feigning disgust.

"Their noses are their superpowers," Merle offered, eyes sparkling.

The park had greened considerably in the week since they'd walked there. The apple, lilac, honeysuckle, and wild plum had all blossomed, punctuating the air with a tantalizing sweetness. The dogs bumped shoulders now and then but mostly steered their own paths, following individual whims and scent trails.

"Look," Merle said as they crossed the meadow en route to the lake. "The wild strawberries."

SB scanned the meadow for tiny white blossoms, and when she saw them nestled with their distinctive sprigs of jagged leaves, she said, "Oh! My!" She didn't remember when she had ever seen more of them open so early across the green.

"Climate change," Merle speculated. When they approached the woody growth that fringed the lake, she said, "The berry bushes are in full leaf now." She seemed in a buoyant mood that must have sprung from something more personal than the flora. Or was SB assuming too much by thinking that?

"I'll have to take your word for it," she said. "I don't know how to recognize any of them without their berries."

Merle stopped and took hold of a slender trunk. "Here's a clump of chokecherries," she said. "The cherry family has these fine, white hash marks on reddish bark. See?"

"Hmm," SB said, leaning against Merle to see better. "Funny, I've never noticed."

"Those are juneberries." Merle pointed a little way distant along the path.

"And all these skinny little thorny canes are wild raspberries. They'd do a lot better if they were allowed to move into the sun without being mowed."

On the far side of the lake, SB felt a sense of privacy. A breeze brushed her face and disturbed the surface of the water. The sky, in reflection, appeared as a penetrating blue, interrupted here and there with ragged white puffs of backscattered clouds.

"You've convinced me," SB said. "I see the potential."

"In what exactly?" Merle asked. She moved closer, eyes teasing.

"Wait," SB said, pausing for comic effect. "Are we talking about plants?"

"I was," Merle laughed. "Are you talking about us?"

"Maybe. I guess I could be," SB said, flustered. "Is there going to be an us?"

"There could be," Merle said. "I think I'd like it. Would you?"

This would have been the time to move in for a kiss, but SB let out a gust of breath. "I guess for me it would mean letting go of Ramona in a way I haven't managed to figure out how to do yet."

Merle backed up slightly, looking disappointed. "How long were you two together?"

"Twenty-one years."

Merle nodded. "That's a long time."

"Seventeen of them with kids. I single parented for the last five."

"That's a big chunk of your life. A lot of strings attached."

"Maybe my judgment isn't so good right now," SB said. "I'm lonely and probably more needy than I even realize. I feel incredibly vulnerable. Likely to screw up, you know? I haven't even thought about getting involved with anyone else until now."

"Hmm," Merle said, her gaze sinking into SB's with a kind of sober gravity. "I guess I feel honored by that."

"You should," SB said. She reached to cup Merle's cheeks in her hands and pulled her into a warm kiss that led to a full-bodied embrace. Merle felt solid, breasts and belly, arms and legs warm and welcoming.

When they disentangled, Merle said, "I mean, life is suffering, but there's also love."

"It's a little early to use that word, isn't it?" SB asked.

Merle frowned and took a breath in deep, "Yeah, but I think I do mean love. You know—as in the gravitational force that holds us in each other's orbits? Also known as the antidote to loneliness? I really want to get to know you, SB."

SB had no answer for that. She started walking again, and Merle followed. They rounded a curve, almost at the end of the wooded part of the path, when Lil gave a beggar's woof and SB noticed the shambling figures of an old man and an old dog headed in their direction.

"Shit!" she said.

"What?" Merle asked.

"Someone I'd rather not run into. A county commissioner. A nasty guy connected to a lot of people who can make things happen."

"Want to turn around?"

"No. He's seen us."

"It doesn't look like we have a whole lot of choice then," Merle said.

Out near the edge of SB's hearing range, Casper Karlsrud chirped to Lil about what a pretty dog she was and what a nice treat he had for her if only she would come to him and let him pet her. When they drew closer he looked Merle and Bernie over and remarked about the "vigorous and handsome" collie as well. He had a treat for each of them. SB made the unavoidable introductions. She stroked the springer's grizzled head.

Casper said, "Susie, I've noticed you haven't followed one bit of my advice on that copper-nickel thing."

"I explained that to you," SB said. "You heard my position."

"And you heard mine," Karlsrud said. His voice became more of a snarl as he went on. "You're walking a very dangerous path!"

"As I told you, I just provide the news," SB said as calmly and reasonably as she could under the circumstances.

Karlsrud looked to be rearing back to deliver another bombardment.

Merle pulled out her phone, looked at the screen, and declared loudly, "Oh, dear, SB! We're late for our appointment!"

SB had the presence of mind to seize the moment. She gathered the slack from Lil's leash and said, "We'd better get going!"

Merle took SB's arm, guided her around the surprised-looking Karlsrud, and pulled her into a hasty exit, shouting back, "Another time, I hope, Commissioner!"

When they got a good way further along, they burst out laughing.

"I owe you," SB told Merle.

"I intend to collect," Merle said. Her sideways glance might have felt salacious if it had been any less welcome. "Sometime I hope you'll tell me the story behind what just happened."

The lines around the corners of her mouth looked vulnerable and sweetly uncertain, and SB would have liked to trace them with a fingertip right then.

"It's a long story," she said, "and one you should definitely hear if you're serious about this community project of yours."

"Suppose you tell it to me over dinner at my house?" Merle said.

"Is that how I'm supposed to pay you what I owe for my rescue?"

"No," Merle said. "Of course not. You owe nothing. Does dinner sound so terrible?"

"When?"

"Soon?"

"I've got to make a trip to Minneapolis on Monday." SB's excuses were beginning to test even her own patience. She knew she'd better get on with accepting.

"Sometime after Monday then?" Merle said. "You're going to eat anyway, aren't you? Let me cook for you. It'll save you some time, and you can tell me the story over dinner."

"You make a good case."

"Come tomorrow."

"Seriously. I've got too much stuff to get ready, and I'm too anxious to be any fun."

"Next Sunday then?"

"Okay," SB said. "We'll confirm by text closer up."

Back at the parking lot, Merle stopped by her car, rolled the windows partway down, and loaded Bernie into the back.

"Okay if I come in?" she said.

SB hesitated.

"Just for a minute?"

In the entryway Merle stood in front of her and bent closer until SB felt Merle's warm breath work its way up one cheek to her forehead, where Merle landed a tiny kiss. She slid her hand under SB's shirt, up to the place where she laid the palm of it across SB's heart.

"It's beating so fast!" Merle whispered.

SB pulled Merle closer and said, "Yours, too."

"We're like a couple of netted birds. We don't know whether to fly or face our fate."

Then, to SB's surprise, Merle pushed away and walked briskly to her car. While SB stood in the doorway breathing open mouthed and watching, Merle popped the driver's side door open and stood behind it. Before she ducked inside, she held up her phone, pointed from SB to the screen, and flashed a mischievous grin.

29. THE COLLABORATORS

EARLY MONDAY MORNING, SB drove past the stand of birch and poplar at the edge of town and caught the highway that would take her to I-35. Thirty-some years earlier, she had traveled this route regularly, back and forth to the university, but traffic had beefed up considerably since then. She purposely avoided Sunday when weekend visitors choked the freeway headed south. She knew she still might find herself in a swell of traffic. That could happen any day of the week, but on a Monday she expected stretches where she could relax and let her eyes take in something more captivating than the road.

She missed the dairy herds and little gaggles of steers and heifers she used to see in their pastures. Cattle sightings had become almost as rare as eagle sightings since farming had gone big, corporate, and south. On the edge of Pine City she watched for the flooded bottomland where a heron rookery appeared in the crowns of a drowning stand of trees. For a long time, SB hadn't noticed the oversized nests, and then one day she did. Now she always looked for the pterodactyl shapes of water birds perched in the bare, gnarly branches.

The pace of traffic quickened just ahead of the fork where I-35 split west and east. She merged onto 35W and took the University Avenue exit, thinking that she might as well resign herself to getting turned around somewhere on the campus. Her familiar movie theaters, late-night cafés, and second-hand bookstores had all been torn down or repurposed. Whole blocks had been razed to make way for a new football stadium, light rail, franchise coffee and bagel shops, high-density apartments, and at least one boutique hotel. Sure enough, a must-turn lane derailed her and looped her around the stadium when she'd wanted to go straight ahead. She pulled over the first chance she got, switched on her phone's GPS program, and followed the know-it-all woman's instructions back to the intersection and the correct lane.

The Witch's Hat appeared on the highest patch of land in Minneapolis. The decommissioned water tower had some other name officially, but people kept on calling it by its familiar name because of its slouching, black, conical roof. Seeing it, she got her bearings again. She knew where to look for the *Record* building, and there it was—a block or so ahead on University—a gleaming, three-dimensional rectangle with the company's logo flashed across the top floor.

From the parking lot, she texted Mel Levine, and he met her in the lobby.

"SB," he said graciously, offering a larger than expected, soft and supple hand. "Good to see you! Great stuff! Is this your first time in our new digs?"

"I don't think I was ever in your old digs," she said. "I did spend a lot of time in Prospect Park over there, though, partying with friends."

She left out the part about her first sexual experience, which happened under the honeysuckle bushes with a sharp-eyed, deft-handed, fellow freshman who wore a Stetson hat and called herself Colorado. SB tried hard to fall in love. They both did, she thought, but it only took a few weeks to figure out that they had nothing in common except willingness and availability—qualities that she learned could sour pretty fast once you realized they were all that you had.

"That's right," Levine said, eyebrows askew. "J-school at the U, right? You forgot to take notes?"

"Maybe we should talk about it over a glass of wine some time," SB responded affably.

"Sure," he said. "When we celebrate our success." On the elevator he told her, "That's one heck of a cache of documents. We're still trying to wrap our heads around what we've got, but what we've seen so far is absolutely dynamite."

"I know," she said.

"Pulitzer quality."

"Well, let's not get ahead of ourselves." She didn't want to jinx them with hubris, and said to undercut the exuberance, "I'm just glad you were willing to partner with us."

"I'm glad Kjell had the instinct to call me," Levine told her. "I hope you know that he's busting his buttons with pride over your work."

"Sounds like Dad," she said as they exited the elevator on the top floor.

Levine led her to a corner conference room, and she saw Chastain Nguyen sitting on the closer side of a long conference table, squinting with her face toward the sun. Windows ran the length of both walls and provided a panoramic view of the green and bushy slopes of Prospect Park.

"You two know each other, don't you?" Levine asked as he watched them share a nod. "And this is Renard Bridges." Levine directed her attention to an investigative reporter whose work she admired. His razor-cut dark hair, coupled with a rakish, Nick Charles moustache, gave him a hard-edged and observant look.

"And here's one of our lawyers, Myles Fulton," Levine said, gesturing toward a barrel-chested man with a shaved head. Fulton reached under his suit jacket, pulled a business card from an inner pocket, and handed it to her. He was billed as a consultant to the *Record*, but his firm's name consisted of a long list of partners that didn't include him.

Levine announced to everyone, "I've already told SB how excited and honored we are to have the chance to work with her on this project. I know I don't have to tell any of you how important and sensitive our work will be. You will surrender your notes and resources to no one outside this partnership. We will hold every bit of information in the strictest confidence until used in a published story, and everything we write will be cleared by me and by Legal before it shows up in print. When that happens, Ladies and Gentlemen, we're going to rock the world! This is the kind of story that we've spent our working lives preparing to write."

SB saw resolute faces all around.

Levine went on, "Obviously the leaked study draft is our first item of business, and it will make the front page soon. Renard has already confirmed its authenticity through reliable, off-the-record sources. We want to go with it this Sunday."

"We've confirmed it, too," SB said, "with an on-the-record source." This crowd was too sophisticated for gap-mouthed awe, but SB did detect some widening of the eyes when she added, "Sunday's not the best day for us. We distribute on Saturdays."

"We'll work that out," Levine said. "You and I can put our heads together later."

SB shrugged. "What about the BeneGeo buyout story? Where does that fit in your mental queue?"

"There's a lot more to be learned about that one," Levine said. "Chastain's working on it."

He cast a managerial look in Chastain's direction, and she responded eagerly, "We're finding evidence in the documents that the BeneGeo buyout was planned from the start, with the original stockholders guaranteed to triple their investments when they handed their holdings over to Worsley. I'm working on following the conversational strands and nailing down the authenticity of the emails and corresponding documents. There's a lot to sort through."

"We might be able to help with that," SB said. "We've found an anonymous company insider who's provided a pile of copied documents for comparison."

"Awesome," Levine said. "Why don't you and Chastain work on it, and keep me in the loop? And then there's Worsley's foundation and the possibility of pay-offs and money laundering. Renard's on that one."

Renard stroked his mustache with a thumb and forefinger before he said, "That's a tangle, too. The financial records need to be cross-referenced with emails and quarterly reports. It's labor intensive, and I'm a long way from getting a firm grip on it. But it looks like lots of officials at different levels of government have been paid off for years through these schemes."

"What are you looking for in terms of evidence?" SB asked.

"Money trails," Renard said. "Ways that payments move around on paper. One money-laundering trick is to pay off officials and book the payoffs as operational expenses backed with receipts from sham providers. A private foundation can be used to channel money, too. For instance, CUNIBelt gives to Green Futures, gets a charitable tax credit, and then the foundation makes a political donation or pays off an official or one of their family members, listing the payoff as some legitimate operating expense. Our source has already provided lots of evidence. We just need to sort it, follow the money, and find ways to confirm that the documents are real."

SB said, "Looks like one of our county commissioners is in pretty deep, taking payments through his campaign fund and his wife's real estate business. I've got some corroborating documents on that one."

"This partnership is smoking!" Levine said with a smile that looked almost devious. "All we need now is time and effort. We're working to shift assignments around on our end to get more people working on this, but we're short-staffed to begin with."

"I'll take on the county commissioner," SB offered. "It's a legacy piece."

"Whatever you need to make it work for you," Levine said. "Here's a tantalizing side note. Turns out the president cancelled the Forest Service study the day after his son and daughter-in-law signed a sweetheart rental deal for an East Side Manhattan condo. Care to guess who owns it?"

"Garman Worsley?" SB said.

"Bingo!" Levine crowed, "Give the astute woman a prize!"

"I think the ones you've already given me will prove quite satisfying," SB said.

"There's more to come," Levine told her. "We're finding evidence that CUNIBelt polluted everywhere they mined, but they've done the most damage in hard rock, sulfide environments. A version of BeneGeo's waste management plan failed in Ontario, and there's some evidence suggesting that someone might have covered it up by arranging an accident that killed a researcher and a journalist. BeneGeo might have known all along that their so-called Mix and Separate barrier isn't impermeable at all. It looks like no currently available material can be expected to perform the way they say theirs will."

"That's still just the tip of the iceberg," Myles Fulton interrupted. He looked around the room, making eye contact with each of them before he went on. "This is highly dangerous stuff. Legal needs you to keep us in the loop. We expect much more information to emerge, and we need to review your corroborating evidence and anything you write before publication. Keep in mind that we'll need time. Probably more than you think. Certainly much more than you would like."

"He's assured me they'll expedite our project as much as possible," Levine added. "Obviously, everything goes through me first. What else do we need to talk about?"

"Cheryl Solem," SB said.

"We'd like to talk to her," Fulton said earnestly. "She could be very helpful in corroborating these documents."

"No kidding," SB said a little too flippantly. She didn't mean it as a retort but realized it came out that way, so she added, "Cheryl's missing. That's why we've got the documents."

"So you don't have any contact information for her at all?" Fulton asked.

"Nothing but her phone number and the voicemail recording that keeps saying her mailbox is full," SB said.

"What else?" Levine asked. After some long, uncomfortable seconds of silence, he said to Chastain and Renard, "Why don't you two get back to it then?"

To SB he said, "Can you stay a few minutes? I'd like to talk to you and Myles."

SB steeled herself for whatever was up.

When the room emptied, Levine said in a resonant voice that SB interpreted as an attempt to assert his alpha maleness, "We need to do some kind of workaround on this once-a-week publication thing."

"What sort of workaround?" she asked. She was not in a mood to give up anything they'd agreed to.

Levine's face softened. "We really need to go with the story on Sunday," he said in a warm, good-guy voice. "That's our highest readership day statewide."

"I understand," she said. "Maybe I should go first on Saturday then, and you could follow on Sunday."

Levine frowned. "Or maybe you could post the story online on Sunday and go to print with it the following Saturday. You'll be getting a byline and full credit in our copy."

"Yeah, but we agreed on simultaneous publication."

"I know, but is that realistic?"

Myles Fulton jumped in, saying with a condescending tone, "Look at the comparative sizes of our markets. You can't really expect us to match your publication schedule."

"You did agree to it in writing," SB said, "so how about if I go to print on Saturday and post online on Sunday when you go to print?"

"Our competitors will eat us alive," Levine groused. "You know it'll be all over the Internet by noon on Saturday."

"Sounds like you'd do best to take it to print on Saturday then," she said.

She noticed that Fulton had a well-groomed hand across his mouth, hiding his amusement at Levine's predicament, she imagined.

"All right!" Levine groaned. "We'll go with a news story on Saturday and an expanded feature on Sunday page one. Will that work for you, SB?"

"I can live with that," she said, "as long as we're fully credited both days per our agreement."

"Ms. Ellingson," Levine said, "has anyone ever told you you're exasperating?"

"I take that as a compliment," she said, "particularly coming from you, Mr. Levine."

30. THE STORY BREAKS

S B AND JACK WAITED in the newspaper office, chatting and running out of words, looking out the window now and then for the truck that would bring the newspapers. The time was not quite five—too early for most people to be out of bed. The sun hadn't rounded the horizon, but its glow spilled like a reverse twilight around the shadows of the downtown buildings. Mesabi Street stood nearly empty, except for the few cars parked in front of bars where, SB assumed, the drivers had walked home or made arrangements to ride with less obviously intoxicated friends. She noticed that Jack sported his annual summer haircut, a severe clip job.

"God, Jack," she said with well-intentioned humor, "even your mutton-chops look like shadows of their former selves."

"It's just once a year," he told her, his grin looking indulgent.

"At least it'll be easy to take care of," she said.

Not that hair hygiene had ever been much of an issue to her—or to Jack as far as she could tell. It was just the kind of bromide that came to mind when she made small talk. She hadn't told him about the front page, and that was on purpose. She wanted to see how he reacted when he saw it.

When the truck pulled up, Lil barked from upstairs, and Jack walked over and propped the door open with the cast iron doorstop that went back to SB's great-grandparents and looked like a black bear standing on its hind legs reaching for something above its head. For the first time in eight months, the pre-dawn air felt mild enough to comfortably walk around without a jacket.

The delivery driver wore jeans and a button-front shirt.

"Just subbing for Bill," she said, wheeling in a dolly loaded with bundles that she proceeded to unload with what looked like ease. "He'll be back next week," she said.

"And you?" SB asked.

The woman shrugged. "Don't know yet. Just subbing for now."

The bundles were tied together with a plastic band about as wide as a line of type, leaving nearly everything above the fold in full view. SB didn't think Jack could miss the banner headline for long.

QUASHED STUDY RECOMMENDS NO MINE

"Holy shit!" Jack yipped. "SB, what did you do?"

"It's more like what I learned and what I had to tell," she said, feeling a momentary flash of concern. If that's how people were going to react, maybe she should get the windows boarded up before the paper hit the streets. But of course she wasn't going to do that.

She filled Jack in with a quick version of the documents saga.

"So that's what you've been dealing with," he said, shaking his head. "What a hot mess! I don't know how you handle all this tension, SB, but you're making me very proud to be part of this outfit. You always have, of course."

"Thank you, Jack," she said. "That's mutual."

"If there's anything I can do," he said, leaving the possibilities open.

"You might regret that offer," she told him. "I don't know how bad things are going to get from here."

"You'll have plenty of people behind you," he said. "Just watch. They'll come out of the swamps and bushes and carry you around on their shoulders once it's all been said and done."

"Maybe."

"For sure."

Dave Maki came in later, predictably red-faced and fuming. SB let herself imagine him as a cartoon figure approaching her with smoke billowing from his ears. It helped make his disapproval feel less personal.

"I warned you," he told her. "Didn't I warn you?"

"You warned me," she said. She didn't think he ought to talk to her like that.

The facts were there for him to read and take into account, and she had the right to make the decisions.

"This could be the last straw for some of our advertisers," he said.

"It's a story that has to be told," she answered. "And it's true."

"Does the truth have to be so in-your-face?"

"It has to be what it is!" She tried to make her voice come out stern and certain so that he would stop and think about who she was and who he was and what part each of them was supposed to play. "I never heard you talk this way to Kjell," she said.

The comparison shut him up for a few seconds, and then he said with a trace of acid in his voice, "I suppose the resort owners and the tourists from the Cities are going to be happy."

"Would that be a bad thing?" she countered.

"No," he said. He hesitated again before adding, "I'm not sure their business is enough to keep a newspaper afloat, though."

"Look, Dave," she said. "We need to pull together on this. If it means rethinking our advertisers, that's what we'll have to do."

"So the fallout lands on my shoulders?" he asked.

"Don't make this a shoot-out with me," she warned. "We can't afford to lose you any more than we can control where the fallout from our research lands. I hope you can live with that. You may have to reach out to some new customers. Start seeing what we can do for the green energy people, the growers, the co-ops and the mom and pop operations. Can you do that?"

He shook his head, more from trying to clear it than from negativity, she thought.

"I guess that's what you pay me for," he said.

"Right," she said, feeling a little relieved. "That's the way I see it, too."

She meant to lock the office door early, but she lingered alone over coffee, chewing over her conversation with Dave.

Marilyn Bednar let herself in, greeting SB with a complaint. "I see that you've gone all the way over to the other side now."

"I'm not sure what that means," SB said, putting down her coffee mug.

"It means you owe the rest of us equal time!" Mrs. Bednar grumbled. SB watched the color deepen in uneven blotches on her cheeks and neck—biochemical rouge that SB couldn't help but think would have amounted to a disastrous tell in poker. If only she could get Mrs. B into that kind of game instead of the tit for tat they were presently engaged in.

"There is no fairness doctrine in this country anymore," SB said, "and if you think there are only two sides to anything, I beg to complicate your understanding."

"I don't need you to complicate anything of mine," Mrs. B retorted sourly. "People around here have been quite tolerant of you and your complications for a long time now. Some of us are getting awfully tired of letting you push your whack-job agendas and personal preferences on us and our kids."

"Letting me what?" SB felt her own cheeks heat up. "I thought we were talking about copper-nickel mining and all it can and can't do for us."

Mrs. B sounded undaunted. "It all fits together out there in far left field where you and your people live, doesn't it?"

"First of all," SB said, rising to her feet, "given what we've learned, it's only our professional ethics that keep us covering this story from as many angles as we do, and I think we do a damned good job, given our resources. If you want more ink from us—which is really what this grievance of yours is all about, isn't it—you can always write a letter to the editor or take out an ad."

Finding SB in her face, Mrs. B rocked onto her heels and sputtered, "Well . . . that's not . . . that's just not good enough!"

"Isn't it?" SB walked to the door, held it open, and told Mrs. Bednar, "I won't look for any more letters from you or your cronies then, and in case you don't already know it, scarier people than you have tried to push me around, and I don't respond well to bullying."

She was ready to add, "so please go," but Mrs. B spun and exited, head held higher than SB thought her chastised expression justified.

SB snapped the deadbolt closed behind her and sat on the loveseat in the lobby for a while, gradually realizing that, despite all, she felt more at peace than she had in years. She felt proud of her work, grateful to the people who had helped her produce it, and more or less ready to face whatever might come next.

Before lunch someone rang the buzzer on the back door, and SB found Alberta on the porch, squinting in the sun.

"That was such good work you did today!" her mother-in-law said, flashing a big-toothed smile. "I'm so pleased with you. I want to buy you a drink down at the Lucky Strike."

"Sounds like I'd be a fool to refuse," SB said.

"Darn right you would," Alberta told her. "Let's go."

At brunch time on a Saturday, plenty of parked cars lined the downtown curbs.

"People are swarming," SB said.

"We can't help it," Alberta answered. "It's the sun and the warmth and the pollen."

The Lucky Strike buzzed with voices. The only two empty seats were stools at the far end of the bar.

"CC and water?" Louisa, the barkeep, asked Alberta when she settled onto one of them.

"And whatever she wants." Alberta jerked her head toward SB.

"A shot of your top-shelf scotch," SB said. "Neat with a water chaser." She felt celebratory and planned to make up the extra cost to Alberta the first chance she got.

When the drinks arrived Alberta lifted her highball and toasted, "Your work!"

"And yours," SB reciprocated. "We're a couple of powerhouses who shouldn't be messed with!"

The scotch filled her nostrils with a smoky sensation. In her mouth it burned briefly and washed like a warm current across her tongue.

Alberta said, "You're warrior to the core, my Other Daughter. Sometimes you'd almost think I gave birth to you."

"Sometimes I almost wish you had," SB said.

A blond man down the bar leaned in and stared. SB thought she caught a hateful flash in his eyes. Toivo Nikko, the Machine Supply manager, would be closing his *Union Voice* account any time now, SB imagined.

"We're being watched," she whispered to Alberta.

"Is that something new?" Alberta laughed. "Let them all look."

SB's phone sounded in her pocket.

"Sorry," she said. "I'd better check this."

"Go ahead," Alberta told her. "I'm not going anywhere."

Merle had texted:

> Kudos and a big salute!
> Do you still want to
> do that dinner we talked
> about? Tomorrow?
> My place?

Alberta grabbed the phone and turned the screen her way before SB had time to pull it back.

"That Merle, huh? You're lucky. She's nice."

"Yeah," SB nodded, "she is."

"You better answer then. I wouldn't make her wait."

The phone chimed again.

Merle had added:

> Lil's invited, too.

"Well," Alberta said, challenging with her eyes. "What are you waiting for?"

SB sat back and returned her gaze. "For one thing," she said, "I was wondering how you'd feel about it."

Alberta looked puzzled, then concerned. "Because of Ramona, you mean?"

SB nodded.

"I miss her," Alberta said, "but she's gone to the land of everlasting happiness or whatever you want to call it. She slipped our grip a long time ago."

"And you're at peace with that?"

"More or less. Does it matter if I am or not? Anyway, we're free to be happy now."

"And you can be happy?"

"Can't you?"

"I'm not sure I know how anymore."

Alberta looked hard at her. "I think you do."

Down the aisle two guys in Miners Union caps seemed to be giving SB the stink eye and grumbling to their tablemates. Across from them, with his back to her, she thought she recognized Arno Toivola's broad shoulders and graying light hair. When she and Alberta finished their drinks and started to the door, he reached out and grabbed SB by the elbow.

"We should talk," he said.

"Any time," she told him.

At home Lil needed a walk. Under the shade of a maple tree in the park, while the dog sniffed and poked around, SB got out her phone and texted her RSVP to Merle.

31. THE DINNER DATE

SORTING THROUGH HER CLOSET on Sunday afternoon, SB marveled at the sorry state of her wardrobe. She pulled out a few of the best options she could find and tried them on in front of her full-length mirror. She had never felt entirely comfortable with the way she looked, and especially not now with her fat deposits shifting under skin that was losing elasticity. In an age of slender, streamlined, and skin-tight, she was thick-muscled, soft in places, and sculpted in ways she didn't necessarily recognize anymore. As a girl she'd enjoyed sports. She was tall and strong for her age, and her long legs had always given her an advantage running. Now none of her clothes felt anywhere close to flattering or up-to-date, even by her personal, relaxed standards. She settled for newer jeans and her least worn cotton shirt, which featured pearl snaps instead of buttons. The shirt fit well, and the pants made the most of her backside, which Ramona had convinced her was one of her most endearing physical assets.

"Those glutes," she used to say with a slap. "Hard to resist, Cowgirl!"

Showered and dressed with her hair brushed, SB loaded up Lil and the expensive, Irish sipping whiskey she'd bought at Liquor Warehouse before leaving the Cities. Her GPS program routed her out of town, down a county highway, and around a sharp turn onto a road in the township of Willow. Near the end she drove along a built-up, gravel roadbed that cut across a tamarack swamp, and then Merle's place materialized from the woods like a cottage in a story—an old farmhouse with a fenced yard situated in a small acreage of trees and meadow. Bernie greeted them from across the fence with a barrage of high-pitched, piercing yips.

In the time it took SB to gather up her hostess gift and open the tailgate for Lil, Merle had appeared at the gate. She stood with one hand around Bernie's snout, holding it shut, and the other on the boards of the gate, holding it open. Her smile looked welcoming in the long, fading afternoon sun, and SB noticed that everything felt emotionally heightened and at the same time smooth, like meeting an old friend in an unfamiliar city. Even the dogs seemed to feel it. They sniffed each other and trotted around without raising their hackles, and SB handed the bottle to Merle. On its closure a toy-sized statue of a horse and rider posed on a bed of wax that ran down the sides of the stopper. The corners of Merle's eyes crinkled with pleasure as she took it in.

"Special reserve," she said admiringly. "Nice!"

SB absorbed Merle's response with a blink and a nod.

Inside, Emmylou Harris streamed on the wireless speaker, the twangy guitars and the singer's voice full of buried sadness and come-hither longing. SB needn't have worried about her clothes. Merle looked equally casual and comfortable, exuding her usual personal radiance in a t-shirt and low-cut denim pants with a wide belt laced through the loops. SB found her eyes studying the solid-looking buckle and its immediate soft and sturdy surroundings.

When she saw that Merle had noticed her gaze, she said, "You look great."

"You do, too." Merle brushed a finger across the snap on SB's cuff on her way to pour the shots. "We best go a little slow with this," she said, eyes aglow at her own double entendre as she handed SB a squat tumbler holding a quarter inch of honey-colored, high-octane hooch.

"Good things," SB said, lifting it.

Merle clicked her glass against SB's and paused there briefly, asking, "Are you a whiskey expert?"

"Oh sure," SB joked. "I smell local notes of foraged plum and dogwood blossoms in this one. Aged, I would say, in charcoaled cedar casks."

"What? No honeysuckle?"

Keeping her face quite serious, SB swished a sip around her mouth and offered, "I'm getting hints of barley malt."

"I think you've nailed it," Merle said.

Outside they sat on canvas chairs beside a kettle grill piled with a pyramid of unlighted charcoal briquettes. The dogs came and lay down on the grass. Merle squirted fire-starting fluid on the charcoal and put a long-nosed butane lighter to it.

"Are you starving?" she asked as the pyramid whooshed into flame.

"Not at all," SB lied. She had ploughed through the Sunday *Record* and then sorted documents through lunch and the early afternoon. She could have eaten a moose if Merle had offered one right then.

Merle said, "I thought we'd just sit here and relax and let our appetites grow while the coals burn down."

"Suits me," SB lied again.

Merle tipped her glass in SB's direction. "Nice newspaper work by the way. You're going to wake up a lot of people around here."

"The story kind of fell into our laps."

"Really? You make it sound like you had hardly anything to do with it."

"Do I? Well, it wasn't that easy, but the documents came to us through a series of events mostly beyond our control."

"You and Gwen made it happen," Merle said. "You should own that. Modesty in women is overrated. There's way too much of it going around. People look up to you with good reason. I hope you know that."

"I guess I do really."

"You should, but there I go. I have a tendency to tell people what to do. I've been told it's not one of my better characteristics."

"It's fine," SB said. "Fair game. I didn't think anything of it."

"Would it be better if I prescribed this?" Merle asked with a puckish grin as she pulled a joint from her shirt pocket and held it upright. "I don't even know if you smoke. We don't have to. It's totally up to you."

"It's been a while," SB said, shifting into a more comfortable position against the back of her chair.

Merle lit the joint with the propane lighter and took the first drag. Her fingers touched SB's when she passed it, and SB felt a charge race up the nerves of her arm. The taste of the herb reminded her of walking with Colorado across the university campus to see the local punk band Hüsker Dü perform at a bar on the West Bank. She felt a tremendous relief just to be there in Merle's company, paying attention to the long, slow unwinding of an afternoon.

"Your place feels comfortable," she said. "Homey."

"So far so good," Merle said. "Eventually I want to improve the gardens and put up a shed and a paddock fence for Dillon."

"So you'd take him from Rocky's?" SB surprised herself by minding the idea so much.

"Not right away. Maybe in a year or two."

"Ah," SB clipped it short, holding in a lungful. She added through exhaled smoke, "How about your edible landscape project? Anything new with that?"

"Some of the city councilors want me to go to the county board for support," Merle said. "Do you think Karlsrud is going to be a problem?"

"I doubt it."

"I mean after our encounter in the park and everything?"

"I wouldn't worry about him."

"Really? I had him pegged as a snake."

"That's probably unfair to snakes," SB said. "But your instincts are right on."

"Hmm." Merle knit her eyebrows in a mystified way and stirred the coals. "Hungry yet?"

"Honestly," SB said, "I'm famished."

"Come on," Merle said. "I could use some help."

Lil jumped up when SB did, and the dogs followed them to the house and back, closely watching the trays of walleye filets and vegetables in hope of a windfall.

The mosquitoes showed up before the filets had cooked to the point of losing their translucence. SB felt the first sting on the back of her hand, followed by a string of them in scattered, vulnerable places. The sun started disappearing behind the tamarack tops, and barn swallows banked around the yard, diving low, after the mosquitoes.

"Let's take the food inside," Merle said.

k.d. lang was singing torch songs in the kitchen. The rest after the fire had finished the fish perfectly, and SB made short, fast work of her supper. Bussing her dishes, she found herself side by side with Merle at the sink. Their arms brushed.

"I'll wash," SB said.

"Leave them. I'll get them tomorrow."

"Are you sure? It wouldn't take long."

Merle reached out and stroked SB's hair. SB felt it in her heart chakra and all the way down her spine.

She confessed, "I'm kind of scared."

"Me, too," Merle said. "Freaking terrified, more like it."

"I'm not even sure I know how to do it anymore."

"It's been a long time for me, too."

"I don't suppose a person really forgets, though."

"We can probably manage to bumble through."

"So are we going to?"

Merle answered with a shy, game grin.

SB slid her hands behind Merle's belt and pulled her close. Merle kissed with creativity, and SB felt all of her perky, little soldiers snap to attention. Her lower back pressed against the bull-nosed edge of the kitchen counter as she felt Merle begin popping open the pearl snaps at a sloth's pace. One by one, they capitulated.

Then Merle pulled back and looked askance. "This isn't very comfortable for you, is it?" she said. "Let's move to the bedroom."

They mounted the stairs like a couple of eight-year-olds, Merle pulling SB by the hand and leading her to the old cast iron bed, where they fell onto thick, clean sheets and moved into a mutual undressing that rapidly gathered speed. Jeans got unzipped, knit things pulled and twisted, and everything was thrown over the edge of the mattress to land in heaps on the floor.

When they lay beside each other fully revealed, Merle maneuvered onto her knees and stroked SB from hipbone to ankle. "Your beautiful, strong legs," she said.

SB pulled Merle's hand to her mouth. She kissed each of her fingers and said, "Your exquisite, good hands."

Before long Merle was on her back, and SB was looking directly into those dazzling, lake-water eyes.

"Seems like it's all coming back to you pretty well," Merle said.

"You're not doing so badly yourself," SB replied.

To stoke the fire of Eros and retreat before stoking it some more felt so completely good that she was beginning to wonder how she could have repressed her desire so long. She positioned herself above Merle and lowered herself until they touched almost completely but with just enough space that SB could reach her hand between them and explore Merle's inner cleavage, tracing the curves and shapes, parting her labia, and fitting her own thigh snugly against Merle's exposed erotic core. She gasped as Merle returned the favor, and they rode together, traveling the canyon rims of their slowly growing preludes to orgasm, shivering, backing away from the chasm, and pressing on.

They had tumbled over the edge and were working on coming around again when the door burst open and Bernie charged in, yipping his high-pitched complaint. Lil came along behind and leapt onto the bed.

SB and Merle fell apart laughing, and Merle said, "God, no! Spare us this!"

"Dogs," SB said. "They always do us so proud, don't they?"

Merle got up and put them out. She closed the door, and SB saw her pull on the knob to test that it had latched properly this time.

Night hadn't quite fallen. They were in the ten o'clock, mid-summer last light, and Merle looked beautiful—smooth-muscled, well propor-tioned, blushed with arousal.

When she saw SB looking, she said, "I knew I was falling for you that first day we went riding."

"Really?" SB said. "For me it was your bare feet under the massage table. I wanted to know how the rest of you moved and how you would feel in my hands."

"And now you know," Merle said as she climbed back into bed.

"And now I think I have a lot more to learn," SB said. She kissed Merle's throat and let her kisses wander a slow trail southward until she heard Merle cry, "Oh god!"

Was it a prayer or surrender? Maybe both, SB thought before she re-membered to try to stop thinking. The answer didn't matter as long as she could be there with Merle, feeling those strong, tender thighs open for her.

32. THE MORNING AFTER

SB ARRIVED HOME IN the broad daylight of seventy-thirty in the morning. She parked in her usual spot and sat for a few minutes with the radio off, hoping to clear her head of the mind fuzz she'd been experiencing since she left Merle's bed. Post-coital, perimenopausal, or whatever, she could still feel the warm weight of Merle's goodbye kiss through her entire body. What was she going to do about it? That was the question. Already, she craved more from Merle, even though she still had plenty of misgivings. She thought a shower might clear her head, but first she took Lil off leash to the grassy spot at the end of the alley. In the shower she lingered longer than usual and felt a little clearer when she headed down to the office to make coffee.

Since Gwen hadn't arrived yet, SB had the place to herself. She went to open the front blinds but when she got close enough to feel the solar gain passing through them, she decided to leave them down until she was ready to unlock the door.

The ways that Merle had touched her kept running through her head. The freshness of the things they said and did were something new to her and to the world, parallel in some ways to the things she had said and done with Ramona, but a completely new creation. Lovemaking confounded her in that way—only so many basic mechanics but seemingly endless variations in delivery, spirit, giving, and taking. She had no clue what she would answer when Gwen asked the inevitable question about how her date with Merle had gone. She spent way too much time practicing her answer and was surprised when Gwen came in and didn't show any of the curiosity she had expected.

Instead, Gwen's eyes went straight to meet SB's gaze with a stare that looked both surprised and disbelieving.

"You haven't seen the graffiti out front then?" Gwen asked.

"What?" SB asked, suddenly derailed, and then, once she had found her traction again, hurtling out the door to see for herself.

And there it was, sprayed across the new window and freshly sand-blasted brick façade, a crazy quilt of supposed witticisms from some self-appointed, grammatically challenged harasser.

RUG MUNCHERS RAG

GREENIES WITH NO WIENIES

REDSKIN LIES SPOKE HERE

DYKE CENTRAL GIRLS WANTED

There were more—a dozen or so. SB felt her pulse accelerating and told herself to keep her breath going deep, out completely, and in again.

She said to Gwen, "Whoever did this pretty much covered all of my sweet spots."

"I'd say about sophomore level at best," Gwen offered, shaking her head. "Would you like me to make some calls about cleanup?"

"Not right now," SB barked. "I'm going to shoot some photos and post them online. People need to see this."

"What about him?" Gwen asked, jerking her head to direct SB's attention across Mesabi Street, where she could just make out the bulkier of the BeneGeo goons, watching from the shadows in the entryway of the old Merchants and Miners Bank.

"What do you suppose he's up to?" Gwen said.

"I don't know," SB answered. "Something, though. You can bet on that. I've got to get my camera. It's got a much better telephoto than my phone."

When she returned, he was gone.

Gwen said, "I'm calling 911."

"Go ahead," SB said, "for whatever good it will do."

She busied herself with long shots and close-ups and then walked around the exterior of the building, checking to see if she could spot any other damage. Finding nothing, she went indoors and tried some shots of the window glass looking out through the graffiti.

When Sgt. DeMarco arrived, she approached SB and said, "Sorry for your trouble here."

"It's getting to be kind of a habit, isn't it?" SB told her.

"Well, it's a repeat anyway," the sergeant said. "Did you by any chance install that surveillance camera I recommended after the rock incident?"

"No," SB said, feeling unapologetic. "I didn't really think I needed it."

The sergeant gave about a quarter roll of her eyes and then pointed out, "It sure would have come in handy now, though, wouldn't it?"

"I'll grant you that," SB said, "but I don't really need any rubbing it in at the moment."

Later, after she and Gwen had been alone in the office, SB allowed ruefully, "The timing on this just stinks, doesn't it?"

Gwen looked puzzled at first, and then her eyes brightened with realization and she said, "Oh, because of your date with Merle?"

SB nodded but didn't smile. She tried not to give too much away.

"Did it go okay?" Gwen asked.

"Yeah, I'd say so," SB answered, "for now, anyhow."

"Good for you," Gwen said with a relieved-looking smile. "She seems nice. I hope it works out just beautifully for both of you."

"Thanks," SB said. She guessed she hoped so, too.

Around lunchtime Arno Toivola came in, dressed in work khakis and a baseball-style cap, all embedded with fine, red dust.

"I've got a couple of union volunteers outside with paint thinner and rags," he told SB. "We'd like to clean this place up if you don't mind."

"Really?" she asked, looking out the window to see a pink-cheeked woman and round-faced man unloading buckets from the bed of Toivola's pickup. "I wouldn't have thought . . ."

"It wasn't us," Arno said. "I mean some of our guys are outrageous and mad, but some of us figure we owe you. You've showed us how we've been had, and we figure if the bosses lie about who owns the company, they're lying about a lot of other things."

"So you think the union might be coming around about copper-nickel mining?" SB asked.

"Oh god, no," Arno said, shaking his head. "Most of 'em still don't have a clue. They think you're the one who's lying to sell your papers. They figure you Ellingsons got rich and keep getting richer at their expense. You've got a lot of convincing to do."

"Really?" SB said. "Do they actually read the *Voice*?"

"Mostly no," he admitted, "but a lot of them talk to somebody who does."

"Well, that's something," she said.

By one o'clock the front of the building looked mostly restored. Later that afternoon a small man in blue jeans and a polo shirt struggled into the lobby carrying a heavy looking cardboard box. He walked with it against one hip, which threw him off-balance and might have contributed to the appearance that he was lame in a knee or hip or both.

"Can I help?" she asked, getting up from her desk.

"My name's Vick," he said, swinging his box up and onto the counter. "Peter Vick. A friend told me someone from here called him. He doesn't want his name used, but from what he said, I think I might have some papers you'd like to see."

"What kind of papers?" SB asked.

He looked around. When he saw that they were the only two in the office, he confided in a half whisper, "Stuff from Commissioner Karlsrud's office."

It sounded too easy.

"Did Casper send you?" SB asked.

"Absolutely not," Vick said, recoiling in what looked like genuine insult. "Why would he?"

"You never know," she said. "I have to ask. Please sit." She and Gwen would look into his background later. For now, she wanted to hear what he had to say.

She patted the seat of the chair beside her desk, and he took the box into his arms again, hobbled over, and started a slow descent. The last few inches he dropped like dead weight to the seat. There was no time for her to reach out to catch his arm, and he probably wouldn't have wanted her help. His unflustered look told her it was business as usual for him.

"You won't have to use my name, will you?" he asked.

"No," she assured him. "We have ways of handling that."

"Good. I can't afford to lose my job or make any enemies."

"Understood," she said. "None of us can. Now, suppose you tell me what you've got here and how you happened to get it?"

"I'm the weekend custodian at the courthouse. Midnight to eight. It screws up your sleep cycles, I'll tell you, but nobody bothers you much. I get plenty of cleaning done and time to read the paper on Saturday nights. The news has been pretty interesting lately."

"It's always nice to talk to an appreciative reader," she said. She'd long since learned the value of returning flattery when it was offered.

"Something strange happened last Saturday," he said. "Around two in the morning, the commissioner came down to the basement. I didn't even know he was in the building. I was taking a break in the furnace room, and I don't think he saw me. He looked like he hadn't slept in a while, face white as a ghost. I watched him empty a file box into the paper-shredding bin. It took a while because the lid is locked, you know. He had to stuff his papers in by the handful through a two-inch slot. He's always been a strange duck, but even for him it was an odd time to be dumping papers, and there's a shred bin in his office. I don't think he's ever carried a box to the basement himself before this."

"Who has the key to the bin?" SB asked.

"Just me." Vick said.

His eyes shone briefly in a proud way, and SB got the impression he saw himself as doing something worthwhile.

"Did you get a look at the papers?" she asked.

"Enough of one," he said. "I knew something funny was going on, and I saw enough to know I was right."

"Funny how?" SB asked.

"Funny crooked," he said. "Money getting asked for and promised here and there."

"Between Karlsrud and who else?"

"Lots of names I don't know and some I do, like BeneGeo."

"Is it okay if I take a look at these papers?"

"You can have 'em," he said. "That's what I come for. I figured you'd know what to do with 'em. Just keep my name out of it."

"That I can guarantee, Mr. Vick," she said. "We protect our sources here. How about if I call you a person familiar with the matter?"

"Sounds pretty okay to me," he said, offering a large-knuckled hand to shake on it.

TUESDAY MORNING, RIGHT after SB flipped the "closed" sign to "open," the man who had forgotten his wallet showed up again. She had barely sat down at her desk when he came through the door and stood at the counter, smiling and looking around the newsroom in that relentless way he had of taking in details that people on the level knew better than to scrutinize so obviously. His behavior put SB on high alert. She found herself sizing him up physically and thinking she might be a match for his reach but not for his heft. She determined to stay out of range of his hands.

He told her, "I'd like to buy an ad."

"What kind?" she asked from her desk.

"A car ad."

"Classified or display?"

"Classified I suppose."

His grin really grated. She got up from her desk and approached the counter, keeping a reasonable distance between them.

"I see you've got your watchdog here," he said, looking at Lil stretched across her cushy bed in the lobby.

Lil was used to customers coming and going and only raised her head after he said the word "dog."

"Does he bite?"

"Only when needed," SB answered.

She had heard the question a few times before when she was walking with Lil or some other dog in the long string of Lil's predecessors. Now and then some man she didn't know had appeared on some path or sidewalk and asked. She always gave the same answer. It just seemed prudent to leave the possibility open.

The man resumed grinning as if everything was all the same to him.

Standing at arms' length behind the counter, SB grabbed the form he needed and slid it in front of him, instructing, "Fill in your personal information, and write what you want the ad to say in the space at the bottom."

"Sounds easy enough," he said, keeping his eyes on her and not lowering them to the form until the front door swung open again, and Sergeant Angela DeMarco came through in her City of Iron police uniform.

"I've got an update on your graffiti perpetrator," she said to SB.

"Already?"

"When you're able to hear it," the sergeant said, rolling her dark eyes toward the man at the counter.

"We'll be done here shortly," SB told her.

The man wrote in a hurry then and wanted to know, "What now? What do I owe?"

"That depends on the number of lines," SB told him. "Let me see it."

He had listed his name as Evan Winter. He wanted to sell a Ford pickup at what looked like a decent price. He could be reached at an Iron landline exchange. She counted the words.

"Looks like three lines," she said. "Forty-five dollars."

"Cash OK?"

"Or we can take a card."

"U.S. dollars," he said, pulling out a leather wallet and producing a fifty-dollar bill that he practically flung at her. As he turned to leave, he ordered over his shoulder, "Keep the change."

When the door closed behind him, SB asked Sgt. DeMarco, "Was that guy a little off, or is it just me?"

"Hard telling," the sergeant shrugged. "Weird smile, but it takes all kinds."

"I guess," SB said.

"I wouldn't turn my back on him, though."

"No. That was my thought, too."

In the right light the sergeant's eyes might have seemed attractive, SB thought, but there was nothing soft or easy about them at that moment, just hard flint, honed to a sharp edge. She steered Angela around to the subject she'd come to discuss.

"What's up?"

"We've got a juvenile who's confessed to doing your most recent vandalism," Angela said. "He admitted to spray-painting the front of your building last Sunday night—or technically in the middle of the night early Monday."

"What can you tell me about him?" SB asked.

"He's fourteen."

"Local?"

"Yeah. A townie."

"Got a name?" SB said.

Angela answered abruptly, "We don't release juveniles' names unless a judge orders them tried as adults."

"And we don't print them as a matter of principle and style," SB answered back. "I'm asking for my own personal information. There'll have to be some kind of victim impact statement and compensation process, won't there? You know how this town works. I'll find out everything eventually."

"He apparently acted on his own volition," Sgt. DeMarco offered, "but at his age that doesn't excuse his parents from responsibility."

"I understand," SB said. "I'm a mom, too. Come on, Angela."

The sergeant straightened in her chair. "It's Jared Bednar."

"Marilyn's son?"

"Yes."

"Did she have any part in it?"

"He said it was all his own idea. After I left here on Monday I checked at Hardware Hank up the street. You know the owners, Jeff and Candy Olson."

"Of course." Another of the multi-generational, business-owning couples in Iron.

"So Jeff remembered Jared coming in and buying paint. He printed a copy of the receipt, and when I took the kid in and showed it to him, he spilled his guts right away. He swears he's sorry, and I think he's probably telling the truth about that."

"I suppose it'll stay in juvenile court," SB speculated.

"Right," Sgt. DeMarco said. "This isn't the kind of thing they waive juvenile jurisdiction for, but someone should be in touch with you. They're doing a lot of restorative justice work in cases like this now. They might want to you to participate if you're willing."

"Feel free to have them call me," SB said. "And Gwen. She was impacted, too."

"I'll mention you both in my report," the sergeant said. "In the meantime, this goes nowhere else, right? I've got your word on that?"

"Nothing we've said leaves this office," SB promised.

Later Gwen listened to SB's account of the visit and said in a disappointed voice, "I don't know Jared all that well, but I always thought he tried to be a good egg."

"It kind of figures, though, doesn't it?" SB said. "What with public life being the way it is right now and his mom being the way she is?"

"I guess," Gwen said, her face drooping slightly. "I guess I hadn't realized how low we've sunk. I mean I did, but I didn't. I must be living in a huge, sugary bubble."

"You're not sounding like yourself," SB said. "Did you spend the night poring over the money laundering files by any chance?"

"God, yes," Gwen told her. "Rebecca Lyon's papers are matching up almost down the line with Cheryl's documents, but there's still so much to sort through. The more I read, the more connections I see, and the more I wonder if I can put it all together."

"Did you come across any more pieces of the Karlsrud money trail?"

"A couple of donations to his campaign account match against CUNIBelt expenditures, and a payment from the foundation to his wife's real estate business got chalked up as rental expenses. I wish I had more. Are we still shooting for Saturday?"

"That's the plan."

"That might be a stretch."

SB picked up Peter Vick's box and held it ceremoniously in front of Gwen. "Before we give it up, I've got a surprise for you," she said. "A gift from the gods. Papers from Karlsrud's files. I'll start going through them right away."

Gwen looked flabbergasted. "How did you get them?"

"From a man who knew a man," SB said. "Thanks to your phone calls."

When they went back to their research, Gwen looked appropriately reenergized. Sorting through Vick's papers, SB found that, since they had gone into the recycle bin by handfuls, bunches of them came out of the box arranged by sender, date, and subject. Things were fitting together, making sense, corroborating Cheryl's documents. In the midst of the push, Mel Levine called.

"Renard and Chastain have put a lot of pieces together on the political payoffs," he said. "We can't wait to take it to press."

"We can't, either," SB said.

"I mean literally," he told her. "We want to go to print tomorrow."

"Wednesday?" she said. "You know that's not our agreement."

"Look," Levine argued. "We've managed to fit a ton of evidence together, and you'll get our story to post. There'll be plenty left for a follow-up on Saturday and for weeks after that. These money trails lead in so many directions. We can help you with that county commissioner of yours."

"We've got that covered," SB said. "The only thing is I don't know if we can pull it off by tomorrow. I don't even know how we'd do it. We'd have to put out an extra, which is something I've never done."

"Time's of the essence," he pressed. "There is a tide which taken at the flood . . ."

"Oh Christ, don't pull out the bard as an authority. You know what I hate most about this whole argument, Levine?"

"What?"

"That you're probably right."

She saw Gwen looking at her with a creased brow, eyes troubled with doubt.

"We're going with what we've got," SB told her. "Let's get writing. Levine needs to run our copy past Myles Fulton by five o'clock. If we can't get our extra to the printer by eight, we'll have to go digital only."

ARLY WEDNESDAY, SB STOOD talking with Gwen and Jack while they
waited for the extra edition to arrive. Dawn in high summer just
stateside of the forty-ninth parallel meant that SB didn't have to bother
to switch on the lights. The blinds were open. The sun had been providing
plenty of illumination since four-thirty.

"Care to caffeinate?" she asked the other two.

"God yes!" Gwen answered. "The usual strength, I hope."

"It's the least I can do," SB said on her way to the coffeepot. "I know you
two pulled out all the stops to make this happen. I'm grateful."

"Don't mention it," Jack said with a jaunty lift of his chin. "I'm nothing
if not a chivalrous dude."

Gwen chortled, "So that's what you're all about?"

"No doubt," he said. "Impressing you ladies."

"And we thought you were just a heck of a good team player," SB joked,
pretending to be serious.

When the papers arrived, the banner screamed in all caps:

DOCUMENTS POINT TO PAYOFFS

Jack read the next headline aloud:

Records Link County Commissioner to CUNIBelt Payments

He swallowed wrong at the end and launched into a coughing jag.
When he recovered enough to try to talk, he was barely able to choke out,
"What did you two do now?"

"Don't worry," Gwen said. "It's all carefully researched and documented.
You'll see when you read it."

"Oh, man," Jack mewled. "I trust that you two know what you're doing.
But oh, man!"

SB had worries she kept to herself. The special edition was bound to set loose plenty of demons determined to drag her to ruin. Besides the reporting she and Gwen had done, Renard and Chastain provided detailed accounts of at least a half dozen elected officials in the state—including two members of Congress—who received questionable campaign contributions and payments. They laid out the details of the financial trails they'd followed to show how money moved between CUNIBelt, BeneGeo, the Worsley Green Futures Foundation, and the officials. Some of it flowed through businesses that appeared to exist in name only. Congressman Lubovitz's wife, daughter, and son-in-law had taken in more than three million dollars doing business as six different limited liability corporations. Green Futures paid more than four hundred thousand dollars to Casper Karlsrud's wife's real estate business.

By noon readers and trolls had jammed the *Voice's* website. Roughly half wanted SB to apologize, recant her lies, go directly to jail, and/or die, preferably by some excruciating and specific method of execution. The rest wanted Karlsrud and the others to resign, pay back their grifted money, face the hostile mob, and/or commit suicide out of recrimination and shame. The few people who occupied nuanced ground seemed odd and mealy-mouthed by comparison.

After lunch, Karlsrud's lawyer called. SB put him on speakerphone while Gwen recorded.

He said in a condescending baritone, "My client has instructed me to sue you for everything you've got. We need an immediate retraction and apology, or we'll close down your paper and see that it never reopens. We'll liquidate your holdings and haul away your personal belongings in a moving truck. When we're through you won't even have your Labrador to console you. I intend to be at the courthouse this afternoon to file."

SB and Gwen exchanged a fiery look.

"New York Times v. Sullivan," SB told him. "Truth is an absolute defense to libel, and don't call me again. You can direct any further communication to my attorney, Myles Fulton, at the *River Cities Record.*"

She disconnected, and Gwen high-fived her.

Later, Chase Monahan stopped in and said, "Ladies." His roan hair had grown enough to curl at the edge of his collar. He brushed it with his hand and said, "I'm impressed! I never thought I'd see the cover blown so completely off the bullshit and corruption around here."

SB said, "You started it."

"I had no idea," he said. "I just wanted to find out what happened to Cheryl."

"And we haven't done that." Acknowledging it, SB felt failure settle like a weighted blanket around her shoulders.

After lunch Gwen reminded her that Chuck would be coming in and the two of them would leave right at five o'clock to make their dinner reservation at the new Caribbean restaurant in Ely.

"I hate to leave you," she said, "but it's so hard to get in. We've had the reservation for weeks."

SB heard the guilt in Gwen's careful explanation. She didn't want that and said cheerfully, "Let me know if it lives up to its reputation."

"For sure," Gwen said. "Maybe you and Merle could double with us there sometime."

At the same time SB said, "That might be fun," she squeezed her face to convey uncertainty. What she didn't articulate was that she didn't want to feel hemmed in about future plans with Merle. She didn't want anyone, including Gwen, to assume anything about where their relationship might be heading—not until she and Merle had figured it out for themselves.

Chuck arrived at five to five. He came in through the back, looking golfer tanned and nicely turned out in creased trousers and a crisp, blue shirt that nearly matched the color of his eyes. The curious thing was his worried frown.

"I've got to tell you gals," he said. "I saw a guy sitting in a car in your parking lot. I don't know what he's doing back there, but I got the impression he might be watching this place."

"Are you kidding?" SB asked.

"I wish I were," he said uneasily.

The three of them went directly to the back entryway. Chuck stood in the doorway and pointed out the SUV. The tinted windows made seeing inside difficult.

"I'll bet it's one of those BeneGeo goons," SB said. She waved to see if he would respond.

"Want me to go talk to him?" Chuck offered.

"No," she said. "You two go and have a good time. If he doesn't leave soon I'll call the cop shop and ask if someone can come and check it out."

"We should stay," Gwen offered. "We'd be glad to."

SB insisted. "Go! Have fun! Merle's bringing dinner. We'll be fine."

It wasn't long before Merle arrived, carrying a brown paper bag that smelled of overheated salt and oil.

"Lucky Strike?" SB asked.

Merle nodded. "Burgers and fries. The Strike's hopping. Everybody's talking about your stories today—a lot of it positive."

"Really?" SB asked dubiously.

"For sure," Merle assured her with a hint of a smile. "Or maybe fifty-one percent. But even the complainers are allowing that you've got guts."

"More than brains probably."

Merle smiled bigger, and that slender, toothy aperture set off a bio-chemical rush that flashed SB back to Sunday night.

"Are you hungry?" Merle asked.

"Famished," SB said, leaving it there even though she was tempted to make a little sex joke.

After dinner Merle cleared away the takeout containers, and SB carried them down to the outdoor recycle bin so that she could check out the parking lot.

"Nobody there," she said when she came back.

"Why?" Merle asked. "Was there someone?"

"Earlier." SB feigned a casual shrug. "One of those BeneGeo security guys."

"Doing what?"

"I don't know. It's a public parking lot."

Merle walked behind her and hugged her around the shoulders. "You're really tight."

"I know," SB said. "Are you surprised?"

"After a day like today?" Merle left the question hanging as her thumbs dug into SB's deltoids.

"Ah," SB said, feeling some of the tightness go slack. "That helps."

"Good," Merle said. "After I get you loosened up, I've got to get home and feed Bernie. Then we can come back and spend the night if it's okay with you. I'd like to."

"I don't know," SB said. "It may not be the best time."

"Hmm. Seems like I've heard that before somewhere." Under Merle's gaze, SB felt seen through and uncomfortably exposed.

"Sorry," she said. "I guess I'm just out of sorts."

She didn't want to talk about the danger. Alone again, she went to the closet in Arte's room and felt around in the dark, back corner until her hand touched the wooden curve of Arte's softball bat. She pulled it out, carried it to the staircase, and leaned it in the corner. Then she went down two flights to the basement. Tools cluttered the workbench counter. She would have had to clear a space to work if that's what she had wanted to do, but she was only looking for the carpenter's hammer. She spotted it hanging on the pegboard and took it in her hand. On the way upstairs she swung it around to remind herself of its heft and balance. She opened the outside door to have another look at the parking lot. Her car was the only one in sight, and evening was settling in. The sky had darkened from robin's egg to lapis. Indigo wouldn't arrive and reveal the full cosmic light show until well after ten o'clock. Inside, she flipped the deadbolt and leaned the hammer against the doorframe.

When Lil barked, SB went to the window and saw Merle and Bernie walking toward the back door. Merle had a bag in her hand, and Bernie pranced off leash ahead of her. SB went down and opened the door.

"Staying away just felt wrong," Merle explained. "Can we come in?"

"It's not a night for romance," SB warned flatly.

"For sure," Merle acknowledged. "It's not a night for you to be alone, either."

In bed, SB had trouble falling asleep. She had the sense that Merle might be lying awake, too, but she didn't want to ask in case she was wrong. Sometimes they turned and touched just slightly, sometimes not. Finally, SB opened her eyes and found Merle looking back at her.

"Have you slept?" SB asked.

"Not much," Merle said. "You?"

They started talking then about lying awake at night and the things that kept them from sleeping, which led to stories about families, jobs, past loves, mistakes they suffered through and learned from, and what a decent person was supposed to do in the face of what looked more and more like a backwards slide into crashing systems, shared insanity, mass denial of responsibility, and chaos.

Finally Merle said, "We've got to stop talking, or we'll never get to sleep."

SB replied, "I don't think I'm going to be able to sleep no matter what."

Merle looked like she wanted to say something, and then she did. "Maybe if I hold you. Like a friend."

Somewhere in there SB lost track of consciousness.

She woke to loud, barking dogs scrambling to the back of the apartment. She wasn't sure if Merle had been sleeping, but as SB pulled on her own shirt and jeans, she sensed that Merle was up and moving, too. Nearing the back door, she heard Merle's footsteps close behind her.

"Keep the dogs inside," SB directed. Too late! Speeding down the stairs, dogs underfoot, she shouted over her shoulder, "Grab the bat!" At the door she picked up the hammer. She looked back and saw Merle two or three steps behind, weapon in both hands, parallel to the ground as if she was thinking about bunting.

She heard people shouting outside—low, gruff, men's voices, she was pretty sure. She heard blows landing and the sounds of scuffling and of someone—maybe more than one person—grunting with pain.

"What's going on?" Merle asked.

"I'm going to open the door and see," SB said. "Okay?"

"Ready!" Merle affirmed, shifting the bat to swinging position.

SB took her own hold low on the handle of the hammer so that if she needed she could deliver maximum power from the increased mechanical advantage. She eased the door open.

Three men wrestled on the pavement in front of them. Two, she began to see, were the BeneGeo security goons. They had someone on the ground, and they were trying to do something to him while he tried to get loose. He was on his stomach, and the slighter of the goons was swinging something silver in the air. A light chain of some sort?

"Stop that!" SB shouted. "Let him go!" She felt emboldened by Merle's backup and made herself look as puffed and menacing as she could.

The beefier of the goons looked up at them, widened his eyes, and ordered, "U.S. Marshals Service! Put the weapons down, Ladies!"

And then the thing she had seen swinging from the smaller man's hand came to rest against the wrist of the man on the bottom, and it began to look like a set of handcuffs. Gradually, she saw that the goons were trying to get the cuffs on the prone man who was wriggling on the ground, trying to slip their grip. It wasn't until they had him cuffed and pulled to his feet, one on each side of him, pinning his arms, that she recognized Evan Winter. He looked mussed and worse for wear, with a split lip and a trickle of blood running the length of his chin, but he still had that trace of an upturn at the corners of his mouth—a grin made all the more disturbing under the circumstances.

"I'll need to see some ID," SB demanded of the larger man.

He frowned and directed, "I'm giving the orders, and I need you to put the weapons down! Now!"

"Maybe we should," Merle whispered. "SB?"

"U.S. Marshals," the big man repeated. "You don't want to make us tell you any of that again!"

An SUV sporting the Red Stone County Sheriff's insignia turned into the parking lot in a hurry. No lights. No siren. The driver pulled beside the three men and braked hard. Walker Hayes climbed out of the driver's seat and gaped at SB and Merle standing with their makeshift armaments. His face turned stern. SB dropped the hammer. She heard Merle's bat land with a crack on the pavement behind her.

The goons seemed to have Mr. Winter under control. In the headlights SB saw that, besides the bloody lip, he sported a broad stripe of road rash on one side of his face from forehead to chin. Walker opened the back door and stood by, looking ready to assist if needed, while the security men pushed Mr. Winter into the caged backseat. Staring out from inside, his eyes looked cold and dead. He smiled on all the same, like anybody's idea of a sociopath. SB regretted that she hadn't thought to grab her phone. She was missing some great photos.

"What's going on, Walker?" she asked, hoping to get an answer for once.

"I'm transporting a prisoner," he said, "assisting investigators from the U.S. Marshals Service."

The bigger of the self-proclaimed marshals got into the front passenger seat without saying anything more to SB, and Walker got into the driver's seat and pulled the SUV out of the parking lot. He headed in the direction of the county jail and the highway junction. She couldn't say for sure where they were going.

"Here," the slighter man said with what sounded like exasperation.

He was pushing something toward her, and she saw that it was his wallet, held open so that she could see a badge and a photo ID card. He looked like the man in the photo, Criminal Investigator Geraldo Luna with the

United States Marshals Service. He had dark, intense eyes, now that she could see them, and a slender, roman-nosed, ultra-serious face. Right then, at that moment, he had a sore-looking, bloody scratch and a swollen bump across the bridge of that nose. His mirrored glasses lay twenty feet or so away on the pavement, twisted into an almost unrecognizable shape.

"Satisfied?" he asked SB in a voice that resembled a wounded growl.

"Surprised," she said. "Confused. Were you under cover all this time?"

"I can't tell you details," he said. "Read into it what you will."

"What about your buddy?" she asked.

"My partner," he corrected.

"Who is he?" SB shot Luna a look that should have told him she was prepared to wait as long as it took for an answer. "A marshal?"

"CI Terry Masterson," Luna divulged. "We're not all marshals."

"What have you two been doing here?"

"Working an investigation," he said. "I really can't tell you more."

"What about that man you arrested, Evan Winter?"

CI Luna frowned. "He's a man of many names. Sy Borgman is the one listed on his birth certificate."

"What was he doing here?"

Luna shrugged. "I only know that he's a fugitive under indictment in a murder-for-hire case up in Sudbury, Ontario. The provincial authorities want him for possible prosecution in the deaths of a reporter and a researcher."

"Hired by whom?" SB asked.

"I can't tell you," Luna said, "but off the record I think you should count yourself lucky about this morning, and you and your team are on the right track."

"About what?" SB asked.

"I've probably said too much already," Luna told her before he turned his back and walked away. He picked up the mangled glasses and didn't look back.

SB hollered after him, "What is it about you law men? You think you can turn things upside down and then just disappear?"

"What just happened?" Merle asked.

In the dim light cast by the lone streetlamp, SB could see that her lover's shirt was buttoned wrong. Merle stood on the pavement barefoot and rumpled, a handful of gingery cowlick standing on end from contact with the pillow. Adorable. That's what SB would have said, except that she felt responsible for the troubled look in Merle's eyes.

SB told her, "I think they just took away one of Garman Worsley's paid assassins."

Merle's eyes widened. "What was he here for?"

"I don't know," SB answered. "Maybe for me."

"CASPER KARLSRUD," SB said after glancing at her caller ID.
"You're not going to answer it, are you?" Gwen asked.

"God no. This one can go directly to voicemail."

"I don't imagine his lawyer would want him talking to you, anyway."

"Do I care?"

It was late on Monday morning. A light rain muffled the traffic sounds on Mesabi. The postman came in wearing a hat with a plastic covering. He dropped a stack of mail on the counter while SB scanned her inbox, looking for an email from Marc Tremblay, a journalist in Ontario who was investigating the deaths of a hydrologist and a reporter. She had never met Tremblay, but she had known the postman a long time. A craggy-faced, hardworking, local boy, he was still young, and his job hadn't inflicted enough injuries to dent his disposition.

"A nice spring rain," he said cheerfully.

"Oh," SB responded, coming around from her techno thrall. "I guess so. I hadn't thought of it that way."

The postman seemed uncomplicated, as if that could be true of anyone. She pegged him as pretty much the same in his depths and on his surface, happy enough with his job, satisfied with his wife, and smitten with his four kids.

"Anything good in there?" she asked him.

"Oh, you know," he told her, "that's not for me to say. I did see a hand-written letter."

"I don't get many of those."

"Nobody does anymore," he said on his way out the door.

The journalist whose message she awaited wrote for *L'Etoile du Peuple*, a weekly newspaper in the far northern city of Sudbury. In the Red Hands file of the documents from Cecilia Baez, SB had found a series of

Tremblay articles looking into the case of a colleague of his who disappeared along with a research partner of Cheryl Solem's. They had been missing seven months when their bodies were found by divers practicing cold water scuba in a water-filled mine pit owned by CUNIBelt. SB wanted to know what, if anything, Tremblay knew about the connection between Garman Worsley and Sy Borgman.

Eleven days had passed since she and her partners broke the story of the suppressed Forest Service study. Each time they brought out a new article based on the papers from Cecilia Baez, they posted all of the supporting documents online for anyone to see. Someone on Instagram dubbed the collection DocuDrop, and the name went viral. The Global Coalition of Investigative Journalists asked to work with SB and her partners, and the revelations just kept multiplying.

Tremblay hadn't replied, and SB's mind kept straying to that letter. She got up and sorted through the pile of mail until she found a grayish, cotton bond envelope that stood out among the white and manila mailers.

It was addressed to "SB Ellingson," correctly spelled and unpunctuated, she noticed, and written by hand in a sinuous, flowing cursive. There was no return address on the front or back. The stamp was postmarked New York City. She held it in both hands and was just turning it over, savoring the possibilities, when she heard the door fly open behind her.

Gwen gasped.

SB felt a pair of hands take her by the neck. Whoever it was spun her around roughly, and she found herself staring into Casper Karlsrud's deluded and desolate eyes. He had her by the plackets of her shirt by then, and she knew she was in trouble when he began to shake her. Her top button popped off and flew. In the background, sounding very, very far away, was Gwen's voice, saying something SB couldn't make out because Karlsrud was shouting over everything. He was too close, much too close, breath smelling of stale tobacco and ash.

"You've gone too far this time, dragging my wife into it! I warned you to drop this craziness! This personal attack is a pure vendetta! You can't say I didn't tell you!"

He had her pressed against the service counter with the full force of his body. She had seriously underestimated his strength, goosed, as it now seemed to be, by whatever psychosomatic stew his hormonal system had cooked up. Just her toes touched the floor. She couldn't get purchase, let alone space to wind up a counterpunch or deliver any kind of kick to his vulnerable locations.

"Gwen," she was able to squeeze out, "Call 911!"

"Already done. They're on their way!" Gwen said, her intensity rising with each phrase. "Get off her, Casper!"

"Shut up, you old witch!" he ranted. "You're next! You ingrates are going to get what you deserve!"

SB felt one of his hands release, but before she had the wits to lift her free arm in self-defense, his fist crashed against her cheek. She had heard about boxers seeing stars, but until then she had always assumed it was just another metaphor.

"Ruined by a couple of dykes," Karlsrud bleated. "And an Ellingson to boot!"

"Let her go," Gwen ordered. "Back off, Casper! Sit down, or you're going to be the one with regrets!"

SB's head drifted, afloat, awash. Another blow drove her lips into her teeth, and a split second later she heard a thud and a near-simultaneous crack, followed by Karlsrud falling against her and then to the floor, shrieking, "My arm! You broke it! It hurts! My god! What is wrong with you two harpies?"

"Oh shut up," Gwen said. "You had it coming!" She stood with her feet wide apart, gripping the doorstop at its narrowest point, fingers wrapped around the upright bear's hind legs. She looked ready to strike again if needed. "Now sit down," she added, "unless you want to feel this thing crack your skull!"

Karlsrud got his legs under him and pushed up from the floor with help from his functioning arm. Grimacing, he retreated to the loveseat and collapsed on it like a broken puppet.

"I did get those new surveillance cameras installed already, didn't I?" SB said. Her head was still swimming. She knew that much. She clamped the counter for balance.

"Yes, you did," Gwen said, taking her by the elbow.

They exchanged a look that asked, "What have we done?"

"Let's get you to your desk," Gwen said.

The police arrived. The round-bellied Sgt. Petersen directed his subordinate, Luke St. Jean, "Get some photos. I'm calling for the EMTs. We'll take statements if we can."

"Does my wife have to know about this?" Karlsrud croaked. "I think it would be a big mistake to tell her. She's not involved, and I'm not saying anything without my lawyer present."

"Why don't we sort out the damages first?" Petersen said. "Everyone stay right where you are."

"Do you mind, ma'am?" Luke asked before snapping shots of SB's face. "Any other injuries or bruises?"

"How should I know?" SB said.

When the EMTs arrived they loaded Karlsrud into the ambulance bound for Duluth and suggested that Gwen drive SB to the urgent care clinic in Iron. The nurse practitioner on duty shined a light into each of SB's eyes. She looked to be at that early-to-mid-fifties turning point where SB found herself as well, egg count dropping or altogether depleted, blond hair silvering, body shifting to a broader, more resigned center of gravity.

She asked SB to count backwards in threes from a hundred and looked satisfied enough by the response. She asked, "Do you feel dizzy or nauseated?"

"Neither," SB said, "My face hurts when I talk."

An X-ray showed that SB's cheekbone wasn't broken. The NP numbed her lip and put two stitches in deep and three on the surface.

"Lips are pretty resilient," she said. "They usually heal fairly well, but you might have a small scar. If you like, you could see a plastic surgeon."

"Why bother?" SB said. "It'll only enhance my reputation."

By the time Gwen got her home, she felt like her mouth had been tied with leather laces and allowed to dry in the sun. Gwen walked her upstairs, filled a baggie with ice, and handed it to her, wrapped in a hand towel.

"Alternate between your cheek and that lip," she ordered.

"*That* lip," SB said through what felt like a mouthful of feathers. "You're right! It doesn't feel like my lip."

"Is there anything else I can do for you right now?" Gwen wondered.

"I don't think so. I'm just going to lay low."

"Good idea. Get some rest."

"Wait!" SB remembered. "Could you bring up today's mail? Just the letter, actually. Not the whole pile."

"What is it?" Gwen asked when she handed the envelope to SB.

"Poison pen letter probably," SB said.

"Looks pretty nice for that."

"Right." SB stuck her index finger under the seal flap and ripped. If it was a hate letter, the writer had broken all of the genre's stereotypes. They had used the same painstaking cursive throughout. No cut-and-pasted print, no block lettered threats, no clipped illustrations of weapons or crude, cartoonish drawings of her body spattered with red ink.

She turned to the second page and looked at the signature.

"Holy!" she trumpeted, wincing with the pain she'd forgotten to anticipate. "It's from Cheryl Solem!"

Gwen came quickly and stood close, reading over SB's shoulder.

36. DEAR MS. ELLINGSON

FIRST, THANK YOU. PLEASE know how grateful and indebted I feel to you and your reporting partners. I understand something about the risks you faced bringing your fine, invesitative stories to light. In a more perfect world, I would meet you face to face, cook you a good dinner, and tell you in person what I'm about to reveal to you in writing. As things are, though, my handlers (as I like to call them) warn me that it's still too dangerous to let me go back to living my own real life. By "handlers" I mean the people in the U.S. Marshals Service who run the Witness Security Program. Thanks to them I'm safely tucked away amid the anonymity of a big city—not necessarily the one that appears in the postmark of this letter.

You may or may not know that the two criminal investigators you met had been working undercover at BeneGeo Corporation as part of a special operations unit. They'd been trailing the fugitive Sy Borgman and helping to investigate his links to Garman Worsley for a long time when they came knocking at my door. That was in March. They told me that federal authorities had the word of an undercover informant that Mr. Worsley hired Sy Borgman to arrange an "accident" for me. They thought they might be able to tail Borgman, gather more evidence about his contact people and activities, and protect me at the same time, but he gave them the slip somewhere between the Iron airport and Moose Horn. You can imagine my shock when they showed up at my doorstep and told me that my life was in danger unless I went with them immediately. Everything happened in a rush. They offered me placement in their Witness Security Program and told me that I needed to pack a bag. When Paul caught those images that you published from his trail camera, they were fetching things that I needed from my house. You might be relieved to know that I have my cat with me now, thanks to some special arrangements they were able to make.

I appreciate the work you and your partners have done with the documents I collected. I know the evidence I managed to gather was incomplete, but you've made the most of it. I've watched the stories spread online, and I know that you and so many other journalists are still working to piece together the rest of the story. Some of the remaining unknowns, I think, will take a long time to bring to light. I do believe that many of them will be revealed through criminal investigations driven by prosecutors with the power to subpoena witnesses and financial records.

I doubt if you know it, but your reporting has revived a Justice Department probe that bogged down under what I think was resistance from political appointees who wanted to protect their bosses. These things can be nearly impossible to unravel and even harder to prove under the law. What you've done through your articles is awaken the public and the public servants. I'm told that we can expect news of federal grand jury indictments within the next few months. Plea deals and trial dates should soon follow. When they do, I think we'll see some very large fish landed with the usual small ones.

Sadly, it almost goes without saying that none of what I have told you can be attributed to me. Not yet anyway. I simply offer it as information from a source familiar with the investigations.

With my highest regards and hopes for your continued success,
Cheryl Solem

37. LONGEST DAY

THE AGE-OLD LAWN AROUND the infinitely younger Carnegie Library had hosted weddings, evening concerts, and Fourth of July picnics. Maybe some of the Dakota and Ojibwe storytellers could speak of gatherings and ceremonies in more distant times, but there'd been nothing in recent memory like the summer solstice party Gwen Groveland organized to celebrate SB's success. The peonies blessed the affair by blooming all along the row that ran like a hedge around the library grounds. At the entrance points from the sidewalk, Alberta and the Grandmothers had fashioned archways of woven willow. They'd placed vases of yellow rocket, lupine, paintbrush, columbine, and wild clematis as centerpieces on the long, folding tables. The Mojigangas wandered the grounds. At the moment SB happened to see them, they were engaging a crescent-shaped cadre of amused-looking union members gathered around Arno Toivola.

The drum group sang and pounded a rhythm near the feast tables. Alberta had somehow managed to reunite the Renegades. She had recruited the Martineau girl from the Lucky Strike to take Ramona's place, pouring her voice and strong arm into the songscape that floated like a dreamy mist over the green space.

Artemisia carried around a smoking braid of sage and sweetgrass. She used a cupped hand to steer smoke toward one person and then another as SB heard her chant, "Oh, Great Goddess, mother of desire and fulfillment ..."

The singing, the drumming, the smudging and the heavy, intoxicating sweetness of the peonies gave the whole scene a transcendent quality that made SB think there could be such a thing as heaven on Earth, and she could live in it and be happy and grateful for however long it lasted.

Across the green Merle stood in all her radiance beside the tables where food and drink were laid out in plenty, and people milled around, filling their plates and exchanging greetings. Merle laughed, quite comfortably it seemed, from the distance at which SB was observing her with Arte and Arte's genderqueer, possible paramour and certain friend, Cayenne. Those two had schlepped the pork and the salad fixings from Hog Heaven Farm, and Kjell had paid to have the rest of the feast catered by his friends at the Iron Country Club. Jared Bednar, the skinny going-on-fifteen-year-old whom SB had come to know as hapless, clueless, and teachable, was working off part of his community service arrangement under Gwen's supervision. SB watched him move with youthful grace as he grabbed a shrimp puff, popped it into his mouth, and swiveled around some party guests with a comment and exchange of smiles. He seemed to be enjoying the company and the hoopla as he ferried a tray of empties to the library basement.

Merle's hair had grown shaggy. It fell around her collar and shaped her face in a way that emphasized the sunlight on her cheeks. SB had been trying to work her way across the lawn to join Merle, but someone or other kept grabbing her sleeve or stepping into her path to offer congratulations or to remark on how surprisingly not bad her face looked now that it was almost healed. The latest was Mel Levine.

He pumped her hand and said, "I'm still amazed. I can hardly tell you how lucky I feel that we were able to partner with you on this one. The DocuDrop just keeps on giving."

"We couldn't have done it without the *Record*," SB told him. "Is anyone else from the team here? I haven't seen Chastain."

"Are you kidding," Levine said, searching the crowd with his eyes. "She's covering this soiree. Renard's here, too, somewhere. My god! Is that Kjell?"

SB turned in the direction of Levine's gaze and saw that the tall, poised man heading toward them at a steady and deliberate, if slightly stiff-jointed, pace was indeed her father. His blond-haired, lookalike, younger companion appeared to be taking shortened steps in an effort not to outstrip him.

"That's Kjell alright," she confirmed. "The other one's my son, Skye.

I think we might be setting a modern record for the number of Ellingsons and former Ellingsons in Iron at one time. Some of them actually had to rent rooms."

"I'm going to say hello," Levine told her. "Catch you later?"

"For sure," she said, grateful for a chance to make more progress toward Merle.

A few steps shy of her goal, Paul and Jessi Mattson walked up to her, looking scrubbed and polished with no sign of potter's mud.

"I guess it's worked out pretty well," Paul said, "except for Cheryl."

"I have a feeling she's going to be okay." SB told him.

"Walker Hayes came out and got her cat," Jessi said. "He told us he had a foster home for her. I don't know why he wouldn't just leave her with us."

SB felt considerably inadequate and two-faced. She wished she could have been more open.

As soon as possible she headed in Merle's direction. This time Gwen grabbed her arm and said directly into her ear, "The speeches are going to start when the drum group finishes. That should be any minute now. We'll want you up near the front."

Gwen had borrowed a real sound system from the Lucky Strike. The floor mic stood stooped like a shy guest on the far side of the tables. Artemisia waited up there with her lover, Sam (formerly for Samantha, now maybe just for Sam). They both had plates in hand and were taking in the scene and chatting with Jack Bono and Dave Maki.

When SB reached Merle's side, she wanted to fall down on her knees and testify. The energy that zipped between them still felt so compelling that all she could do was beam and put an arm around Merle right there in front of the Great Goddess, the Creator, and everybody. Arte looked like a twelve-year-old, holding the hand of her lover or whatever they would end up calling whatever Cayenne would end up becoming to her. Skye came and stood beside his mom, breathing in the festive atmosphere and breathing it back out as life-giving energy.

"Who is this handsome stranger?" SB said, embracing her son.

When Gwen began her "testing, testing" routine at the microphone, the honking and shouting started from a parade of cars and pickups that had been gathering on the street. They circled the block, up the avenue, back around through the alley, down the avenue on the other side, and back around on the street. At the entryway to the grounds, Walker Hayes stood in civilian khakis and a cotton shirt, watching the procession. Kent Nowak's pickup passed with some little people who might have been his grandchildren sitting on straw bales in the truck bed, waving various sized versions of the stars and stripes. SB recognized Marilyn Bednar and her husband marching with a "Save Our Schools" banner. Some of the union miners and their families carried "Mining Forever" signs, and Toivo Nikko drove his Machine Supply van with a "We the People" banner fastened across its side.

Merle screwed up her mouth and shook her head disapprovingly.

"Oh, come on," SB said. "You knew they wouldn't let us have the last word if they could help it. This disagreement isn't over."

Gwen upped the volume on the sound system, and said, "Welcome, everyone!" The speaker proved potent enough to carry. She said, "Thanks for coming to honor Susan B. Ellingson, her partners in crime, and all the people who helped bring to light what's been happening around here. I just want to say how lucky I feel—and how lucky we all are—that SB wants to live here and keep the *Union Voice* alive and committed to finding the truth and telling it. She's a first-rate reporter, a first-rate business operator, and a first-rate friend and family member, and I know you all know it."

Alberta walked with light steps to the microphone, accompanied by countermelodies of car horns and cries of "Miners' Lives Matter" and "Greens will not replace us."

She leaned into the microphone and said, "A shout out to Gwen Groveland for organizing this feast. And to the Renegade Singers for traveling from many faraway places to be here with us. This place, for thousands of years, has been home to the Anishinaabe/Ojibwe, the Dakota, and the ancient ones going back to the First People. In Anishinaabe culture women are the water protectors. I thank the Creator for the warrior spirits in people like SB and Gwen and those strong grandmothers out there who help us preserve and protect this land and this water. We're still here, and we're not going anywhere, so please keep in mind the history and the importance of this place and these people. You are standing on Indigenous land. All our rivers run into the world."

Kjell Ellingson mentioned how proud he was to be one of the founders of the feast.

"Ouch!" Merle whispered to SB. "Gwen's going to feel bad about forgetting to say that."

"He should have just let it go by," SB answered.

Kjell went on, "It's good to be back in this hometown that my grandfather and great-grandfather helped to build and shape. I'm so proud of my daughter and the work she's carrying on at the *Union Voice*. The old rag is still making an impact, and she's kept it alive at a time when a lot of papers have gone broke."

"I guess women get to run businesses now," SB muttered to Merle.

"And now I'd like to shut up," Kjell added, "and get out and talk one-on-one with as many of my old friends as I can."

Gwen directed Chase Monahan to the microphone.

He adjusted it and began with his usual urgency, "We've won some points, but we have to stay vigilant. We can't let up the pressure. BeneGeo's plan might be dead, and it might not, but the ore is still here. The veins still run through sulfide rock, and the demand for it isn't going away. If you need any reminder that plenty of people don't agree with us, there they are, out on the street right now, telling us that they're not going anywhere, either."

Artemisia got up and said, "When Alberta talked about my daughter's warrior spirit, I knew I'd done something right. When I was a girl, the role models for women like me were hidden from us. We had to go searching for them. Now our children are becoming our role models, and we have a duty to help them change the world."

Mel Levine recounted how Kjell and SB brought the DocuDrop to the *Record* and how the project had mushroomed to include journalists, sources, and readers around the world. He ended by stabbing a pointed finger, and declaring, "Next year the Pulitzers!"

"There we go with the exaggerations," SB whispered to Merle. "I'm afraid he'll jinx us, setting expectations so high."

"Oh, I don't know," Merle replied. "Twenty-twenty has a nice ring to it."

"Maybe it does," SB said, letting herself feel a little dreamy. "I guess it's bound to be a good year."

AUTHOR'S AFTERWORD

Clouded Waters tells a fictional story, and Iron, Minnesota, is an imaginary town full of made-up characters. In some ways, Iron resembles Hibbing, Virginia, and Ely, the bigger towns on the actual Minnesota Iron Range, but in many other ways it's unlike all of them. BeneGeo and CUNIBelt, the mining corporations in the story, are not real, either, but the Range, the concrete, physical landscape of the place, remains as contradictory as I describe it—promising, tortured, and tragically beautiful.

In these cold, wet, rocky slopes and woodlands, Indigenous people have enacted their stories and made their own history for thousands of years. The two-billion-year-old, eroded mountain range, once taller than the Rockies, tops out at just under 2,000 feet now, and within it we find Misaabe Wajiw, the Anishinaabe/Ojibwe's Big Man Mountain, identified on contemporary maps as the Mesabi Range. In the late 1600s, French voyageurs, fur traders, and loggers began to play their parts in the history of this place, and then the rest of the immigrants—cooks, trade unionists, robber barons, plyers of the tourist trade, and all. The social and economic story of the Range, as told through SB's eyes, reflects the real place, as accurately as I could do it, based on research and lived experience.

When I started writing this novel, I'd been aware for years that mining companies sought to dig and process copper, nickel, and other precious metals just a little over an hour's drive from my own stomping grounds in Duluth. That part of the story is real, along with the fact that the mining companies' proposals and the objections to them have been debated and fought at many levels—official and public—and the argument continues. BeneGeo's oxymoronic mining waste disposal plan, Mix and Separate, is a product of my imagination, made up for the purpose of telling this story, but the spotted environmental record of copper mining is a fact. As of this writing no company has yet cleared the necessary regulatory and judicial hurdles to begin mining.

Not yet.

The pressure to begin and the points of contention are real. Given the state of existing technology, we need copper, nickel, and other rare metals if we want to create a clean energy future. Just as clearly, we need to learn how to handle mine waste without mistakes. The rain that falls here travels wide, and water remains essential to life on earth.

Managing the conflict isn't helped when small city newspapers like Iron's *Union Voice* really do struggle to survive. In the U.S., thousands of local news sources have reduced print runs, let journalists go, sold out to larger conglomerates, curtailed local reporting, or given up altogether. According to the *New York Times*, 2,500 American newspapers have stopped doing business since 2005, and more than 300 have closed since just before the start of the COVID pandemic. The loss of local investigative reporting has led to a decline in accountability at all levels of government. We find ourselves less informed, less understanding of one another, and unequipped to separate facts from falsehoods or agree on what needs to be done.

As SB experiences, Lesbian, Gay, Bisexual, Transgender, and Queer-identified people are still not safe from hateful rhetoric, harassment, and violence. In the past seven years, mass shootings at Pulse, a gay nightclub in Orlando, Florida, and Club-Q, an LGBTQ club in Colorado Springs, brutally underscored that fact, just as Matthew Shepard's beating death did in Laramie, Wyoming, in 1999. Even the nonviolent, everyday grind of petty judgments, critical comments, and restrictions takes a daily toll on LGBTQ people and their loved ones. Now we see new and proposed state laws restricting drag shows, drag story hours, school library books, lessons, and even gender-affirming therapy. In some states, parents are threatened with child abuse charges for providing affirming support to their trans children.

In many places, including Minnesota, Indigenous women have taken leading roles as water protectors. They teach, organize, lobby, write books, and create events like protests, art exhibits, fundraising concerts, and walks for water. Under existing treaties, the Ojibwe/Anishinaabe (also known as Chippewa) retain the right to hunt, fish, and gather across many of their Minnesota homelands, even when they no longer own the land. They tell us water is a sacred gift and cultural responsibility, essential for preserving human life, wildlife, and plants. Manoomin, the traditional Ojibwe staple that some of us call wild rice, grows in water and is particularly threatened by sulfate pollution, according to recent studies.

The fictional DocuDrop, Cheryl Solem's leaked document collection unveiled by the reporters at the *Union Voice* and the *River Cities Record*, reflects real world document drops like Daniel Ellsberg's famous Pentagon papers and the much more recent and extensive Pandora papers. Released by the International Consortium of Investigative Journalists in 2021, the Pandora Papers include nearly 12 million records that expose how wealthy people around the world keep their financial dealings secret, avoid taxes, and cover up political corruption. Such evidence suggests that the world needs a lot of reporters like SB and Gwen following a lot of money trails right now. Let's hope we get them.

ABOUT THE COVER ARTIST

SARA PAJUNEN is a composer-improvisor and an audiovisual artist based in what is now called Minnesota (USA). Trained as a violinist and employing locally-responsive media ranging from field recordings to drone imagery, her work is motivated by interactions between her ancestral roots, American cultural histories, and connection to our environments through sound. Her long-term project "Mine Songs: Sounding an Altered Landscape" uses violin, environmental recordings, image and archival material to reframe the altered landscape of Minnesota's Mesabi Iron Range—the artist's childhood and ancestral home. *www.sarapajunen.com*

ABOUT THE AUTHOR

DIANNA HUNTER is the author of two nonfiction books, *Wild Mares: My Lesbian Back-to-the-Land Life* (University of Minnesota Press) and *Breaking Hard Ground: Stories of the Minnesota Farm Advocates* (Holy Cow! Press). Both were finalists for the Minnesota Book Award. Her short fiction, journalism, essays, and book reviews have appeared in national and regional publications, including the *In These Times* Rural America blog, the Rural Women's Studies Association blog, *Peregrine, Feminist Collections, Hurricane Alice*, and *Earth Matters*. A former farmer and retired teacher of writing and women's studies, she currently writes, gardens, and forages in the rocky green spaces of Duluth, Minnesota, where she lives with her wife, Deb. For more information, visit *diannahunter.com*

Printed in the USA
CPSIA information can be obtained
at www.ICGtesting.com
JSHW021448041223
53222JS00002B/19